JUST DESSERTS

JUST DESSERTS

J.M. Gregson

Severn House Large Print
London & New York

This first large print edition published in Great Britain 2005 by
SEVERN HOUSE LARGE PRINT BOOKS LTD of
9-15 High Street, Sutton, Surrey, SM1 1DF.
First world regular print edition published 2004 by
Severn House Publishers, London and New York.
This first large print edition published in the USA 2005 by
SEVERN HOUSE PUBLISHERS INC., of
595 Madison Avenue, New York, NY 10022.

British Library Cataloguing in Publication Data

Gregson, J. M.
   Just desserts. - Large print ed. (A Lambert and Hook mystery)
  1. Lambert, John (Fictitious character) - Fiction
  2. Hook, Bert (Fictitious character) - Fiction
  3. Murder - Investigation - Fiction
  4. Detective and mystery stories
  5. Large type books
  I. Title
  823.9'14 [F]

  ISBN 0-7278-7421-7

Printed and bound in Great Britain by
MPG Books Ltd, Bodmin, Cornwall.

To Fred and Paula Soutter,
whose splendid restaurant provided the
setting for this sinister story

One

Everyone seemed to like him.

That is normally a good thing, an admirable thing. In this case, it would eventually make things very difficult for the police. But no one was thinking about policemen at the time.

Patrick Nayland was a model employer. Both his workforce and his customers seemed to think that. And this was the kind of business where there was plenty of evidence.

Nayland owned a small golf course outside the old market town of Oldford, in that green and pleasant part of England between the rivers Severn and Wye, where Gloucestershire runs into Herefordshire. It is a quiet and beautiful area, with the mellow stone villages and rolling hills of the Cotswolds to the north and east and the high mountains of the Brecon Beacons to the west.

This was not a pretentious golf course: it had only nine holes, and a short and undistinguished history. In the early nineties, when the proliferation of golf courses was being encouraged by a government anxious to emphasize the new leisure which was to be a feature of life in the years ahead, Patrick Nayland had obtained planning consent for a new golfing development.

With this secured, he paid a grateful farmer what seemed an extravagant price for a piece of difficult agricultural land. It had been suitable only for sheep yet Nayland had paid well above the going price for pasture land. The Gloucestershire man who had farmed this hillside since he was a boy grinned gratefully as he took the money: here was another city-dweller who had made his money too easily and spent it too freely, he decided.

But Patrick Nayland knew what he was doing. The land was beside the main road from Gloucester to Oldford. As his modest development took shape, with the forthcoming golf course proclaimed on a large sign beside the road, there was considerable interest from passing motorists. Nayland kept the changes to the minimum, using the natural contours of the land wherever possible, using the earthmoving equipment he hired just to level some areas for greens and to gouge out the small number of bunkers he thought necessary.

He planted a hundred saplings, which in due course would become quite large trees, fringing the fairways, but not narrowing them too much and not near enough to the greens to cause serious golfing problems. He did not want a course that was too difficult. 'Challenging', that word beloved of more ambitious golf-course architects, was not for him. This development would be mainly for beginners and novice golfers. The game itself was quite challenging enough for them. Patrick Nayland knew his market.

He had his nine holes ready for play within fifteen months, and the customers flooded in. At first, the grass on the fairways and the greens was rather coarse and patchy, but it steadily improved with mowing. Soon you could see the shape of the holes and the landmarks provided by the bunkers, which he filled with striking, near-white sand. The place began to look like a real golf course.

And everyone liked the man who owned it.

The people who played at the long-established courses like Ross-on-Wye and the Rolls of Monmouth turned their noses up a little at the modest new nine-hole venture, but even they had to acknowledge that the new course served a useful purpose. It enabled people who had never played golf to try out this intriguing but often infuriating sport to see if it suited them. They could even hire clubs, if they couldn't find a relative's discarded ones in the attic or the garage. They could introduce themselves to the game without the considerable expense of joining the waiting list at an existing high-profile club or of purchasing shining new golfing equipment.

The venture prospered over its first ten years. Nayland gave it an impressive entrance and called it Camellia Park Golf Club. As the trees grew and the greens improved, the land matured into quite a nice-looking little course, pretty enough to attract golfers of both sexes and all ages, but modest enough in length to flatter their often limited abilities. Patrick Nayland even played it occasionally himself, waving to his patrons with a lordly proprietorial air, though he retained his membership and played his more serious golf at the nearby Ross-on-Wye Golf Club.

He visited Camellia Park regularly, keeping a fond and sometimes critical eye upon its development, but he did not manage the place himself. He employed a manager who kept a daily check on the takings and the outgoings and supervised the staff. He had found exactly the man he needed in Chris Pearson, who at forty-seven years old was just two years younger than Nayland himself.

They shared other things as well as their generation. Patrick Nayland had been a captain on a short-service commission at the time of the Falklands. He had seen active service in that curious backwater of a war, and become a major as a result. The promotion hadn't prevented him leaving after five years of the military life to pursue a career where individual initiative was not restricted by Army rules.

Yet perhaps he retained a respect for the qualities instilled by military discipline, for when he was looking for someone trustworthy and reliable to run Camellia Park, he was swayed by the Army career and the impeccable references of Christopher Pearson, who had risen through the ranks to become a warrant officer class 2. That was the rank enjoyed by sergeant-majors, and perhaps Nayland unconsciously assumed that his relationship with his manager would be that of officer and senior NCO.

Whatever the psychology involved, the partnership worked well as the new business venture developed. Pearson was a tough, no-nonsense manager of the office, the modest clubhouse, and the labour taken on as the course developed. Tough but fair: the course and domestic staff learned that they would get away with very little, but that good work would be recognized and rewarded.

And the owner of the enterprise, who had distanced himself from the day-to-day problems of the course with Pearson's appointment, remained popular with staff and customers.

On one of the last days of November, Nayland and Pearson were walking round their golf course together, devising a programme of winter work for the green staff. When the need for cutting the grass was gone, there would be time to trim trees back, to lay one or two new stretches of path, to repair the edges of bunkers which had grown shabby and unkempt with summer use. The list grew, for both men wanted the busy little course to be as neat and as fair as was possible; Chris Pearson kept a note of everything they agreed as they walked the fairways purposefully among the golfers.

There were plenty of those, for this was an unseasonally benign, mild day at the end of November. The temperature was scarcely lower than that of August, and only the early twilight and the myriad shades of red and gold on the trees and hills reminded you that autumn was well advanced. The man who owned the course and the slightly taller figure at his side did not hurry their work, for it was a pleasant day to be out in the open, and both of them knew there might not be another day as benign as this until the spring.

They agreed and marked the precise point where a flowering cherry was to be planted behind the fourth green, decided that the tee behind the sixth should be extended and that the one on the eighth should be given extra drainage to enable it to stand up to the traffic it was now carrying with the success of the course.

Most of the golfers recognized the manager if not the owner of the enterprise, and the pair received many greetings and not a few compliments on the condition of the course as they proceeded. It was the kind of day which made people happy with life in general and philosophical about the deficiencies of their golf. Even the two men who were so familiar with this scene, who knew every rise and fall of the land, every patch of grass on the little course, took a moment when they had finished their work to gaze at the crimson of the sunset and the black profile of the maturing trees against the horizon.

There was an agreeable interval of silence before Chris Pearson said, 'I thought we might consider taking young Barry on fulltime. The takings warrant it, and with the number of regulars we now have, I'm sure the winter green fees will be up on last year.'

Barry Hooper was a young black man they had employed for the last six months, initially part-time, then full-time, but only on a temporary basis. Patrick Nayland said, 'It's not a good time to take on new outdoor staff, with the winter coming up. There isn't the same work on the course as when we're mowing every day.'

13

'There's enough for two men, with the winter programme of works on the course we've just agreed. The drainage and the new paths are quite big projects. I don't think Hooper will have time on his hands, but if he has, I can always get him to give a hand with the catering or in the bar at the weekends. Young Barry doesn't mind turning his hand to anything, and he lives near enough to come in whenever we want him. He has his own transport.'

'But are you happy to take the lad on permanently, Chris? It's not easy to get rid of labour, after the probation period. And Hooper had a pretty chequered employment record before he came to us.'

'I know that. But he's settled in well here. He loves the outdoor work. And he's not a shirker. He gives full value for what we pay him.'

Nayland grinned. 'With a greenkeeper like Alan Fitch and a manager like you, he won't get much chance to slack, I'm sure.' He had made the proper noises, asked the ritual questions expected of the man who paid the wages, but he had always been going to accept the suggestion about this latest addition to the permanent staff. Hooper was a good worker and in truth they paid him not much above the minimum wage.

The decision made good commercial sense. He would give the lad a small rise,

14

when the pace of work quickened on the course in spring. 'All right, you can tell him he's now on the permanent staff, a proper member of the team.'

Chris Pearson wondered if it was a residue of Nayland's Army officer's training that made him constantly stress the importance of the team ethic. But it was appropriate enough, with the small, carefully selected workforce they employed. He said, 'It will be a nice surprise for the boy, with Christmas not too far away.' Barry Hooper was twenty-two, but both he and Nayland had reached the age where they thought of such men as lads.

'Speaking of Christmas, I thought we might take the staff out for a meal some time in December,' said Nayland. It's ten years since this little enterprise began, and a modest celebration seems to be in order.'

'Good idea!' said Pearson promptly. 'Did you have anywhere in mind for this little party?'

'I thought we might push the boat out. Go to Soutters Restaurant in Newent.'

Pearson whistled softly. 'That would cost a bit.' Soutters was quality: well worth the price for its food and its ambience, but not cheap.

Patrick Nayland grinned. 'We can afford it, once every ten years. And it's a small, intimate place, just the right size for us. We could take over the whole restaurant for an evening for our little party. They're pretty fully booked in the run-up to Christmas, but I've already reserved an evening for us. I'll confirm it, and you can let the staff know next week.'

It sounded like a most agreeable evening. It should have left Chris Pearson with a warm glow of anticipation as darkness fell and he was left alone in the office behind the reception area.

He could not work out quite why he felt so apprehensive about the evening at Soutters. Celebrating the first ten years was a splendid notion, and could only encourage everyone to pull together in the months ahead. It could only help to make the boss more popular still.

For, after all, everyone liked Patrick Nayland.

Two

'We'll have a nice meal together. Open a bottle of wine and relax over it. It's a while since we did that.' Liza Nayland's words to her daughter rang falsely bright and cheerful in the big modern kitchen.

'Can't do Saturday. I go out on Saturday nights.'

'I know you do, dear. We'll make it Sunday then. We'll eat around six thirty. I'll get some of that fillet steak you like in the morning.'

'He likes, you mean.'

'Not "he", Michelle. "He" has a name, you know. I don't know why you can't just call him Dad.'

'Because he's not. That's quite simple, Mum. I've got a dad, and it's not him.'

Her mother sighed wearily. 'You've got to move on, Michelle. You've got to face facts. You've got a new life now.'

'You have, you mean. Don't pretend that I have. It wasn't my choice. I wasn't even consulted.' Michelle Nayland knew she wasn't being fair, that she was behaving more like a child than a woman of twenty-three. But at that moment she had no desire to be fair.

Her mother forced herself to remain calm: they had been down this road often enough before, and things would only get worse if she showed her anger. 'You *were* consulted, dear. And I know you didn't see things my way. That's a pity, but I had to go ahead and make my own decision. You may think I'm ancient, but I've got a lot of my life still to live, I hope!'

Michelle grinned, forced herself to relax. 'Of course you have, Mum. I can't disguise the fact that I wish you'd chosen to live it with someone else, but it's not fair of me to go on moaning about it. Look, make that meal fairly early on Sunday evening, and I'll be there and smiling!'

'It's a deal. And I bet you don't leave the steak, whatever you say.' They were happy with each other again, increasingly so as they moved on to other and less emotional things.

Michelle told herself that this wasn't the moment to reveal her news. Instead, she must steel herself to be nice on Sunday evening.

Her mother obviously still didn't know about Patrick.

Alan Fitch, the greenkeeper at Camellia Park, was one of Chris Pearson's 'finds', one of the reasons why the modest little golf course had been so successful in its first ten years.

Fitch had spent eleven years in the Merchant Navy, a period which he claimed was responsible for the versatility which everyone remarked in him. He could turn his hand to most things, and his willingness to do so had been his most valuable quality in getting the new venture off the ground and into eventual profit.

He was not only good at operating the various machinery needed on a golf course, but good at maintaining it. He had serviced the mowers and the chainsaws which had been bought second-hand in the early years of the course. When the old tractor – which was their single powered vehicle in the early days – broke down, Alan Fitch had usually been able to diagnose the problem. He had even been prepared to tour the scrapyards of Gloucestershire in pursuit of cheap replacement parts, and he had fitted them himself.

His title had recently been elevated to Head Greenkeeper, for he now had Barry Hooper as his workforce. Fitch was a stern taskmaster, prone to hark back to those early days of the course, which became ever more attractive in retrospect. When Barry had arrived as a junior and temporary employee, Alan had been frankly suspicious of the black boy and his motives. How much of this was down to racial prejudice, even Alan

Fitch himself could not have determined. He had trained himself not to think deeply about such things, having had for many years to accept the decisions of those around him. He had worked with a variety of nations during his days at sea, but that was a long time ago, when white British people on British ships had just accepted that 'the foreigners' would not be promoted beyond a certain level.

Barry Hooper won him over. Whatever the wiry young lad really thought, he accepted his boss's early strictures without complaint. 'Keep your head down and get on with it, whatever you might think. You're not paid to think,' Alan Fitch had said to him on his first morning. To the greenkeeper's secret surprise, Barry Hooper did just that.

'Right, boss,' was his standard response to any command; then he went away and did it. But he was not cowed. Barry did not always understand exactly what was necessary, but when he needed advice he asked for it. The nature of the work meant that the pair were a two-man team, which was supplemented only on those rare occasions when an outside contractor was brought in for some specialist task. Most of the work on the course they did together, with Alan Fitch always as the senior and directing partner.

They made an unlikely pair, the stocky, powerful 55-year-old, with his heavily lined forehead and his tattooed arms, and the slim, swift, young coloured man who responded to his every suggestion. But they had some things in common. Hooper, who had never had the opportunity to work in the open air in his chequered pattern of previous employment, discovered that he loved the outdoor life and the wide skies above him as much as did the man who had spent eleven years at sea.

Fitch, who had been born and bred in Gloucestershire, taught his protégé about the birds and the wild flowers which were their friends and the coarse grasses and weeds which were their enemies upon the course. And Barry Hooper thrived upon every minute of it. He grew to love the changing seasons and the way they manifested themselves in his new small world of the golf course. He had revelled in the long days of summer, and in the months to come, even the winter rains and frosts would be welcome to a young man who had chafed in a factory and sweated in a slaughterhouse during previous periods of employment.

He was enjoying this unexpected period of calm, sunny days at the end of November, as much as any weather so far. It was too late to be an Indian summer, but it was a balmy autumn bonus, before the trees were stripped of leaves and the water froze on the little pond on the third. Barry Hooper sang as he went about his work, and Alan Fitch smiled a happy inner smile, even as he pretended to rebuke this relentless cheerfulness in his workforce.

On this last afternoon of November, they were extending the tee on the fourth hole, and Barry was enjoying the learning process this involved for him. They had levelled the ground weeks ago. It had seemed flat and ready for the new turf to Barry, but Fitch had explained that the ground needed to settle before they could even think about laying turf. They had left it for ten days, then come back and raked and trodden the patch again, with the older man full of amusement at his assistant's impatience to have the job completed.

Now they gave the ground its final preparation, with Fitch using a spirit level attached to a plank to get the ground exactly level, setting a standard which he knew the younger man would adhere to in the years to come. 'Half an inch below the existing level, remember!' he said sternly. 'Remember, two hours spent on preparation saves days of work on reparation.' He was rather proud of that maxim, which he had invented for himself.

'You said the new turf was an inch thick. Surely that means an inch lower!' said Barry triumphantly. He'd show the boss that he'd been paying attention to everything he said:

if he could catch him out at the same time, that would be doubly satisfying.

Fitch smiled into the eager, mischievous young face. 'We lay half an inch proud of the existing tee,' he insisted. 'There'll still be some settlement as the new turf beds in, and that and the many feet that are going to tread upon it will lower our new patch by about half an inch. That's the theory, and those are the measurements we work to. But full marks for paying attention!'

Fitch looked at the sky as they finished the work. 'This weather looks settled for a while longer yet. We'll get the turf laid, day after tomorrow. With a bit of luck, the roots will get a hold before the real winter sets in. This new patch'll be ready to use by next May. We'll put the tee right at the back for the club championship. Bit of extra length will suit lads like you, with more brawn than brains!'

He grinned affectionately at Hooper, who had recently been introduced to the mysteries of golf, but the young man's face clouded suddenly. 'I might not be here then,' he said dolefully. Six months was a long time ahead in his young life. He had never held a job for that long until now, and he realized suddenly how much this one meant to him.

Fitch smiled a knowing smile, but kept his news until they were back in the green-keeper's shed, with the kettle coming to the boil and the milk ready in the beakers. 'Got something to tell you,' he said. He didn't look at the younger man, being beset with a sudden and uncharacteristic diffidence because he had good news to deliver.

The owner had confirmed the appointment with his manager, and the manager had told his greenkeeper. Now the greenkeeper was to communicate the tidings to the young man it most concerned. That was the way things operated at Camellia Park; it reinforced the unstated hierarchy of the team, but gave each tier of it in turn a little pleasure.

Fitch was pouring the boiling water into the teapot by the time he said, as casually as he could, 'I've got some good news for you, young Hooper. At least I hope it's good. Job's yours on a permanent basis if you want it, and there'll be a small rise for you in the new year.' He delivered his tidings all in a rush, finding the good news was suddenly an embarrassment to him, instead of the pleasure he had anticipated.

Barry for his part could scarcely contain his joy. He made a brief attempt to accept the news in the matter-of-fact, man-to-man way in which it had been delivered, but his unlined black countenance shone with a pleasure he could not disguise and his smile stretched towards the ears at the sides of the slim face. 'I won't let you down, Mr Fitch!'

he said tremulously, when he could finally trust himself with words.

Alan Fitch thought of pointing out that it wasn't his decision, that all he could do was recommend the appointment. He wanted to say that this was no more than a hard-working and conscientious employee deserved. Instead, he said nothing, and the two men drank their tea in a comfortable silence, their world as perfect as the autumn weather outside the shed.

It would be a long time before either of them felt quite so comfortable again.

Joanne Moss had never thought the job would develop as it had. When she had taken it on seven years ago, 'Catering Manager' had been a grandiose title. She had worked part-time then, serving a few refreshments at weekends in the tiny wooden hut which served as a clubhouse for the little golf course in its early days.

But the demand for after-golf amenities had grown with the success of Camellia Park, had even outstripped the growth of the course. For the last three years, she had operated in a new brick-built, one-storey building behind the office where the green fees were taken and golf equipment sold. Now there was a bar and a weekend steward; Joanne had a new and well-equipped kitchen, and the Sunday lunches provided for members and guests were one of the features of the club which made it most popular. 'Just like a real golf club!' she heard people say appreciatively, unconscious of any irony in the phrase.

Like most of the people at the little course, Joanne Moss was proud of what she had achieved. She had taken the job as no more than a stop-gap, as she collected herself amidst the debris of a messy divorce. She had intended to acquire a little money from it whilst the terms of the settlement were argued, then move on to pastures new: at twenty-nine, there was plenty of time to make a different life for herself.

Catering wasn't even her field of expertise. In her previous working life, Joanne Moss had managed a small but busy office. But she had always enjoyed cooking, and she could manage the rudimentary stuff which was needed – when Patrick Nayland had approached her, the course had only been open for three years and everything about it was still rough around the edges.

Seven years later, she had a full-time job, two part-time staff, the appreciation of the members, and a sense of achievement which made the shattered self-esteem of her divorce seem to belong to another world. She also had a new relationship, which at once excited and frightened her. She wasn't quite sure yet where it was going, but she wasn't planning to opt out of the discovery process. It wasn't going to be easy for Joanne Moss to move on from Camellia Park.

The club now served simple meals at every lunchtime, meeting a demand which had grown as the reputation of the weekend catering spread. Wednesday was the busiest day midweek, but by four o'clock on this perfect November afternoon, the rush was over and Joanne had time to watch Alan Fitch repairing to his favourite greenkeeper's shed with young Barry Hooper, who was listening avidly as usual to his mentor's every word.

Joanne smiled as she watched the pair, reflecting on how good the bond was for both of them, the older man with no son to shape in a dangerous world and the youngster who had taken to the work on the course like a duckling to water. Everyone liked young Barry. He was willing to turn his hand to everything about the place, cheerful and unquestioning without being over-deferential.

She guessed that Alan would be telling him in his lair that he had been added to the permanent staff of the club. Everyone would be happy about that. It was sound economics, not sentiment: you didn't get many people as reliable and hard-working as Barry, not at the kind of money you paid to junior greens staff.

Chris Pearson had come into her kitchen and consulted her before he had decided to recommend to Nayland that Hooper should be made permanent. She had been pleased by the gesture, though she had said that it wasn't really anything to do with her. Chris had maintained that it was only common sense to consult her, because Hooper would be called upon to help her during slack periods on the course. She had been enthusiastic about the young black man, as Pearson had known that she would be. Everyone liked Barry.

The manager came in again as she was switching off all the appliances and preparing to leave. He was a handsome man, mature and confident, just under six feet tall, with dark hair that showed no sign of thinning in his late forties. But theirs was strictly a working relationship. Chris Pearson had never even made a pass at her, which she had appreciated, particularly in those early days when men gathered round an attractive divorcee like the proverbial bees round the honeypot, and she had sometimes felt that she could smell the lust in the air.

Pearson was never less than friendly, and she couldn't recall a single dispute about the way she ran her section of the enterprise. He listened carefully to what she had to say, generally agreed that it made sense, and occasionally added some small suggestion of his own, which was invariably thoughtful and often helpful. But there was a reserve about him which she had grown used to over the years. In the early days, she had been thankful for it; nowadays it occasionally rankled her, for reasons she could not define.

She was aware now, for instance, that he had something to say, that he would not have come into her kitchen for social reasons, but he did not immediately produce it. There would be a little period of social fencing before he announced the real reason for his visit, pleasant enough between two people who liked each other, but unnecessary, and therefore a trifle irritating.

She decided to take the initiative and talk business. 'I assume Patrick will want me to do the usual Christmas dinner for the staff,' she said. 'It means closing the place for our regular customers, but there won't be many complaints in December, so long as we give them a few days' notice. We might even get one of those deluges which means no one is able to play golf on the day, at that time of year.'

'There won't be any need for you to close, this year. We won't be asking you to do our Christmas lunch,' said Chris Pearson. Then, as if he realized he had spoken abruptly, he smiled and said, 'We'll all miss your turkey and trimmings, but I don't expect you will miss all the work.'

'I don't mind the work, not really. And I enjoy watching us all make fools of ourselves, with paper hats and silly jokes from crackers.'

'It's ten years since we started, though I know we'd been going for three of them before we had the good sense to bring you in. Patrick feels he ought to take us all out to celebrate. To Soutters Restaurant in Newent.' He added the name of the place as if anxious to assure her that there was no slur on her own efforts.

'He's pushing the boat out, isn't he?'

'I expect he can afford it, once every ten years.' Alan grinned at her conspiratorially, an unexpected expression which cut through his normal reserve.

'And when will this splendid celebration take place?' Joanne felt oddly put out that she had not heard this news from Patrick Nayland himself.

'On the thirteenth of December. It was as near to Christmas as Patrick could get.'

'Unlucky for some,' she said automatically.

The phrase would echo many times in her mind in the months which followed.

Three

The balmy autumn weather lasted for another week. Alan Fitch and Barry Hooper laid their new turf and saw it begin to knit in with the surrounding grass. Michelle Nayland ate her way through a tense Sunday evening meal with her stepfather and her rather anxious mother without any serious incident. Chris Pearson helped Joanne Moss to mount a lunch for the over-sixties golfers of Camellia Park, which was an occasion of raucous but good-natured fun.

Then the weather changed abruptly. The temperature dropped steeply, the rains came in from the west, and an overnight gale battered the area, stripping the trees abruptly of the autumn glory which had been impressive for a month and more. By the time of the staff Christmas dinner at Soutters Restaurant on the thirteenth of December, winter had taken a sudden grip on the land. The turf on the fairways of the golf course was white with frost in the mornings, and the flags on the greens stood out stiffly in the strong north-east wind, which strengthened throughout the day.

Golfers are hardy and determined souls, but by the middle of this bitter afternoon, the last of them had admitted defeat and were hastening from the course. Camellia Park closed early, and the staff hastened away gratefully to don their finery for the evening's festivities.

Soutters is a small and intimate place: its rooms date back to Elizabethan times and its softly lit restaurant has an atmosphere which makes every meal an occasion. It was exactly the right size for the sort of evening Patrick Nayland planned to give his staff, for its small size meant that he was able to take over the whole establishment for his party.

The bitter cold outside seemed only to add to the occasion. Everyone came in shivering, but within minutes was laughing with the rest of the company round the little bar where the preliminary drinks were served with the roaring log fire in the background. Paula Soutter served them herself and took their orders for the starters and main courses they would enjoy as the evening progressed. Nothing was hasty or unconsidered at Soutters: the place was theirs for the whole evening, and the food and wine would be served and enjoyed in a properly relaxed and unhurried pageant of enjoyment.

Several hours later, when the bulk of the

meal had been enjoyed, Fred Soutter would emerge from his kitchen in his tall chef's hat, smiling and unflustered, his face shiny with pleasure in his work, shyly receiving the plaudits of the customers who now felt almost like guests, standing beside his poised and elegantly gowned wife to answer any questions about the food and the wines. There was a cost, of course, at the end of the evening; quality never comes cheap. But the charges were reasonable for what was given; Soutters' clients paid for four hours of splendid fare in a unique setting, but they got good value for money. *The Times* had given the place a strong recommendation three years ago; its customers nodded sagely and kept rather quiet about such publicity, as if they resented outside opinions and wished to keep this tiny gem of civilized entertainment to themselves.

For all but the man who had devised the evening, the cost did not matter. And Patrick Nayland, circulating among the workers who had become his guests for the evening, gave the impression that cost was the last thing he was considering. He had a word for every-one, from the humblest to the most exalted of his little band, and he had a quality unusual in a boss: he listened to other people as well as to himself. Even the wives, husbands and partners who had never seen him before, who had come along diffidently to this evening which was designed primarily to reward their partners for loyal service, felt themselves a part of it as Patrick chatted to them about their lives, their families, and their concerns in the wider world outside Camellia Park.

Barry Hooper had not brought a partner for the evening. He had no girlfriend at the moment, he repeated patiently to a succession of enquiries. He was such a recent addition to the permanent staff of the golf course that he felt it an enormous privilege to be here himself, sitting in a restaurant which he would never have dared to enter, with a company glittering for the evening as he had never seen them before.

Liza Nayland, elegant in a sapphire-blue dress, had already drawn from him a full account of his work on the course, listening and smiling until eventually his shyness had dropped away and his enthusiasm for what he did and the place where he did it had come bursting through his diffidence. And Barry could scarcely take his eyes off her daughter, Michelle Nayland, dressed more informally in a close-fitting green cotton dress, whose lustrous black hair and clear grey eyes seemed only to grow more vivid as she moved down the steps from the little bar and into the soft lighting of the dining area.

The seating plan had separated Barry from his mentor and friend Alan Fitch, who sat rather awkwardly with his wife at the other end of the table. It was rather a surprise to Barry to see Mrs Fitch at all, since Alan never mentioned her at work and he had almost forgotten that there was such a person. She looked surprisingly animated as she chatted happily to Joanne Moss, a contrast to her rather dour husband. Fitch, who had always seemed to Barry Hooper to know everything in their two-man exchanges on the course, looked ill at ease in this social situation, smiling nervously when spoken to and contributing little himself as the level of noise rose inexorably beneath the beams of the old room.

Joanne Moss had brought her brother as her partner for the evening, a surprising escort for a woman who could surely have had a selection of men to accompany her. She looked younger than her thirty-six years, her dark eyes sparkling but observant in the soft light, her ready smile making her the most radiantly attractive woman in the room; Barry wrenched his gaze away from Michelle Nayland and gave himself up to visions of sexual instruction from a mature woman, one of his favourite recurring fantasies.

The meal was perfect but unhurried, so that there was plenty of time for conversation between courses. Patrick Nayland circulated among his small company, rather like royalty at a garden party, thought Chris Pearson uncharitably, surprising himself with that waspish thought. He allowed Paula Soutter to fill his glass with burgundy for the main course, acknowledging her attentions with a grateful smile. Perhaps he needed the wine to mellow him, to enable him to present the relaxed face which was appropriate to the company at large.

No one was driving; there were taxis laid on for the journeys home at midnight. Pearson watched his wife talking to Mrs Fitch and reflected upon what a handsome woman she was still, poised and in control of herself and the situation. Was that how people thought of him? he wondered wryly. It was the image he strove to present through the working day at Camellia Park. He was proud of his wife, and the sight of her happiness should have cheered him, but he felt flat and watchful amidst the noisy hilarity which now surrounded him. Almost as if he were waiting for something to happen.

Michelle Nayland watched her stepfather as he moved among the company, dropping compliments like winter snow among the people he had invited to his feast. He was good at this, she admitted to herself regretfully. He could charm the birds from the trees, just as he was now charming the partners of his employees, whom he had not met until this evening. No one except her seemed to see through him, and that added to her frustration.

He had got it right, as usual. She had never been to Soutters before, but it was just the right place for this ten-year celebration, combining the quality, ambience and intimacy which made for a memorable evening. This was something special without being at all stuffy. Everyone seemed to be both excited and appreciative, from her mother at the head of things to that slight black boy with the thin, interesting face, who surely must be older than he looked.

A familiar, mischievous notion crept into her mind. She wondered how she could best irritate her stepfather as he moved so confidently among his guests. She inched herself a little sideways and began to speak to the wide-eyed Barry Hooper. 'Looks as if we're here to carry the flag for the younger generation!' said Michelle Nayland.

'It's a great place this, isn't it?' said Barry. He was glad that words, words of any kind, had come to him. He had thought he might become speechless under the dazzling spotlight of this goddess.

'Soutters?' Michelle looked round at her surroundings as if viewing them objectively for the first time, as if his words had surprised her and were worthy of her attention. 'Yes. It's a wonderful place for a function like this. They've got both the décor and the food just right. And they look after you well without pretending to be servile. I like that in a restaurant.'

'Yes.' Barry couldn't think of anything else to say in the face of such sophistication. He couldn't even start to compare one restaurant with another, as this divine creature was able to do. Now, if it came to which caffs served the best fry-ups for breakfast, that would be a different matter. But it never would come to that, he thought glumly.

'I've never been here before. I think I'd like to come again, on a less formal occasion.' She looked round appreciatively at the antique candlesticks, the glitter of fine wines in wine glasses, the log flames which winked cheerfully in the old fireplace.

Barry wanted to say that she should come here again with him, that they should enjoy an intimate evening together in one of the alcoves of this magical place. He made no such invitation, of course; such monstrous presumption was well beyond his powers. He looked away from those large and humorous grey eyes, which seemed to see into his very soul, and said desperately, 'It's very good of your dad to lay on an evening like this for his workforce.'

He had been rather proud of himself for that; with his mind reeling from the sight and the scent and the presence of this magical girl, he had come up with something which seemed safe. And he had managed to deliver it without the air of a sycophant, mainly because it was genuinely felt.

But Michelle's brow clouded for a moment with the idea. She seemed about to say something about it, even to argue with him. Instead, she merely shook her head minimally, flashed him a final, almost apologetic smile, and moved on.

It was both a disappointment and a relief to Barry Hooper. He felt the tension easing away from his limbs as his toes uncurled in his shoes. In a moment, he was answering the more maternal and infinitely less emotionally demanding queries of Mrs Fitch about his work with her husband.

The evening proceeded successfully. The food and the wine were consumed without haste and with much enjoyment. Most people had eschewed the turkey and trimmings which would surfeit their palates in the season to come in favour of the more appealing menu offered by Fred Soutter's kitchen, and there was much comparing one dish with another, even a little sampling of other people's choices. And as the hours slipped by, there was recourse inevitably to the cloakrooms in the basement of the old building.

For better or for worse – and not all clients approve of them – these are a feature of Soutters. Where the ambience above is perfect and nothing rules but good taste, the toilet facilities are designed to shock and to amuse. There is a Hogarthian vigour about the cartoons and other adornments which enliven these normally dull facilities. Many a maiden aunt has been denied a visit to Soutters because of the embellishments which make the ladies' room there so individual. That is no doubt an unjustified estimate of the narrowness of experience of the modern maiden aunt, but old prejudices die hard.

For by modern standards, this vulgar picture gallery is really quite mild. Nevertheless, on the evening of the Camellia Park celebration, the visits to the basement caused much astonished hilarity as the evening proceeded. Whispering behind hands from returning diners caused others to visit the nether regions of this surprising place, only for them to return minutes later with whoops of confirming laughter.

Wine-loosened tongues lost all inhibitions after the startling Rabelaisia of the basement; anecdotes grew ever bolder as the decibel level rose inexorably amidst the impeccable furnishings of the restaurant.

None of this was surprising to Fred Soutter, listening discreetly in his kitchen. When you had developed a place like this and run it for years, there was very little in even the wide ranges of human nature that you hadn't seen before. He listened to the cacophony amongst his customers, judged it with his expertise to be a happy cacophony, and was contented with the evening and the enjoyment his food and his setting was providing.

It was because of the level of noise at the tables that Fred Soutter was the only one who heard the screams.

With the desserts served and the coffee and petits fours ready to serve, the chef was preparing to make his customary sortie among the clientele to ensure that they had enjoyed his food and been delighted with their evening. He had no fears on this night that there would be any complaints.

Then he heard the screams. They came from somewhere in the basement. And they were prolonged, high-pitched, hysterical.

Joanne Moss was standing just inside the open doorway of the gents' cloakroom. That in itself was startling, but what lay beyond her was awful enough to banish any petty thoughts of decorum.

The corpse lay on the floor near the urinal, its right leg twisted unnaturally beneath it. The eyes were open, the expression fixed in a permanent ghastly stare of astonishment and agony. The rigid fingers clutched at a chest from which the blood still seeped into the enlarging pool beneath his side.

Patrick Nayland had not died peacefully.

Four

Superintendent John Lambert had been looking forward to a quiet day. The meeting with the District Crime Squad shouldn't take more than an hour. And the one with the National Paedophile Unit had been cancelled because they had a big secret operation planned for today.

He could spend the morning tidying up the paperwork which he hoped would persuade the Crown Prosecution Service that a GBH case was worth taking to court. With a little luck, he might get away early in the afternoon for nine holes of golf at the Ross-on-Wye club. It was bitterly cold, but a weak sun was struggling to rise over the Malvern Hills as he drove towards the police station at Oldford; perhaps the frost would be gone by lunchtime.

The news of the violent death at Soutters Restaurant in Newent was waiting for him when he reached his desk at eight fifteen on the morning of Thursday, the fourteenth of December. He sighed automatically as the prospect of golf vanished more swiftly than the winter sun. But regret was overtaken within seconds by a sharper feeling: excitement.

Every successful CID man must have a strain of the hunter strong within him. Murder is the vilest crime, but still the most stimulating, to a senior detective. Even a veteran like John Lambert felt the familiar half-guilty elation at the prospect of pitting his wits against a murderer. He knew Soutters quite well, having been there for a number of family celebrations. It was such an unlikely place for a murder that his interest quickened further.

He was already a little miffed that he hadn't been called out on the previous night. When he arrived at the restaurant, the photographer was long gone and the scenes of crime team had almost completed its work. Inspector Chris Rushton, his junior by more than twenty years, looked up apprehensively from his notes as his grizzled chief came into Soutters. 'It's murder all right. No question about that. I've given the "suspicious circumstances" go-ahead to the press.'

'Why didn't anyone fetch me out last night?'

'It was late when the news came in. I didn't get here myself until nearly midnight. I'd have called you from here if I thought it right to disturb you. But there wasn't much we

43

could do last night. Some of the people were drunk; all of them were shocked and exhausted. We took brief statements from all of them and sent them home.'

He had all of the phrases ready. They came out like a prepared statement, but because he was nervous, they came a little too quickly. Lambert knew that Rushton had rushed here hoping for a confession, hoping to find someone standing like a conspirator over the bleeding body of Caesar, literally red-handed. A prompt arrest, a murder solved within the hour, a feather in the cap of the eager and efficient young DI Rushton. John Lambert smiled sourly; twenty-five years ago, when he had been a young man carving out a career and a reputation in the CID, he might have behaved in the same way.

That didn't make it right. He said, 'I may be a dinosaur as far as you and the other youngsters are concerned, Chris, but I'm not quite extinct. When there's a crime as serious as this, I like to be in from the beginning. And you needn't fear you're going to embarrass me in someone else's bed if you call after midnight. I'm not a free agent with lots of offers, like you!'

Rushton's smile was as sour as his chief's had been, for very different reasons. John Lambert had referred to his status as a divorced man, but the handsome and well-

44

presented Inspector carried with him an unfortunate stiffness of manner, which meant that he had found it difficult to create new relationships. He said, 'It's not going to be an easy one, this. I thought at first that it would be, but it isn't.' He immediately looked guilty, as if he had confessed that he had sped here last night in search of kudos.

'What did the police surgeon have to say?'

'Not much.' Rushton shrugged, happy to get back to the routine of an investigation. Chris was good at routine. 'The deceased is Patrick Nayland, who was hosting the evening and paying for everything.'

Lambert raised an eyebrow. 'The Nayland who owns that new golf course on the way into Gloucester?'

'That's the man.'

'I know him. Knew him.' Lambert smiled at himself, caught out in the wrong tense, as shocked relatives often were after a death. He tried not to sound as if he were rebuking Rushton again as he said, 'Corpse has been removed, I suppose?'

'Yes, sir.' Chris had embarrassed himself again: he knew that the older man didn't like to be addressed as 'sir' or even 'guv', but the words continued to slip through his lips on occasions. 'The pathologist said there was nothing further to be learned here, so the meat wagon took the body away at about two o'clock this morning.'

Lambert wondered how much sleep his spruce-looking Inspector had enjoyed last night. Youth was a wonderful thing: you had to be careful not to resent it. 'So how did he die?'

'Multiple stab wounds, sir.'

'Weapon?'

'Not discovered, so far.' He narrowly avoided another 'sir', like a man teetering on the edge of a steep drop. 'I've got two uniformed officers searching the surrounding area.'

But both of them knew that if the weapon hadn't turned up by this time, they were unlikely to find it. Lambert had a sneaking feeling that if this hadn't been such a middle-class gathering, Rushton would have insisted on having the guests and their belongings searched before they left. Even at one o'clock in the morning, the rougher clientele of one of the more dubious pubs in Gloucester might not have been allowed to depart so easily.

The Superintendent stood silently for a few minutes in the basement cloakroom where Patrick Nayland had fallen, trying to visualize the scene at the moment of his death. The scenes of crime team was concluding the task of collecting whatever tiny scraps of evidence it could, even from the urinal near which the dead man's head had lain. There would be plenty of DNA evidence around here, thought Lambert sourly, most of it irrelevant and the mass of it, he feared, tending to confuse rather than illuminate this killing.

He climbed the stairs to the restaurant above, feeling irritated anew that he had not been called out last night. Empty chairs seemed now to stare mockingly at him, the open windows seemed to be encouraging secrets to leak away from the tight confines of the intimate eating place into the empty air outside. He would have liked to have been here last night, studying the shocked white faces in the immediate aftermath of this death, trying to determine which if any of them was not as scandalized as it pretended to be.

People were at their most vulnerable and their least guarded in the hours following a killing. Because few murders were revealed as quickly as this one had been, you didn't often get the chance to see the reactions of suspects in this key period. And he had been denied it.

John Lambert was an anachronism among superintendents, in that he didn't direct a murder hunt from behind his desk at the station. He left DI Rushton to collate the vast mountain of information which poured in from a murder-hunt team, whilst he pursued the investigation directly in the world outside. His methods were tolerated, because they had brought results. And he wasn't going to change now, in the last years of his service.

Rushton was a good officer, Lambert told himself, meticulous to a fault. He wouldn't have missed anything last night. It was egomania in him to imagine that he might have picked up what his Inspector had missed. He tried to silence those mischievous cells at the back of his brain which insisted that Rushton was a creature of routine, not imagination, who would have done exactly what the book said he should do last night, but perhaps missed some reaction in one of the diners in the restaurant which he should have picked up as significant.

He knocked on a door and went through to the private living quarters above the restaurant of Fred and Paula Soutter. Paula was white-faced and shocked, though it was now ten hours after the discovery of the body of the man who had hosted what had seemed such a successful evening. Lambert knew the pair, for he had used the restaurant often enough himself. He smiled at Paula Soutter as encouragingly as he could and turned to her husband. 'Sorry about all this, Fred!' The movement of his head took in the three police cars outside, the plastic tapes around the entrance, the 'Closed until Further Notice' sign by the entrance to Soutters.

'Can't be helped.' Fred shrugged shoulders which had had to cope with all manner of culinary crises over the years.

'We'll have you open again as soon as we can. Possibly as soon as this evening, if the scenes of crime team decide they've gathered everything they can from here.'

'Thanks. It's a busy time for us, coming up to Christmas.'

'You'll probably find it helps your bookings in the long term. Murder has a certain grisly glamour, especially for those innocents who've never been in contact with it.'

'I suppose so. The press boys are already clamouring for pictures of our cloakrooms.' Fred Soutter smiled ruefully.

'I wanted to check a couple of things with you. First, are any of your knives missing from the kitchen?'

'No. I've checked again this morning. And all the cutlery used in the restaurant is still here.'

'Right. And could anyone who wasn't a customer have got into the cloakrooms from outside during the evening?'

'No. The outside doors and the entrance to our own accommodation are locked throughout the evening, when the restaurant is open.'

'So that the only way someone from outside the dining party could have been in there is to have secreted himself beforehand, locked himself in a cubicle, and waited three hours or so for his chance to kill.'

'That's impossible.'

'I know it's unlikely, but—'

'Not unlikely. Impossible. One of the things I try to do while Paula is serving the aperitifs and taking the orders at the beginning of the evening is to do a quick inspection tour of the cloakrooms to ensure that things there are exactly as they should be at the beginning of the evening.'

'And you did this last night?'

'I did. After I'd locked all the outer doors. There was no one in any of the cubicles.'

Lambert nodded, pausing for a moment to let the implications sink in to these people who were not used to murder. Then he turned to the white-faced Paula Soutter. 'You were in and out of your restaurant and close to the diners throughout the evening. I realize it's an almost impossible question, but I have to ask it. Did you notice anyone behaving unusually?'

She made herself stop to think before she answered. 'It's almost impossible, as you say, because apart from Patrick Nayland and his wife, I hadn't met any of them before, so I don't know what their normal behaviour would be. But everyone seemed to be enjoying themselves. There was a lot of laughter, even a bit of shouting. The level of noise rose sharply as the evening went on. But that's

50

what we'd expect, what we're used to.'

'This is important. Did you see any sign of an argument between people at the table? In particular, did Patrick Nayland seem to annoy anyone, or to be upset by anyone?'

'No. I've thought about that a lot during the night, in view of what happened. But I can't recall any disagreements at all, serious or trivial. Everything I heard said to Patrick was complimentary, congratulating him on the success of his evening and so on.' Her pallor was mitigated by the beginnings of a blush; obviously the compliments had included the host's choice of venue and the excellence of the fare his guests were enjoying.

Lambert nodded. 'Keep thinking about it, please, both of you. Ring Oldford CID and ask for me personally if anything occurs to you, however tiny it may seem. Because we've just agreed that it was one of the people enjoying themselves so boisterously at the table last night who went down into your basement and perpetrated this brutal killing.'

At Camellia Park on the morning of December the fourteenth, an air of shock hung over the course. Determined golfers, muffled against the cold, tramped over the frozen fairways, searching for white balls which became more than usually elusive against the white of the frost. Most of them had not known the owner of the course personally, but the news of his sensational death ran swiftly round the place.

When they were finally released from Soutters by the police on the night before, Chris Pearson had told the staff that they could take the morning off, but most of them came in to work, albeit a little later than usual. They all said that they felt at a loss at home, that the rhythms of familiar tasks would take their mind off the tragedy which had befallen them. This was at least partially true. But they were driven also by a natural human curiosity, by a fear that if they stayed at home they might miss further developments in the sensational story which had begun so dramatically for them amidst the splendid glass and china of the restaurant.

Alan Fitch was the first one to arrive. He entered the greenkeeper's shed which was his own small fortress five minutes before his normal time of eight o'clock. He had not slept much overnight. There was not much useful work that he could do on the course on a frosty morning, but he knew what he had to do before anything else.

He took some of the oily rags which he had used in his maintenance of the course machinery and carried them out behind the shed, to a spot at the edge of the course which they used for the occasional bonfire. He built a swift pyramid of dry twigs over the rags, as he had done scores of times before. As if acknowledging his expertise, they burst into a swift, cheerful, blaze.

He looked round to make sure that he was unobserved before he added the stuff he had brought from home in his plastic bag. No one was in sight, not even any of the scattering of hardy golfers he had noted on the first three holes. He watched for a few seconds, saw the flames lap eagerly around what he had fed to them. Then, sure that the fire was established, he piled on the broken fencing panels they had replaced by the Gloucester road and the browning brambles they had cleared from beneath the trees on the ninth.

The flames disappeared for a time beneath an impressive column of smoke, which rose straight and high in the still, cold air. It was like the funeral pyres he had seen in India long ago, which had so impressed him as a young merchant seaman. That image seemed now to belong to another age, to another life which he had long forsaken. For the first time in years, he found himself wishing he was back on a ship, on the other side of the world.

Alan Fitch was not an imaginative man, so it did not strike him as of any great significance that the image which had come to him so powerfully was one of death.

Presently, the flames got a hold on the brambles and his fire raged so fiercely that he had to stand back from it. He watched the flames appreciatively, curling like angry tongues around the material he piled steadily around the centre of his blaze, dangerous, destructive, cleansing.

'I thought we were leaving those brambles until the new year. Letting them dry out for a while.'

Fitch felt himself twitch violently at the words, as if he had for a moment lost control of his movements. He thought he had been keeping a wary eye behind him for any intrusion, but his concentration upon feeding the bonfire had betrayed him. Now even the familiar tones of Barry Hooper had made him start like a guilty thing. He said roughly, 'You shouldn't creep up on a man like that! Nearly made me jump out of my skin, you did!'

'Sorry, boss. You made an early start. I thought we weren't coming in until this afternoon.'

'Why're you here, then?' Fitch heard the harshness in his voice; he was still shaken by the younger man's intrusion upon his private world.

'Couldn't sleep, could I?' Barry Hooper began to drag more of the dead brambles towards the fire. He had apparently noticed nothing that was odd in his mentor's bearing. 'I thought we were going to leave this stuff for another two or three weeks.'

He treated Fitch's pronouncements as if they were some sacred gospel. At that moment, Alan wished his helper didn't remember things so precisely.

He said carefully, 'There isn't much else we could do in this weather. And it's nice to have a bit of warmth on a bitter day like this.' He pushed his fork into the dead foliage at the edge of the fire, and it responded like a living thing, bursting into a seven-foot-high cone of orange flame, causing the pair to step back hastily away from the heat.

They worked in silence for a few minutes, feeding the blaze, gathering in stray scraps of the dead brambles which were now disappearing so quickly. Then Fitch gestured towards the distant clubhouse, invisible behind his greenkeeper's shed. 'Any news?'

'No. Not that I picked up, anyway. Mr Pearson says the police will want to speak to us all individually.'

'Aye. They said that last night.' The words came impatiently, like a rebuke to the younger man's forgetfulness.

Their exchanges were edgy and spasmodic throughout the morning. Barry Hooper noticed it, but he put it down to the shock from last night. That must be affecting all of them; he could certainly feel it still in himself. He was glad when it was lunchtime and they could boil their little kettle in the shed and settle down with their sandwiches.

But even here, they did not become the relaxed pair he was accustomed to. Fitch said suddenly, 'Why do you keep looking towards the door?'

'Was I doing that? I hadn't realized it. I suppose I was wondering when the police will come. Makes you nervous, doesn't it, something like this? I've never been involved in anything like it before.'

'And you think I have?' Fitch's voice was abrasive, accusatory.

'No, I know you haven't.' Barry wanted to say that it was just that Fitch had so much more experience of life in general than he had himself, that he looked to him to be able to cope with anything. But the right words wouldn't come and he said nothing. It was consoling, in a way, that even the man he had come to regard as unshakeable could be affected by something like this.

Barry Hooper had the sense to say very little during the rest of their break. He was glad he had brought the *Sun* in with him, and he pretended now to immerse himself in its contents. When Fitch eventually stood up, he rose with him, obediently and automatically.

'Stay where you are, lad.' Brian Fitch realized how rasping his tone sounded, and made an effort to be friendly. 'You're entitled

56

to another ten minutes yet. Stay here and make us another cup of tea, and I'll go and check on our fire. Just to make sure it's safe, you see.'

He wished he hadn't added the last phrase. It hung unnecessary and artificial in the cold, still air.

He went outside and over to the fire, which had almost burnt itself out. A thin line of white smoke rose straight and unruffled above the grey-white ashes. He raked in a few stray strands of unburned material from around the edges, checked that Barry had not followed him out, and examined carefully the patch which had been at the centre of his fierce blaze.

It was satisfactory. There was no sign of the trousers or the shirt he had put there as the fire developed.

Five

Lambert took Detective Sergeant Bert Hook with him to visit the widow of the dead man.

It was always difficult, the interview with the spouse of the deceased. You had to be respectful of their grief and try not to intrude more than was strictly necessary into the domestic trauma which follows a violent death. Yet the spouse was always the first suspect to be considered in a suspicious death: the statistics dictated that it should be so.

Bert Hook with his stolid, village-bobby exterior, his immediate response to what people were feeling, his anxiety to prevent unnecessary suffering, was a reassuring companion in circumstances like this. The fact that his calm exterior concealed a keen intelligence, a profound experience of human folly, a sharp observation of behaviour, was a bonus of quite another kind. Hook often caught people off their guard.

Lambert had learned long ago not to trust appearances in the aftermath of death. Some

58

people controlled grief better than others. Those who appeared controlled, sometimes even uncaring, could dissolve into paroxysms of anguish when they were afforded the privacy they needed for their mourning.

Mrs Liza Nayland seemed to be in control of whatever emotions she felt. She wore no make-up and her fair colouring should have readily revealed any extremes of grief. She was forty-four years old, dark blonde, blue eyed, and no doubt in happier circumstances an attractive woman. Now her face was pale and drawn, showing the lines of middle age which cosmetics might have concealed. The skin around her eyes was puffy with the tears she had shed through the night.

She took them into the lounge of a comfortable detached house, offered them refreshment as if they had been respectable middle-class visitors, not detectives. I'm almost like the vicar, thought Bert Hook, wondering what his boisterous thirteen-year-old twin sons would make of that image. Bert Hook was a Barnardo's boy; he knew a lot about vicars and well-meaning middle-class ladies: they had seemed in his adolescence to be deciding the path of his life for him.

'How long had you been married to Mr Nayland?' said Lambert, when he had got the preliminary apologies for intruding at a time like this out of the way.

'Ten years. It was a second marriage, for both of us.' She said it as though it was an unpleasant fact that had best be got out of the way at the outset.

'Was he in touch with his first wife?'

'No. Not for years. There were no children from the marriage and the settlement was agreed at the time of the divorce, so there was no need for them to meet.'

'Someone from our team will be contacting the first Mrs Nayland, nevertheless. She needs to be eliminated from the inquiry. I understand that you also have a first husband who is still around.'

'Yes. I can't see how this is relevant to your investigation.'

Lambert gave her his most apologetic smile. 'Neither can I, at this point, Mrs Nayland. But even at this early stage, we know that this is murder. And murder is unique among crimes, in that the victim cannot speak for himself. We have to build up a picture of him, of his virtues and his faults, which he is not able to provide himself. We shall ask all sorts of intimate questions, of other people as well as you. The information which is relevant to this murder will emerge eventually. None of us can decide what is relevant today.'

She nodded impatiently; the fingers twisting the engagement and wedding rings on her left hand were the only sign of agitation.

'All right. Yes, I'm divorced. And unlike Patrick, who never wished to see his first wife again, I still see my first husband occasionally. My daughter wishes to keep in touch with her father, naturally.'

'Thank you. Did your daughter resent your second marriage?'

She felt her pulses racing, told herself firmly that she had known this would come up. She forced herself to smile into the long face and the grey eyes, which seemed all the time to be seeing far beyond the words she was giving him. It was a bleak little smile, but that was surely appropriate for a widow. 'There were a few problems, yes. Nothing too serious. I should imagine they were quite normal, for a teenage girl having to adjust to her mother discarding her father in favour of another man. But you will understand that this is my own and my daughter's only experience of such things.'

It was dismissive, and Lambert thought too well phrased to be thought up on the spot, but he let it go. You couldn't push a grieving spouse too far, and they would be talking to this daughter of hers in due course. He looked steadily at the woman in the dark-blue dress with her hands clasped together in her lap, studying her as closely as ever as he said, 'But your own relationship with your husband was entirely a happy one?'

61

'Yes. I'm glad you've given me the opportunity to emphasize that. Entirely a happy one.'

The repetition of his words sounded curiously formal, curiously controlled, for someone deep in grief. Yet it was spoken with such dignity that Lambert was inclined to believe her. He said, 'Forgive me, but I have to ask. All marriages have disagreements. Most of them, indeed, have major rows, from time to time. Have you had any serious differences with your husband over the last few months?'

'No. And you needn't apologize for asking. I know the wife is always the chief suspect in murder cases.'

He smiled, enjoying her frankness. 'I prefer to state it as "the first person to be eliminated from the list of suspects".'

She wondered if she could ask him if he proposed to eliminate her. Instead, she said, 'And have you a lengthy list in this case?'

Lambert smiled at her again. This woman was shrewd enough and composed enough to have worked this one out for herself. 'Our list appears to be confined to the people who were in Soutters Restaurant last night, Mrs Nayland. There was no outside access to the cloakroom where your husband died.'

She gave a little, involuntary shudder, as the image of the spot where Patrick had fallen flashed briefly before her again. They had tried to stop her going to him, but she had thrust through them, had cradled his head briefly in her arms for a moment before hysteria took over and they dragged her away. Chris Pearson, it had been, who had shaken her back into silence and the dull realization that this had really happened.

She nodded at those grey eyes, which seemed never to blink as they studied her. 'One of us, then. I wonder who would want to do such an awful thing. Who would want to cut Patrick down like that, on an evening of celebration, which he had devised and paid for, which everyone seemed to be enjoying?' She let her bitterness come out as she lingered over the last phrases.

There was a pause before Bert Hook came in and said, 'No doubt someone had a motive to do this. But motive isn't always the first thing we look for, Mrs Nayland. We always begin by considering who had the opportunity to commit a crime. In this case, we know everyone who had the opportunity. The motive may be less obvious. It may mean that we can't discount people who were not present in the restaurant last night.'

'I don't follow that.'

'I mean that anyone with a grievance might have employed someone who was at your table to commit murder for him.'

'That doesn't seem very likely.'

'I agree. It's unlikely. But it's by no means

impossible. People get themselves into all kinds of financial trouble, for instance. Desperate men – and sometimes desperate women – can be persuaded to do astonishing things, if they are assured that it will get them out of a financial hole.'

She could see that, when she thought about it. Patrick was a methodical man, and that might have been the way he would have gone about it, if he had ever needed a murder. She pulled herself up short. How could she be thinking about him in this way, on the day after his death? It must be something connected with the shock everyone talked about. She said, 'I'm learning things about crime, aren't I? Things I'm not sure I want to know!'

There was something brittle about her, thought Lambert, as if once they broke the thin china of her composure she would spill into hysterics. He said, 'Have you any idea who killed your husband last night?'

'No.'

'It might help us if you speculate. It needn't go any further than these four walls, if it proves unfounded.'

'No. I've thought about it a lot since it happened. I haven't come up with a killer for you yet.'

'I see. Please continue to think about it, then. We shall be interested to hear about your thoughts, in confidence.'

'I will, Superintendent. I'm as anxious to see the man who killed Patrick like that put behind bars as you are.'

'Or the woman.'

'Or the woman, as you say. But I shall be surprised if it was a woman who did this to Patrick.'

She looked for a reaction in the long face, but Lambert seemed totally impassive. He said, 'I understand last night's occasion was designed to celebrate ten years of development at Camellia Park. As the owner of the course and the director of policy, your husband must have made tough and unpopular decisions at times. Such decisions tend to make enemies. Do you know of anyone who had a serious grievance against your husband?'

'No. The place has been a success. It's been expanding ever since Patrick took the chance and put his money into it. He said there aren't too many staffing problems whilst that is happening. The real problems come when you have to cut back on something.'

That was true enough. When someone built an empire, other people went up with him, and most people were happy. Lambert had seen it happen, even in the police force. There was one area, however, which often caused resentment. 'Was anyone passed over for a promotion he felt he should have had?'

'No. Not as far as I know. And the kind

of post available in a small organization like that is hardly worthy of multiple stab wounds.'

'I agree. But we have to explore every possibility at present. This killing has all the signs of an unbalanced mind. You might be surprised how much some people brood on small injustices, until in their minds they develop into something much larger.'

'I've seen some of that. I worked in an office with five other women.'

Lambert couldn't suppress a small smile. He'd never have dared to say anything as politically incorrect as that. Then he said seriously, 'I agree with you that other passions can be more powerful than ambition. So I now have to ask you if you know of any relationships which might have had a bearing on this death.'

She found herself wanting to fly at this calm inquisitor, to scratch the flesh on the gaunt face. She must be much more on edge than she thought. Forcing a calmness into her tongue, she tried to be dismissive, but found herself sounding unexpectedly prim as she said, 'You mean, was Patrick conducting an affair with someone, was there a jealous husband involved? No, of course there wasn't.'

Lambert, listening to the manner as well as the substance of the denial, thought that maybe the lady did protest too much. He

66

said, 'How did you meet your husband, Mrs Nayland?'

She wondered if she could refuse to answer, reject the question as the irrelevance she knew it to be. But that would only heighten the man's interest, and he would pursue it elsewhere. He had already indicated that someone would be in touch with the first wife. She said icily, 'I've already told you I worked in an office. Patrick was an executive there. In due course, I became his personal assistant: I believe that he asked to have me assigned to him. Then it was the old story of the boss having an affair with his secretary, if you like. Except that Patrick was already separated. I was the one who was playing away.'

'So there was resentment from the man who was then your husband?'

She forced a smile when she felt like attacking him. 'You'd be barking up the wrong tree there. Malcolm – that's my first husband – certainly wasn't happy at the time. He's now happily remarried, with two small children. He wouldn't want me back if I came wrapped in diamonds.'

Lambert said quietly, 'Thank you. I apologize again for the personal nature of some of our questions, but, as I said, we have to build up a picture of the victim; it usually helps to indicate who might have killed him.'

It was Bert Hook, sitting quiet and watchful, making the occasional note in his note-book, who now looked up and said, 'How would you describe your daughter's relation-ship with the victim at the time of his death, Mrs Nayland?'

She had thought the question would come if it came at all from the tall man whose grey eyes stayed so disconcertingly upon her face through everything she said. Instead, it was this stolid, slightly overweight Sergeant with the curiously innocent features, like those of a small boy imposed on a middle-aged man, who had asked it.

Liza Nayland delivered the words she had prepared during the morning. 'Michelle had a few problems in the early stages of our relationship. It would have been surprising if she hadn't.'

'Yes, you mentioned that earlier. And in our experience, it would be surprising if those problems didn't persist in the years which followed. How would you say Michelle felt about your husband at the time of his death?'

'They were perfectly happy with each other. Michelle had realized that my happi-ness was bound up with Patrick, and had accepted the situation. We had a happy Sun-day evening meal together, only a few days ago. I'm sorry to disappoint you, Sergeant.'

Hook was too experienced to rise to that. He made a note in his notebook, face as inscrutable as a boyish Buddha. It struck him that if you had to note a meal in a household as being happy, there were problems.

The two veteran CID men drove away from the house in the Herefordshire village in the companionable silence which came from working for many years together. They had travelled a good two miles before Hook said, 'She was holding something back, wasn't she? I'm not quite sure what it was yet, but she wasn't being totally honest.'

There wasn't much work for Joanne Moss on the day after the murder. She knew there wouldn't be much demand for her food on a morning like this, when only the hardiest of golfers tackled the frostbound acres of Camellia Park.

But these intrepid souls were rewarded eventually by a thin white sun, and by midday the whiteness had melted from the surface of the course. The men – women were far too sensible to venture out in such Arctic conditions – were jovial when they came into the little clubhouse, as if they had earned the thanks of the world for their bravery in the face of the elements. And they were hungry, eager for the toasted sandwiches, bacon butties and other simple but tasty fare which Joanne could supply from her spotless kitchen.

This little period of brisk activity lasted scarcely more than an hour. Joanne would have wished for it to be longer, for activity meant that she had to concentrate hard on the simple manual tasks of food preparation. That took her mind off the things she did not want to think about, the things which set her mind racing along channels she did not wish it to explore.

But very soon, this brisk activity died away to nothing. Joanne tried to string out the work, taking longer than usual over small tasks, like a machine which runs briefly after it has been switched off. Yet suddenly, she knew that she must move quickly. The urgency of what she must do burst like a wall of water into her brain, flooding away her lethargy, filling her with a sudden urgency which was the very opposite of what she had felt only moments before.

It showed how febrile her brain was, how racing were her emotions, she told herself, as she hurried to her car and drove away from Camellia Park without a backward glance, without even hearing the cheerful farewell called to her by the last of the golfers in the car park.

When she opened the door of her flat, she saw it as she had not seen it for many months, perhaps not since the moment when she had first viewed it and decided to buy it. She saw it not as a home, but as a

70

place which might tell other people things about her, which might reveal more of herself than she wanted to show to these strangers coming into her life. A place which might – the word had sprung into her mind before she could reject it – incriminate her.

Joanne even looked round the place to assure herself that no one had been here, that no one had carried knowledge about her away from the place before she could prevent it. She knew that the idea was stupid, that the people she feared needed search warrants and the paraphernalia of the law behind them. Nevertheless, she checked the beaker on the side of the sink, checked the familiar ornaments and photographs on sideboard and mantelpiece, even went through into her bedroom and checked that the nightdress lay across the pillow exactly as she had left it when she had left the room with her mind racing so madly a few hours previously.

Only a few hours! The time seemed to stretch itself into days; it seemed already weeks since that sudden scream and the shocked faces coming to terms with the unthinkable last night. And yet she could have given no clear and detailed account of what she had done in the time since then. Her movements, her reactions, even her thoughts, seemed today to have a dream-like quality about them, as if she was watching another person doing the things she did.

She shook herself back to reality. Quite literally shook herself, in front of the mirror in the small hall, wanting to feel the vigour of the movement in her shoulders and hips. There was nothing unreal about what she had to do now. She must be at her coolest and most methodical. The minds she was pitting herself against would be like that; they wouldn't be battered by emotions, as she was, but clinical, logical, ruthlessly assessing whatever they saw.

Having shaken herself, Joanne forced a smile at herself in the mirror, rehearsing the part she must play, telling herself that her years in amateur dramatics must give her an advantage. Perhaps the whole untidy collection of parts she had played had been a preparation for this real one which had been so abruptly thrust upon her. On with the motley. Let the clown smile. Let the tears be kept for private release; their public display was an indulgence she could not afford.

She took a black plastic dustbin bag from the cupboard under the sink and went rapidly through the flat. She was surprised when it came to it how well her brain worked. It was as if action eased her mind into its normal efficiency, and she gathered items as if she carried an unwritten list within her brain.

She had not been conscious of any such list

earlier, but now she knew exactly the items she needed, and she moved through the rooms as methodically as a cleaner following a weekly routine. She moved the photographs and the two other items which were on display first. Then she went to the drawers and cupboards, treating each room methodically, surprising herself with her knowledge of exactly the items she wanted to remove.

Joanne was pleased with the way her mind worked: she might be moving like an automaton, but it was an automaton directed by a cool brain. It was only when her task was almost complete, when she was retracing her steps through the five rooms of the flat and trying desperately to think of items she might have forgotten, that panic burst suddenly upon her hyperactive mind. She began to listen for the ring of the bell, to run her eyes frantically along shelves and table and kitchen units to search out the one object she must have overlooked.

This was like being in a Kafka novel, waiting for the faceless forces of the state to intrude upon her small and private world, to discover the small, intimate, forgotten things which would tell the bureaucracy of the state more about her life than she wanted it to know.

But there was no ring at the bell, no watching eyes as she peered right and left from the door before taking her dustbin bag of evidence out to the car. How small and light it felt. How slight were the remembrances of emotions which had been so fierce, which had changed the pattern of her life.

Joanne's plan was simple enough. She knew the area of Gloucester where the bin men operated on Thursdays, for she had lived there herself before she bought her flat. She would simply drive around until she saw the Biffa lorry, with its steel jaws at the rear, which ground whatever was fed into them into merciful oblivion. She would then drop her own small dustbin bag into those jaws and watch a section of her life disappear for ever.

The finality of that would be satisfying, in its own way: she knew she needed to re-assure herself by witnessing the physical destruction of the evidence. If she merely dumped the bag for collection, she would be afraid that someone would investigate it and discover her secrets, even at the eleventh hour.

There was an interlude of black comedy, in which she drove round street after suburban street without locating the familiar lorry. She began to wonder if the rotas had been changed, or if the men had started early and already finished for the day. But they couldn't start so early, not at this time of the year when there was not full daylight until

74

eight o'clock. A kind of panic began to gnaw at her, as vista after quiet vista revealed no Biffa lorry.

Then, just when she was ready to give up, when she was wondering where she could most safely leave the bag she certainly couldn't take home with her, she saw the shiny black bags piled at the corner of the street ahead, twenty or more of them. She almost laughed aloud like a child at the sight, her elation reminding her again just how much on edge she was. The men had collected the bags from individual residences and piled them there; the lorry could not be far away.

She saw it when she reached the corner, moving slowly along the road within a foot of the kerb, the powerful motor of the destructive mechanism at its rear drowning the noise of its engine. She drove past it carefully as it came towards her, parked her car on the opposite side of the road, and slid from the driving seat with the black plastic bag in her hand.

She would wait for her moment, wait until the men feeding the bags into the maw of the monster at the rear of the lorry went off to collect another pile of bags in the next street, and then fling her own small contribution into extinction. She wanted to disguise herself in some way from any observers, was tempted for a moment to adopt a limp. Then she remembered a production of *Oh What a Lovely War!* she had been in years ago, where the boys had been asked to simulate wounds as they came away from the front in the 1914–18 war. They had all decided to limp with the right foot; their ragged company had even limped in step with each other, and the rehearsal had collapsed into hilarity. She grinned at the remembrance of it, and decided she had much better walk naturally.

'Get rid of that for you, m'dear!'

She started like a guilty thing, feeling her heart leap into her mouth, unable because of that to frame the words of a reply.

He was a large, cheerful black man, the Gloucestershire accent falling oddly from his broad lips. He smiled at her, his broad white teeth seeming suddenly to fill the whole of his face. She became aware that he was holding his hand out to take her small burden from her.

She found her voice at last. 'It's all right, thanks. I can chuck it in myself. It's – it's an unofficial one really. I'm not from round here.' She was telling him things, when she wanted to withhold information, not spread it. He was surely harmless, with his broad and innocent black face, his cheery helpfulness. But other, more sinister, people might talk to him, other people might wheedle from him any information she volunteered now.

'Not allowed, that, m'dear. Public not to feed our mechanical dog, in case they injure themselves.' He laughed at the absurdity of that notion. His chuckles seemed to Joanne to echo up and down the street, calling attention to the strange couple, the powerful black man with the boxer's build and the slim middle-class Englishwoman with the dustbin bag held incongruously in her hand behind her.

He reached forward, took the bag gently but insistently from her. For an awful moment, she thought he was going to investigate the contents. But he merely turned and walked to the corner. When he was a good ten yards from the pile of bags, she caught her breath as he flung her own slight contribution onto the top of the pile with practised expertise.

He looked back at her with a reassuring smile, and Joanne Moss lifted her hand briefly in acknowledgement of his service. She sat in her car and watched the slow progress of the Biffa lorry, knowing she could not leave without the physical evidence of the destruction of her past.

Two young men who seemed little more than boys flung the pile of bags into the steadily churning steel jaws at the back of the lorry, moving with such sudden swiftness that she was not sure which was hers in the hail of bags which suddenly peppered the machine. Two minutes later, the Biffa lorry drove past her stationary car, its steel machinery still turning steadily at the rear, though everything fed into it at the corner of the street had now disappeared.

It was done. A section of her life had been suddenly obliterated. A section which had held much happiness before the final brutal sadness which had shattered it.

Joanne Moss felt drained and empty rather than relieved.

Six

They were going to have another cold night. Bert Hook could see the frost crystals forming on the hedges already as they drove through the lanes towards Cheltenham. It was seven o'clock on Thursday evening, exactly twenty-four hours since the guests had assembled in Soutters Restaurant for their fatal celebration.

Chris Pearson looked slightly nervous when he opened the solid door of the house in the old village and faced them. There was nothing remarkable about that: murder investigations made even the most innocent of people nervous. It would be the only time in this exchange when he showed any trace of apprehension.

He looked at them for a moment, their faces lit by the light from the hall behind him, and said, 'You'd better come in.' Then, as if he realized that sounded grudging and ungracious, he added as he led them through the hall and into a dining room at the front of the house, 'You're working late on the case.'

79

Lambert smiled as he took the chair Pearson indicated to him in the small, neat, room. It had prints of Middle Eastern scenes upon the wall, possibly reflecting Pearson's Army service, though there were no pictures of the South Atlantic. It had the air of a room little used, with its neatly set dining-room furniture, its sideboard with family photographs, its display cabinet of china and cut glass. The Superintendent said, 'We work all kinds of hours when we're on a murder case. It makes its own rules, murder. And even chief constables tend to forget about the overtime budget, when the media get excited about a murder case.'

Pearson nodded. 'Has to be solved quickly, doesn't it? I seem to remember some statistic about most successful murder investigations being concluded within seven days.'

'Statistics can be misleading at times. That one is a little warped by the number of domestic killings, where we usually have a confession within a few hours. Still, we like to interview the people who were close to a murder as soon as possible after the death, whilst their memories of what happened remain clear and vivid.'

'Physically close, in this case. I suppose I wasn't more than a few yards from where Pat Nayland was killed, but I haven't a clue why anyone should have wanted to kill him.' His voice was calm, his suntanned skin seemed odd amidst the pale faces of December. His deep-set eyes were at once watchful and unrevealing.

Bert Hook flicked his notebook to a new page and said, 'You will understand that everyone we have seen so far has expressed similar sentiments, Mr Pearson, and I have no doubt we shall hear the same thing from all who were at last night's meal. But one of the people at least will be lying. One of them is a murderer.'

Chris Pearson looked from one to the other of the earnest faces confronting him. 'I suppose there can be no doubt of that?'

'None whatsoever,' said Lambert quietly.

'It's just that it seems so incredible.'

'You find it so? I was hoping you might have some ideas which would help us. We know almost nothing about the victim, as yet, whereas you had worked closely with him for ten years.'

Pearson looked for a moment as if he was about to take offence. Then, as if recognizing the logic of the thought, he said slowly, 'I suppose I did know Pat pretty well. Probably as well as anyone outside his family.'

'Then you can help us. You're the first person outside the family that we've spoken to.'

'Apart from the questioning conducted last night by Detective Inspector Rushton and his officers.'

'Apart from those short formal exchanges, yes.' They noted the precision of his correction, the fact that he remembered the name of Rushton, even from the chaos following last night's sensational discovery. Lambert, switching his ground suddenly in the hope of discomforting this citadel of calm, said, 'You were a regular Army officer, I believe, before you took up your present post.'

'No. I served in the Royal Artillery, but I wasn't commissioned. I was a warrant officer.'

'And you served with distinction, it seems. You were commended for your actions in the Falklands War.'

'It was a strange war, that. I'm not sure how history will pronounce upon it. At the time, you did what you had to do, as a serving soldier.'

'Did you come across Patrick Nayland during your service?'

'No.' Then, as if trying to mitigate the bluntness of this prompt negative, Pearson said by way of explanation, 'The Army is a big organization, even in these days of cutbacks. Unless you're in the same regiment, you're not likely to meet other individuals.'

'When was the first time you met Patrick Nayland?'

'When I responded to his advertisement for a Manager of the new golfing enterprise he'd started with his Army gratuity. It was not then known as Camellia Park. We began with two large fields and a bulldozer. We decided on the name about six months later. The post was on offer at the right time, in the last month of my Army service, when I was wondering what to do with the rest of my life. It was a modest enough development, and financially I could have done better. But the idea of being in on the ground floor, of helping to create something new, appealed to me.'

He had given them far more than he had been asked for, had sounded faintly defensive about applying for the job as Nayland's right-hand man. Lambert wondered if he had wanted to distract attention from his Army service. But he had no reason for returning to that, having been told that Pearson had never met the dead man in those years. He said, 'How would you describe your relationship with Patrick Nayland?'

Pearson looked him straight in the eye, recognizing the challenge in the question. He gave the tiniest shrug of his broad shoulders before he said, 'Excellent. I've no means of comparing it with similar situations, since this is my only important civilian job. But it was a small enterprise, and we worked closely together. There haven't been many things we've disagreed on over the last ten years; when we did, Patrick's view prevailed: it was his money which was financing things after all.'

'Can you give us an example of such a disagreement?'

Anger flashed briefly across the weather-beaten features, suggesting in that instant that Chris Pearson would not be a good enemy to make. But his face was impassive again in an instant, his voice perfectly calm as he said, 'You're barking up the wrong tree if you're looking for bitterness between Pat and me, Superintendent. The most radical divergence in our views came about eighteen months ago, when I felt that we should be looking to add a further nine holes to the course, to give ourselves an eighteen-hole layout. Pat thought we should concentrate on improving what we had, on making the most of what he called the "cheap and cheerful" golf market.'

'And his view prevailed.'

Pearson nodded calmly. 'As was only right and proper. As I say, it was his money which was financing the enterprise.'

'And you say you took such disappointments in your stride?'

'I did indeed. Patrick had a perfectly valid point of view. It will take at least ten years to say who was right on that one. But, even if I'd felt very strongly that he was wrong, it wouldn't have affected our relationship. I think it helped that we were both used to chains of command, from our Army days. We both knew and accepted that Pat would make the ultimate decisions.'

Policemen have suspicious minds; it is a result of prolonged exposure to the seamier parts of human nature. Lambert wondered if Pearson was being rather too insistent about the easy way these two senior men had worked together, if their relationship had in fact been more strained than he was allowing. Perhaps other people who had worked with the pair would clarify that issue, in due course.

He said, 'Would you give us your account of exactly what happened last night at Soutters Restaurant, please?'

This time Pearson's shrug was obvious and unhurried, as if he wished to show that he was not at all worried by his part in these dramatic events. 'There isn't much to tell. We were all enjoying an excellent evening. As a matter of fact, I was just thinking how well it had gelled, how worthwhile an enterprise it had been in bringing the staff together, when we heard Joanne Moss screaming. We all rushed downstairs and – well, you know what we found. Joanne screaming in the open doorway of the gents' loo and Pat lying dead behind her.'

'What happened next?'

'It was all rather confused. We could hardly believe our eyes. It was so unexpected that I remember wondering for a second whether it was some elaborate practical joke. One look at Pat soon got rid of that idea.'

'Did anyone touch the body?'

'Yes. Liza Nayland cradled him in her arms and tried to revive him. I detached her, as gently as I could, and checked the carotid artery to make sure that he was dead. That was a formality; you could see from a glance at the face that this was a dead man.'He spoke as calmly as if he had been a doctor, steeled to the everyday experience of death. Perhaps it was his military experiences which had given him this quality. He was the only one they had spoken to so far who did not seem to be deeply shocked by this death, but his calmness could be masking his deeper feelings.

Lambert said, 'You are very much the same age as Mr Nayland was.'

Pearson nodded. 'Pat was in fact about two years older than me. I think he was forty-nine; I'm forty-seven. We had a common military experience to draw on, and perhaps that helped us to think on similar lines. I'm certainly glad I took the post of General Manager ten years ago, and I think Pat was happy with his appointment.'

'And what will happen now that Mr Nayland has been removed so abruptly?'

The deeply furrowed brow darkened for a moment, as if he was angered by the directness of the question. 'I don't know. It's too early to say. This death has stopped all of us in our tracks. Camellia Park is prospering, and I imagine Mrs Nayland will want to retain possession of it and see it go forward, even if she isn't as "hands-on" as Pat was. But obviously I haven't spoken to her about that. I've hardly considered it myself. We're all too shaken by Pat's murder to think straight at the moment.'

That seemed a rather belated recognition of the shock and grief that Nayland's death had brought to him. But perhaps he had been merely striving to be objective, to stifle his personal feelings in the interest of helping the police inquiry.

'When did you last see Mr Nayland alive?' Lambert saw no reason to apologize for the bluntness of the question, since this man seemed to pride himself on being so much in control of his emotions. He would normally have started his questioning with the details of the previous night, but he had adopted a more oblique approach to the meeting with this watchful and composed man, in the hope that he might reveal a little more of himself.

Chris Pearson smiled grimly. 'At the table. Smiling, laughing, enjoying himself, as the host of a successful evening. But everyone is going to tell you that. Presumably one of us will be lying.'

Lambert gave him an answering smile of

acknowledgement, as if he realized an opponent worthy of his steel. It was in fact a surprising relief to be able to speak so openly to this balanced figure, after having to pick his way so carefully through the emotions of the grieving widow, controlled though Liza Nayland had seemed to be. 'At least one person will be lying, yes, Mr Pearson. Perhaps more than one: we can't rule out the idea that there may have been collusion in this killing, until we know more of the facts surrounding it. Did you visit the cloakroom yourself during the evening?'

He fired the question in abruptly again, but again Pearson showed no sign of being ruffled by it. 'I think we all did, at some time during the evening. It was a very pleasant and relaxed meal, and as a result quite protracted. There was some hilarity also about the rather risqué decorations in the toilets, and I remember the ladies in particular felt that they had to go and inspect the illustrations on the walls of their loo.'

'How long before Mr Nayland's death was your visit to the basement?'

'I should say about half an hour before the *discovery* of the body. I do not have the technical expertise to say how long Pat had been dead before I got to him.'

How absolute the knave is, thought Lambert ruefully. He smiled, recognizing that it was the kind of correction he might have

88

made himself. 'Half an hour, you say. How sure are you about that?'

'I'm not at all sure. It's an estimate I made this morning. None of us thought such things would be important, at the time.'

'No doubt other people will be able to confirm the time. Have you had any serious disagreement with Mr Nayland over the last few weeks?'

This time Pearson's smile was a grim one, and there was something like contempt in the deep-set dark eyes. 'Why not just come out and ask me if I killed Pat? It's what you mean, isn't it?'

'If you had killed him, you would deny it, no doubt as vehemently as the most innocent person at the table last night. I'm asking you if you'd any serious area of resentment with your employer.'

Again there was the briefest flash of anger across the tanned features, so fleeting that it would have been missed by anyone studying them less intently than Lambert. 'You're probing to find why I might have killed Pat.'

'I'm trying to find why he died. Either someone had something to gain by his death, or someone hated him enough to drive a knife into his chest repeatedly. We shall explore these areas with everyone who was in that restaurant last night, until we find who was holding that knife.'

'All right. I accept that, of course. It's

difficult to find myself as a murder suspect, that's all. It's never happened to me before.'

'I expect that will be the case with everyone who was at Soutters last night. Do you know of anyone there who had reason to dislike or resent Mr Nayland?'

He hesitated. Whether that was because he was giving due weight to the importance of the question, or because he was considering whether to hold something back, Lambert found it impossible to tell. He was a cool, composed subject, this one. Neither he nor Hook was sure yet how sorry he was about this death, or whether he regretted it at all.

Eventually, Pearson said, 'Pat was a good friend to me. He was a good employer to everyone, from me down to our latest recruit, Barry Hooper. As far as I know, we are all happy in our posts. I can't see why anyone should have wanted him dead. If you consider the situation now, we are less certain of those jobs than we were before he died.'

Bert Hook had not spoken since the first minute of the interview. Now, responding to a tiny nod from Lambert, he shut his notebook and said, 'Please go on thinking about this death, Mr Pearson. If anything occurs to you which may be of significance, please speak to us immediately, in confidence, at Oldford Police Station.'

They were safely in the car, negotiating the

unlit Gloucestershire lanes, before Hook said to Lambert, 'I notice that he said Nayland was a good friend and employer. He didn't say anything about his qualities as a husband and stepfather.'

Sitting with the sandwich and his mug of tea, John Lambert's face had what his wife called 'his murder look'. Christine had grown used to it over the years.

It was a look which reflected suppressed, half-guilty elation. Only the major crimes brought that air to him, and even among the major ones the only certain trigger was murder. The hunter is an essential part of the make-up of all CID men; it was most apparent in her husband when he was faced with a homicide which had no obvious solution, when he was pitting his brains and deploying his team against someone who had perpetrated the oldest and direst of crimes.

A generation ago, when they had argued about his work and he had buckled it about him like some secret armour, Christine Lambert had hated this quality in him, this grisly fascination with the darkest part of the human mind. She understood it better now. It still frightened her a little to see him so animated by evil, but she recognized it as a necessary part of his detective equipment. What she saw now was the same old elation, combined with a new factor that had only intruded in the last two or three years: fatigue. She had thought last year that he would be retired by now, but his Chief Constable had succeeded in getting his service extended, 'in view of his outstanding record in bringing criminals to justice'. The *Gloucester Citizen* had rolled out that phrase; it had added to John's already considerable local reputation and caused him no little embarrassment.

But watching him now, apparently relaxed in front of the television, she saw the lines about his eyes etched more deeply than she could ever remember them before, the corners of his mouth drooping downwards. He still had a good head of grizzled hair, but the back of his head was streaked increasingly with grey. Christine watched him as diligently as she had watched her children all those years ago, as fondly as she now watched her grandchildren. Presently his chin dipped, as she had known it would, and he drowsed in front of an excited Jeremy Paxman and a squirming politician. She removed the cooling, half-empty mug of tea from the arm of his chair and took it into the kitchen.

Twenty minutes later, he blinked at her as she removed *The Times*, unread, from his knees. 'Not going to be easy, this one,' he said with that small, intimate smile which he had always seemed to preserve for her. It was his attempt to allow her into his world, to share the experience he had once hugged so tightly to himself, and both of them recognized the moment. They had become closer with the passing years, closer still with her operations for breast cancer and a heart bypass in the last few years, when he had thought that he might lose her. She was restored to full health, an energetic woman in her early fifties, but her husband found it difficult to accept that.

The murder at Soutters was sensational enough for her to have picked up the lurid details from press and television. She grinned into his tired face, pleased that he was making this small attempt at a discussion of his work. 'I thought you might have had a confession pretty quickly for this one. Somehow, it doesn't seem organized. Not planned and executed with precision. A spur-of-the-moment thing.'

'Yes, though perhaps that was the way it was intended to look. Perhaps someone had in fact thought it through very thoroughly, but wanted to make it look like a desperate, impulsive thing.'

Christine didn't press him. She was happy to have him soundly asleep before midnight. It took her a little longer to sleep herself, but she fell soon enough into a deep, untroubled rest.

At five thirty, two hours before the late winter dawn, in that darkest time for humanity, when sick men die and the soul is beset by despair, John Lambert was staring at the ceiling of his bedroom and planning how he should tackle the suspects he had not even met so far.

Seven

Michelle Nayland was doing well in her first year of teaching. It was a probationary year, but there would be no problem for the head teacher in certifying her competence at the end of it. She was bright, resourceful, full of ideas, and with excellent control of herself and her charges. The head teacher told Sergeant Hook as much when he rang to ask when would be the best time to see Ms Nayland.

Bert Hook couldn't help thinking that sounded like an excellent personality for a murderer. It made you cynical, this job.

Michelle taught in a Herefordshire comprehensive school, at Newent, no more than five miles from where Patrick Nayland had died thirty-six hours earlier. The head teacher had volunteered his office for the meeting, to ensure that it would not be interrupted. She told the two plain-clothes men that she was surprised to see Ms Nayland back in the classroom so early; it showed just how conscientious she was, how she put the welfare of her pupils above her personal grief and suffering.

Lambert began with that. 'No one expected to see you back at work so quickly after a tragedy like this.'

She was cool, slim, dark-haired, with large, clear grey eyes and a mouth which seemed about to relax into a smile even when she was at her most serious. She looked very unlike her mother; her looks must have come from Liza Nayland's first husband. She would quite certainly be the subject of adolescent fantasies among some of her older pupils, Hook decided. She said, 'My mother is very upset, but perfectly in control of her grief. I spent yesterday at home, but found I wasn't any use to her.'

'But what about your own grief? It must have been a terrific shock to you, what happened on Wednesday night.'

'It was. But I'm better at work. I'm talking to you in a free period, but I shall see nearly two hundred children of various ages today. It doesn't give you time to mope, a schedule like that. In your first year in the job, you're too concerned with survival!' She gave them the wide, brilliant smile which had threatened since she came into the room, and Lambert found himself responding to it.

'I gather from people who know that you are doing far better than that. In which case, we'd better be brisk, so that you are ready to carry on the good work when the time comes.' His own grey eyes were more cautious than hers, had narrowed a little with thirty years of police experience. But they sparkled a little above his answering smile.

'I'd appreciate that.' Michelle thought that this might after all be less taxing than she had feared. She felt on her own ground here, even though they had been accorded that holy of holies, the head's room, for their exchanges.

Lambert said briskly, 'Tell us what you can recall of Wednesday evening, please.'

She took them calmly through the excellent fare and ambience provided by Soutters and how the company had gelled there. She had not seen most of the people who were there before, but they had soon got on famously together. She was not naïve enough to ignore the part that good food and wine had played in that, but an occasion she had rather feared in prospect turned out to be much less of an ordeal than she had expected. To be positively pleasurable, in many respects.

So far, so good. She managed to deliver what she had prepared with a fair impression of spontaneity, though she had expected them to interrupt more, to help her along with the narrative by some friendly questions. Instead, they both watched her closely and listened intently, as if registering the manner as well as the matter of what she said, and she found that more disturbing than direct interrogation. As any attractive woman is, Michelle was used to being a point of attention in a room, to being conscious of people watching her even when they were outside the immediate circle of her conversation. But this unembarrassed assessment at close quarters was something quite new to her. She became more self-conscious, and eventually found herself faltering unexpectedly in the account of events she had prepared for this moment.

She was approaching the startling climax to the evening when Lambert said suddenly, 'You visited the basement yourself, no doubt. How long was that before your father's body was discovered?'

'Stepfather.' Even here, in this context, she had to make the correction. 'It was probably about twenty minutes before that woman who works at the golf course – Joanne Moss, isn't it? – found Patrick.'

'Did you see anyone else down there?'

'No.' She allowed herself the ghost of a smile as she said, 'Of course, I can only speak for the ladies' cloakroom.'

'And the door of the Gents was shut at that time?'

'Yes, I think so. Yes, I'm sure it was. If it had been open, I'm sure I'd have remembered, because I'd have had a quick peep into the forbidden area: I'm as curious as the next person.'

'Your stepfather might have been behind that closed door. Or do you recall that he was in the restaurant when you returned?'

'I can't be sure. I don't remember seeing him, but he was probably there. I wasn't talking to him but to other people.' She wondered if she was being too cool, too detached. But she wasn't going to simulate a grief she didn't feel. That wouldn't fool these calm, observant men.

Lambert nodded. 'No one seems to recall Mr Nayland leaving the table and going downstairs.'

'I see. Well, I'm not surprised at that. There was a lot going on by that stage of the evening. Lots of shouting and laughter. But presumably one person saw him go, followed him downstairs and killed him. But he won't be volunteering that information, of course.' She was surprised how calm she felt as she made the suggestion. Tight situations had always brought out the best in her.

Lambert said nothing for a few seconds, studying her with an expression which seemed almost one of admiration. 'The killer might have simply waited for his victim in the basement, of course. He – or perhaps she – could have been down there for quite some time without arousing suspicion. Perhaps as long as twenty minutes.' He lifted his eyebrows a fraction, letting the implications of the idea impact on Michelle Nayland.

She kept her cool. 'I suppose that's quite possible. But it wasn't me who stabbed Patrick on Wednesday night.'

'Describe your relationship with your stepfather for us, please.'

It was that heavy, blockish-looking Sergeant who had issued that command. He was sitting with his pen over his notebook, studying her as impassively as the Superintendent had done from the start. Perhaps they thought the change of interrogator would ruffle her, especially when combined with this abrupt introduction of the one area she feared.

Michelle made herself control her indignation before she said, 'I suppose you have to ask about these things. I think you raised it with Mum, when you spoke to her yesterday, didn't you?' It wouldn't do any harm to show them that she'd compared notes with her mother about what had been said on their visit to her on the previous day; they must surely be used to people doing that.

Hook said stiffly, 'Your mother indicated that you and Mr Nayland had certain disagreements.'

'Did she, indeed? Well, I don't mind admitting I had a few problems accepting Patrick when he first came into our lives. I love my dad, still see him as often as I can. It doesn't help when you're a teenager and you find your dad suddenly gone and another man in bed with your mother. I gave Patrick a hard time, at first, and I'm sure he thought I was a right little cow. But those days were a long way behind us. By the time of his death, we were getting on perfectly well. I've taken his name, after all, haven't I? He was very good to me, was Patrick, very sympathetic to my problems when I was training to be a teacher.'

She had delivered it well, she thought. It didn't seem to have the ring of a prepared statement. And for almost the first time, she was glad that she'd allowed her mother to persuade her to take on the Nayland name. That had been a good touch to offer to these suspicious men.

They seemed now to be weighing what she'd said, to be wondering where to go from here. It seemed suddenly very quiet in the room. She heard the phone shrill in the adjoining office, and the school secretary answering some query. But she couldn't catch the words: it was just a distant buzz, reminding her of that other and more innocent world outside.

It was Lambert who eventually said to her, 'I'm sorry if you consider this line of questioning an intrusion. But I hope you see that we need to know about your relationship with your stepfather. You will understand that we have to explore any enmities a murder victim may have had.'

'I understand that perfectly. There is no need for any apology.'

'I am glad that you see no need for evasions. Let me say therefore that you do not appear to be either shocked or grief-stricken by this death.'

He flustered her for the first time with this prompt frankness. She wanted to spit some defiance at him, in response to what seemed like a calculated insult. But she made herself pause, telling herself that she had brought this upon herself, that it was perhaps even a sign of how successful she had been so far that he should wish to break her composure.

'Appearances can be deceptive, as you must know, Superintendent. I was certainly shocked by both the death itself and the manner of it. But I have had thirty-six hours to come to terms with that shock. And as for grief, you are probably right. Patrick had been good to me and we'd worked out a way of getting on well with each other. But it wasn't like the death of my real father would have been. I found yesterday that I was sorry for my mother, not myself. And I'm not going to simulate a misery I don't feel.' Pride flashed into her face with that declaration, and it took her a moment to recognize the emotion as ill-timed and banish it.

Lambert studied her with that steady, impassive assessment she had grown used to by now. Then he gave a small nod and said, 'Who do you think killed your stepfather, Miss Nayland?'

'I don't know. Someone he'd offended in his business dealings, I should think.' Then, recognizing how waspish this had sounded, she added, 'That seems the only possible explanation to me, you see, because I know no one in the family would have killed him. But I told you, I don't know most of the people who work at Camellia Park. I hadn't seen most of them until Wednesday evening.'

They let her go then, with the usual injunctions to get in touch if anything occurred to her which might have a bearing on the death of Nayland.

They must have stayed to talk to the head for a few minutes, for she saw them sitting together in the police car a quarter of an hour later, when she looked through the window of the classroom whilst taking the third years for English. The class were doing some written work, so she was able to watch the car, whilst trying to give her pupils the impression that this was no more than a casual gazing through the glass above the radiator. The two detectives conferred with each other for a couple of minutes, before they drove slowly out of the car park and through the big gates: she would have loved to know exactly what they were saying to each other.

She was very excited. It was like the buzz you got after examinations, when you had given everything you had, but couldn't wind down without nervous chatter with other people who had suffered.

Michelle Nayland knew she couldn't talk to anyone about this. Not even her mother: least of all her mother. But she felt she had done well. She was sure she had given the impression of frankness, without really being frank.

The police hadn't come up with anything to tie her in with the murder, to put her in that basement at the moment when Patrick Nayland had died. And she was sure they didn't even suspect the fierce motive she had for murder.

The full written post-mortem report had been delivered by the time Lambert and Hook arrived back at the police station in Oldford.

This would normally have been received with at least a very lively interest by the team allotted to a murder inquiry. In this case, no one expected to find much that was surprising or helpful in the PM report. It told them that Patrick Nayland had been in excellent health for a man of forty-nine. He had died when his left ventricle had been pierced by a heavy knife. Death had been almost instantaneous.

There was some interesting but probably useless information about the instrument of his death. It was a double-edged knife blade, probably some seven inches long from its point to the beginning of its handle. It was quite a heavy knife, but not necessarily a tool designed for use as a weapon. Similar blades would be found in many kitchens, especially those establishments where food was professionally prepared.

The first thought was obviously the kitchen of the restaurant where the victim had died. But Fred Soutter had already confirmed to Lambert that none of his kitchen implements was missing. An extensive search of the area, widening out from the buildings immediately around Soutters Restaurant to take in the whole of the small market town of Newent, had so far failed to turn up anything which answered to this description of the murder weapon.

Lambert and his colleagues knew the score: if the weapon had not been found by now, the probability was that it never would be.

There was one interesting feature in the report about the manner of this death. There had been so much blood surrounding the corpse by the time the police arrived that Rushton and his men had assumed this was a multiple stabbing, which suggested a picture of someone thrusting a knife repeatedly into Patrick Nayland's torso, in a frenzy of hatred, or a desperate panic, or a combination of both.

There were in fact only three stab wounds, of which the first one might well have been fatal. That was impossible to determine for certain, since the blows had been administered in rapid succession. These facts were certainly of interest to the CID team. Contrary to popular opinion, it is rare for someone to die from a simple stab wound; the human body has been known to survive as many as forty abdominal and chest stabbings, with the benefits of modern surgical techniques.

Patrick Nayland had been stabbed not many times but only three. It helped to explain why no desperate cry for help from him had pierced the cheerful cacophony in the room above, why no one had been conscious of what had happened until Joanne Moss's repeated screams had announced it. No one could be sure exactly how many minutes Nayland had been dead at that moment.

The accuracy of the mortal wound also raised an interesting possibility. Did it mean that the person who had murdered Nayland had some specialist knowledge, either of martial arts or of medical matters, which had enabled him or her to apply the blade to the precise point where it would ensure instant death? Lambert spoke to the pathologist on the phone, but he confirmed that he could not be sure if the first wound was the fatal one, which would have supported the thought of a killer with special training.

Nor could he be drawn into even an opinion as to whether the fatal wound represented a specialist attack or was merely the result of luck accompanying a more random blow. 'All I can say is that this was a serious weapon. With a heavy, double-edged knife like that, it wouldn't need much luck to kill someone.'

DI Rushton set about cross-referencing the pathologist's report with the findings of Sergeant Jack Johnson and his scenes of crime team. But the peculiar nature of this crime meant that the SOCO findings on this occasion tended to confuse as much as illuminate the picture.

The team had diligently gathered material from the corpse which had originated with other people at the gathering. There were fibres from other people's clothing, several human hairs which did not belong to Nayland. But his wife had cradled the dead man in her arms, Pearson had touched the throat of the victim to make sure that he was dead, and other people had no doubt left fibres of their own clothing behind in detaching the hysterical widow from her hold upon the dead man.

Moreover, Patrick Nayland had passed freely and eagerly among his guests earlier in the evening, shaking hands with wives, patting people like Barry Hooper on the back. It was difficult to see how anything found upon the body could be used to incriminate anyone at the gathering, and even more difficult to see how the connection could stand up to examination in court by an experienced defence counsel.

All this is what the team would have expected. It was not until later that day that the surprising fact emerged. Rushton had made sure that a sample of Patrick Nayland's blood had been submitted for comparison with samples on the National DNA Database, which retained the DNA of people convicted of previous crimes. No one expected a match, but the routine had to be observed.

In this case, it was destined to provide the murder team with an astonishing fact about the dead man.

Eight

Alan Fitch found the presence of the young man at his side irritating today. Normally he was glad of the company: the maintenance of the small golf course could be a lonely job, and the presence of a protégé who listened eagerly to his every word was usually much to his taste.

Barry Hooper had been a welcome addition to his world, and he was surprised how pleased he had been when the young man was confirmed as a permanent appointment. But today he found the young black man's company a burden, his eager questions an imposition. It was like having a devoted but demanding spaniel puppy at your heels all day, when you wanted a bit of privacy for your own concerns.

It was too cold to do much work outside. Even the pile of soil they had been riddling to make a spring dressing had frozen overnight and had to be left to thaw out. They spent the morning servicing the gang mowers, which would not be used on the fairways for the next three months. To be accurate,

Brian Fitch serviced the machinery, whilst his willing acolyte passed him tools and asked him a series of increasingly irksome questions.

They lunched together in the familiar shed, glad of the old electric fire between the two shabby but comfortable armchairs. It was not their usual companionable meal. Barry chattered on about life in general and the delights afforded by his new motorbike in particular, seeming not to notice how his senior's replies became increasingly surly and monosyllabic. He didn't mention the murder investigation, and as Hooper's manner became increasingly febrile, Fitch wondered for the first time whether his incessant chatter was an attempt to distract himself.

Alan Fitch was relieved when, early in the afternoon, he found a genuine chance to be rid of Hooper. He sent him into Gloucester to get replacements for two worn bolts on the mowers, making him wrap the worn parts carefully in old sacking and take them with him, to make sure that he got identical replacements. He listened to the sound of Barry's powerful motorcycle engine diminishing as his assistant rode away, then sat down for a moment in an agreeable silence. He needed to gather his thoughts.

He was raking over the remnants of yesterday's fire, making sure that there was nothing to see but a few innocent twigs which had not burned, when he heard the police car coming up the unpaved track to the big shed where the course machinery was housed. He left the charred earth hastily and went back to the gang mowers, which lay in pieces on the concrete floor. He was wiping his hands on an oily rag and preparing to sharpen the blades when the two CID men came into the shed.

The one who was introduced to him as Detective Sergeant Hook said, 'We need to ask you a few questions. Is there somewhere where we could sit down in privacy for a few minutes?'

He took them to the familiar room at the end of the shed, where the electric fire still burned, and pulled up a third, rarely used armchair from the edge of the space. His offer of tea was refused; the two big men folded themselves comfortably into the shabby armchairs and looked at him steadily, in a way which he was already finding disconcerting. This place which was so familiar suddenly seemed alien to him, transformed by a police presence it had never endured before.

Hook seemed to be trying to put him at his ease as he said, 'Merchant Navy man, weren't you, Mr Fitch?'

He wondered how they knew that. He was sure he hadn't said anything about it in the brief statements they'd all been required to make on Wednesday night after the murder. Perhaps they'd been studying the employment files in the Camellia Park office; they surely wouldn't have deduced it merely from the tattoos on his forearms. He found the idea that they might have prepared themselves for this talk more thoroughly than he had was disconcerting to him.

His voice sounded gruff and forced as he said, 'That's right. Eighteen years I did. Seems like a different world, now.' That was a comment he often made to people; why then should it sound so false in his own ears now?

'Almost joined the service myself once – probably a few years after you'd gone to sea, it would be. I was a Barnardo's boy, you see. The Merchant Navy was one of the careers they always urged us to consider, in those days.' Hook was trying to encourage a man not normally required to be articulate to speak freely.

'It was a good life, a lot of the time. Made me grow up quickly, it did. But I told you, it seems a long way behind me, now.'

'Saw quite a bit of violence, I should think, in those days.' Hook obstinately stuck with a subject the man wanted to leave.

'Learned to look after myself, to know whom I could trust. You looked out for each other, once you knew who your friends were.'

112

'I expect you did. And I expect these things stay with you. I should think that even when you were back on land, you knew how to look after yourself. Learned not to take any nonsense from anyone, I should think.'

'I keep myself to myself, most of the time,' said Alan Fitch cautiously. He didn't have to use words much nowadays to get the things he wanted. He was desperate to change the subject now, but he didn't know how to do it subtly. He said bluntly, 'This is a waste of time, isn't it? You've come here to talk about what happened on Wednesday night, not about what I did in the distant past.'

'It may or may not be a waste of time, Mr Fitch.' Lambert came in so promptly that he caught his man by surprise. Alan wondered for a moment if the two were working together, had set things up to catch him out before they came into his shed. It made him feel yet more uneasy, even as he repeated to himself what he had said a hundred times before they came, that he must keep calm, that there was nothing they could uncover if he kept his nerve. He just needed a few seconds to gather his resources.

But Lambert was going on. 'Until we know otherwise, everyone eating with Mr Nayland on Wednesday night has to be a suspect. Once you have accepted that, I'm sure you will see that the more we know about all of you, the better it will be for our

113

investigation.'

Alan did see. He wanted to argue, but all he did was to say woodenly, 'I didn't kill Mr Nayland.'

'I'm glad to hear it. In that case, the sooner we can eliminate you from suspicion, the better it will be for all of us. My advice to you if you are innocent is to be as frank and straightforward as possible with us.'

'That's what I always meant to be.' That sounded better, Alan thought, a little more defiant.

'So you can start by being frank about that violent past which Detective Sergeant Hook was exploring with you.'

They knew, he thought. They'd done their homework before coming here. He should have expected it, but somehow he hadn't.

The shock made him do the wrong thing. 'I don't know what you're talking about. There were times when the fists flew a bit, in foreign ports, as I've already said. Nothing serious. Nothing which makes me a candidate for killing Nayland.' He'd dropped the 'Mr' in his excitement. Somehow his hatred seemed to him to ring out far too clearly with his simple omission of the title.

'Nothing serious, you say. You wouldn't call a conviction for causing an affray something serious?'

Alan fought against a rising panic, telling himself that he should have known they'd turn this up, that it made no difference to the present situation, however it might look. He tried to banish the dryness from his mouth. 'I only got a suspended sentence.'

'But you were guilty. Your captain spoke for your previous good conduct. The impression from reading about the court proceedings is that he didn't want to sail with a crew one short.'

He hadn't bargained for this. Not for them knowing all the details, as they seemed to do. He'd almost forgotten about the conviction himself, over the years: the probationary sentence had come in his own mind to seem almost like a 'Not Guilty' verdict. But it wasn't; if it had been, they wouldn't have been able to look up the details and come at him like this with it. 'It was a long time ago. A silly seamen's fight in a bar. I didn't even start it. It was something and nothing. I've put it aside and forgotten about it.'

'Very wise, Mr Fitch. In that case, I may need to remind you that you were extremely fortunate to escape a much more serious charge of Grievous Bodily Harm.'

'There was no evidence for that.' Alan spoke like one in a dream; his own voice seemed to come from far away.

'That's not how they remember it in Cardiff, Mr Fitch. DS Hook spoke to CID records down there. It was only because they couldn't get the man you injured to bear witness that you didn't face the charge, and a probable prison sentence.'

'He was as guilty as I was.'

'Never tested, that, was it?'

'No. But he was. He knew he—'

'You attacked him with a knife, I believe.'

His mind reeled. He had never in his worst moments thought they would get as far as that. He shut his eyes, trying fiercely to concentrate. 'I had a knife, yes. I didn't hurt him with it. Not seriously.'

Lambert let the seconds stretch, making the most of his advantage. When the brown eyes in the weatherbeaten, experienced face opposite him opened, fear filled them like a tangible, liquid presence. He said, 'You realize how this looks, in view of the way Patrick Nayland was killed.'

'I – I haven't carried a knife for years. Not since that night in Cardiff. Even when I was still on the ships, I didn't—'

'You haven't got a knife around here, have you?' Lambert looked slowly round the room, then at the dark oblong of the doorway, which led into the recesses of the huge shed beyond it.

'No. Well, of course, there must be the odd knife about, in a place like this. We do a lot of our own repairs to vehicles and the other course equipment, and—'

'We haven't found the murder weapon, you see. Not yet. We're satisfied that it's not been left anywhere near the scene of the crime.'

'It's not here.' Alan knew he should say something else, should deny any connection with the knife that had killed Nayland. But his tongue was suddenly too big and too dry for his mouth, and words would not come. And just when Alan wanted him to speak, this long-faced inquisitor, who had recently been so eager to interrupt him, chose to remain silent and study him with those grey, unblinking, pitiless eyes.

Lambert next ran those eyes thoughtfully round the room, letting them rest for a moment on the battered old cupboard in the corner. Alan panicked for a moment, trying desperately to go through the contents of that innocent container in his mind. Was there anything still in there which he would find hard to explain? He wondered if they needed a search warrant to go through this private working domain of his. Did they need a warrant just for your home? Could they move methodically through this place, examining things at their leisure? For a moment, he thought Lambert was going to ease his long frame out of the sagging arm-chair and stroll over to the cupboard.

Instead, the Superintendent returned the scrutiny of those clear grey eyes to his man's face and said quietly, 'Did you kill Patrick Nayland, Mr Fitch?'

'No.' He wanted to shout more words, to

say the very idea was absurd, but all he could manage was the blank monosyllable. It seemed to him far too small to refute a monstrous charge like this.

'You see why we have to consider the matter, don't you? He was killed with a knife, possibly applied with some skill and knowledge of human anatomy, the postmortem report tells us. You are the only one of the people in that restaurant who has a previous history of knife crime.'

The man was throwing all these long words at him, as if to point out the inadequacy of his one-word denial. Alan sought again for the phrases which would cascade out in anger, reinforcing his outrage, flooding away the calm logic which seemed to be rising like a tide to engulf him. Nothing would come. He shook his head dumbly in a hopeless, inadequate denial.

His fear had come as a surprise to him. He had expected this meeting would be taxing, but he had never thought he would lose his nerve like this. He was Alan Fitch, the reliable, unflappable guardian of the golf course, the man whose competence was evidenced in the acres where he plied his trade, the man whose calm answers and assurances about what he was doing and what he proposed to do were accepted without question by those who surrounded him. He had acquired a reputation for calmness and unflappability, an image he had begun to believe in himself. He had never expected to find the blood pounding in his temples like this, to find the capacity for rational thought slinking away from him, like a faithless dog.

They were asking him now about the events of Wednesday evening, with the Sergeant recording everything he said. He had expected this, and he had the answers ready. He was relieved when they came automatically to his lips. Yes, he'd been down to the toilets earlier in the evening, had been surprised by the bawdy pictures in there, had enjoyed a bit of a laugh with the others when he came back upstairs. He couldn't say how long that was before Nayland died. He didn't know how long the host had been missing before his death was discovered. So far as he could remember, he hadn't spoken to him during the evening.

He faltered a little when they asked him if he knew of anyone who had any reason to kill Patrick Nayland. Some small, troublesome part of his reeling brain told him that this was a chance to divert suspicion from himself, to tilt the scales a little against that damned knife from all those years ago, which they had discovered and thrown into the balance against him.

But he was in no condition to pit his mind against these calm, ruthless adversaries. He

119

confined himself to as few words as possible, to being unhelpful rather than actually trying to mislead them. And surprisingly quickly, it was all over, and they were telling him to get in touch if he thought of anything which might be helpful, and not to leave the area without giving them an address.

They went out with him into the cold of the world outside, where there was a light wind from the north beneath a deceptively blue sky. It was over, he thought, wishing them into their car and off the premises. They moved with irritating slowness, and he had to moderate his pace to theirs, so that he could pretend that there was nothing here to hide, that he was as relaxed now as they were.

They strolled past the dead embers of the fire he had lit yesterday, then stopped together, as though they were puppets operated by a single string. The Sergeant with the countryman's face stared at the ground, then stirred the ashes with the toe of his shoe, neglectful of the high shine he was impairing. He watched the white dust float away on the breeze, then sniffed the air like an inquisitive Labrador. 'Quite recent, this, isn't it?'

'The fire? Yesterday. I burned some old timber which had too much rot in it to be any use again. And some brambles we'd cleared from the course. And some broken chairs from the dining room in the club-house. And some old rags we'd used to clean the tractor and the mowers.'

His tongue was suddenly working again: he had relaxed when he had thought that the ordeal was over. He was now saying too much, as if by cataloguing the ingredients of the fire he could make it a more innocent blaze.

The two CID men stared down at the black circle with its grey remnants, and Alan had to resist a ridiculous impulse to leap forward and cover the evidence from their scrutiny. There was nothing here to see. He had checked it earlier himself. But some weird and mischievous goblin tried to convince him that the eyesight of these predators was more than human, that they would swoop upon the scorched earth and hold aloft triumphantly some incriminating thing he had thought consumed for ever by the flames.

He said stupidly, 'It was a good day for a bonfire, yesterday. I was glad of the warmth.'

'You were alone when you lit the fire?' This was the Superintendent, seizing on the singular pronoun as if it were the final piece in some obscure jigsaw which would send Alan into a cell. He had almost thought 'send him to the gallows', his mind springing in fear back to the recesses of some childish nightmare.

Alan said, 'I think I was alone when I lit it, yes.' That was stupid: they would realize that he knew perfectly well whether he was alone or not. And if they were interested in the matter, as it seemed now they surely were, they would check it out with other people. 'I lit it first thing yesterday. Barry didn't come in until later.'

'First thing yesterday. Only a few hours after you'd left Soutters Restaurant and the body of Mr Nayland, then.'

'Yes. I couldn't sleep. I came in early.' He wondered how they contrived to make every question seem like an accusation, whether they did that with everyone they interviewed. He had a moment of inspiration. 'The fire was one of the things I could do on my own, you see.'

'I see,' said Lambert. He took a step forward and stirred the grey-black ashes, as Hook had done before him. He looked into Alan Fitch's face again, as intently as he had done for twenty minutes inside his shed. He nodded a couple of times, gave him a brief smile, and said, 'We must be on our way.'

It was the first conventional, meaningless phrase Alan had heard from him during their meeting. He stood and watched them drive down the unpaved track and back to the main road, watched the police car until its roof disappeared between the hedges, oblivious of the keenness of the north wind.

They had come with the knowledge of his violence of years ago, and disconcerted him with that knowledge. And when he had thought they had done with him, just when he was relaxing, they had found the remnants of his fire and challenged him on that.

But they hadn't discovered anything, and they couldn't reverse the process of destruction. They could think what they liked about the fire, but it had done its work.

Nine

Barry Hooper had only had the Ducati 620 for six weeks. It wasn't new, of course – he could never have afforded that – but it was in splendid condition. When he had finished polishing it, you would never have thought that it was three years old.

The bike was still an exciting novelty rather than a mere means of transport to Barry. He loved the sensation of the engine roaring into life between his knees, delighted each time anew in the sudden surge of power as he eased the bike on to the road and away from the kerb.

He even enjoyed getting ready to go out on it, the donning of the leathers, the careful fastening of the helmet strap beneath his chin, the slow pulling on of the big gauntlets, which seemed to make his slim hands so much more powerful than they had been without them. Two years ago, he had been riding a moped, a late developer among bikers, the centre of friendly laughter among the boys he met at nights. Now he had moved swiftly from youth into manhood. Now he was the subject of envy among his peers, not derision.

When he was riding the Ducati, it took all of his concentration. Once astride the Ducati, he could forget the dramatic events of the last few days, could thrust away for a time the apprehension which had beset him since the death of Nayland.

But it seemed that on this day he was not going to be allowed to forget. He rode carefully along the road into Gloucester, slowing obediently to thirty miles an hour as he went through the village of Highnam, where everyone knew the cameras would get you if you did not crawl along. He had almost reached the junction with the A40 when he saw the police car.

They passed each other slowly enough for him to see the occupants, a driver with a rather florid face and a tall, grave-faced man, who seemed to Barry's young eyes quite elderly, though he was probably only in his fifties.

In that moment, Barry Hooper knew as certainly as if someone had whispered the information into his ear that these men were plain-clothes detectives, driving to Camellia Park, investigating the death of Nayland. Very probably they were going up to the familiar greenkeeper's shed to interview Alan Fitch. They hadn't interviewed him yet, and though his boss had said nothing, Barry knew that he was anticipating a visit from the fuzz. He even knew that Alan Fitch was nervous about it; Barry wasn't as dim or as inexperienced as the older man thought he was.

Barry's mother had been used to say when he was a small boy that money burned a hole in his pocket, that he just couldn't wait to spend it. The phrase came back to him now, and with it came the absurd fantasy that the thing he had kept in the pocket of his jeans since the night of the murder was beginning to burn its way into the flesh beneath it. He slid his right hand for a moment from the throttle to the small bulge beneath the denim on his thigh, as if he needed reassurance that the thing was not a red-hot brand; even through the thick sausage-fingers of the gauntlets, through the black leathers which encased his limbs, he could tell that it was not so.

But he needed to be rid of it. He had known that since the night of the murder, but he had done nothing about it, his will atrophied by his fear of discovery. With the sight of those policemen on the way to Camellia Park, his resolution was confirmed. He began immediately to implement it.

The bolts which Alan Fitch had sent him to purchase could wait. He'd think of some explanation as to why it had taken him so long in due course. That wasn't his primary concern now. He must get rid of the watch.

He didn't go into Gloucester. He took the by-pass, then roared along the complex of new roads which had been built to connect with the M5. But he ignored the turnings which would have taken him away to the north towards Birmingham or south towards Bristol and the West. They were unknown lands to Barry Hooper. He wanted somewhere as far from home as possible, but somewhere where he had been before. He couldn't venture into completely unknown territory. Not with what he had in the pocket of his jeans. Not to do what he had to do to get rid of it.

He opened the throttle and roared up Birdlip Hill, exulting in the power beneath his slim frame, crouching with his head low to the handlebars, staying in the overtaking lane as he passed a stream of heavy lorries as if they were standing still, slowing in the last fifty yards to walking pace as he came to the roundabout at the top of the steep rise.

He had intended to take the turning for Cheltenham just after the roundabout, disposing of the watch at a shop there which he knew took such things. But something told him that he wanted to do this further from home, that the more miles he put between him and the place of the murder, the less likely he was to be discovered. If he went to a shop he didn't know, that would somehow give anonymity to the transaction, and anonymity was essential to secrecy.

He rode on to Burford, that delightful little Cotswold capital which was full of antique shops, which was sure to offer him the facility he needed. Yet the town, so full of tourist crowds which would absorb his presence in the summer months, was quiet on this bitter December Friday. Barry cruised quietly down its main street, feeling far too conspicuous, feeling as if the bow windows of the old shops were themselves observing him. He did not dismount, but turned swiftly at the bottom of the hill and accelerated back up the High Street and out of the town.

He needed the faceless streets of a city. He tried not to panic as he got stuck for three miles behind the back of a huge van on the narrowest section of the A40. Alan Fitch was going to wonder where on earth he had got to, was going to demand an explanation for his absence. He would cross that bridge when he came to it: he had problems enough to contend with before then.

It was a relief to get to the miles of dual carriageway which ran past the old town of Witney. He accelerated up to eighty, ninety, a hundred, passing a succession of Mercs and Jaguars and BMWs, feeling the mastery which his speed and acceleration gave him. Then he eased back the throttle and moved at a steady eighty; it would never do to be stopped for speeding, with the watch in his pocket.

It took him longer than he had thought to find the place he wanted in Oxford, because of the one-way system. But he found a spot to park his bike at the end of the street. He looked briefly into the small window of the shop. It was full of rings and jewellery and, reassuringly, had two trays of timepieces, old and new. He marched quickly through the door, before he could lose his nerve.

It was dark within the shop, as he had expected, and he blinked to adjust his eyes to the dimness after the brightness of the street outside. What he had not expected was to be confronted by a young woman. He had somehow expected an aged figure, full of knowledge, bent with age, shocked by nothing, and not asking him too many questions.

'What can I do for you?' Above the small, professional smile, her face was bland, deliberately impassive. This was obviously the greeting she offered everyone who entered the shop.

'I've a watch I want to sell. A good one.' He fumbled in the pocket of jeans which seemed suddenly too tight, had to set down his helmet and his gauntlets awkwardly on the floor to give himself the use of both hands.

'We might be interested.'

Barry glanced automatically towards the

three brass balls in their triangle above the door on the street, but they were now invisible behind him. He had thought these places bought anything and everything, hadn't anticipated a lukewarm female like this to bargain with. He said as confidently as he could, 'You'll want to buy this, when you see it. It's a good one.'

He produced the watch at last, set it down on the tray she pushed towards him across the mahogany counter. It looked good, gleaming softly yellow and expensive in the dim yellow light.

She stared down at it, her expression still impassive. 'It's a Rolex.'

Barry thought she sounded impressed, despite herself. That gave him a little more assurance, and he said boldly, 'Didn't I tell you it was a good one?'

'Is it genuine?'

Snotty cow. 'Yes, of course it is.'

'There are a lot of fakes about, you see. There always are, when the genuine article is as costly as a Rolex.' She did not look at him. Instead, she turned the watch over, reached to her right, produced a powerful overhead light and an eyeglass. She studied both the front and back of the watch intently through the eyeglass. Then she put the eyeglass down and finally looked into his face. Reluctantly, to his mind, she said, 'This appears to be the genuine article.'

'I told you it was.'

She smiled a mirthless smile. 'In this business, you have to be certain. I'm sure you'll understand that we can't just take anyone's word, however genuine he might appear.'

Barry could tell that these were phrases she used all the time. Yet he thought he caught a note of irony in the way she had used them to him, thought he caught her glance straying to the helmet and goggles he had pushed behind his feet. Saucy little minx! He'd like to have her on the back of his bike, take her up to the ton, see if she still felt like putting him down with a wind like that howling up her skirt. She was older than he'd thought at first, probably nearly thirty. There were no rings on her perfectly manicured fingers, which seemed odd in a place where she was surrounded by them. He said, 'I understand that you have to be careful. But this is a Rolex all right. What's it worth?'

She smiled at him, and this time he was sure it was a patronizing smile. 'You mean, what are we prepared to pay for it, don't you? We have to make a profit. Costly items tend to hang about for a long time, when we've had to lay out our money for them.' It wasn't true in this case. The serial number said the watch wasn't more than eighteen months old; a Rolex as new as this would go within days, at the right price. 'Have you any provenance for the watch?'

'Provenance?' He stared at her, trying not to look stupid, and failing.

'We like to know something of the history, when we take in a Rolex watch.'

'It belonged to my grandfather. He died last month. He always said the watch was coming to me. I'd like to keep it, but I need the money.' He had prepared this story in case anyone asked him how he had come by the watch. Now it had all come tumbling out too suddenly, the phrases piling up on top of each other, when they should have been delivered in a much more relaxed fashion. He wished he was anywhere but in front of this cool woman, who seemed to see through everything he was saying and find it amusing. But he stuck to his guns: it would be as bad anywhere else he took the watch, he was sure of that now. At least he had overcome his fears and brought himself here; he was going to tell his tale and stick stubbornly to it.

He glanced down at his leathers and said, 'I've just bought a new bike, a Ducati 620. They don't come cheap, you know.'

The woman gave him that thin-lipped, knowing smile again. 'I'm sure they don't. What did you want for the watch?'

He'd thought they would be anxious to get hold of such a valuable piece, that they'd give him a price and he might be able to get them up a little by cool bargaining. He could feel the blood rushing to his face; even the tops of his ears felt hot. He said, 'You know the value of these things better than I do. It must be worth at least a thousand, surely?' But he knew even as he spoke that he had let the uncertainty creep into his voice.

The woman frowned. 'We certainly could not go as high as that. Not without a provenance. No offence, sir, but we only have your word for how you came by the piece. In the circumstances, I don't think we could go above...' She paused, glanced down at the watch again and shook her head gently. 'Three hundred pounds.'

'It's worth more than that, surely?'

'You're welcome to take it elsewhere, sir, of course. Someone else might think differently, but I doubt whether they'll offer you more than that. Not without any provenance.' She shook her head, with more certainty this time, and eased the tray with the watch upon it an inch in his direction.

'Four hundred.' Barry stuck out his jaw sullenly.

The woman smiled, knowing that the argument was over, that the bargain was going to be resolved heavily in her favour. 'If it will help you, sir, I'll go to three fifty. But that has to be our final offer.'

'All right.'

She nodded, approving the wisdom of his decision. 'I'll make you out a cheque.'

'I'd prefer cash, if you don't mind.'

This time she did not trouble to disguise the condescension in her smile. 'That's not how it works, I'm afraid. We don't hold large sums of cash on the premises nowadays – it's against all police advice. We'll give you a receipt for the watch, which covers you against any sharp practice on our account. But I can assure you that our cheques do not bounce.' She smiled her first open, wide smile at the absurdity of such a notion.

Barry took the cheque and the receipt, stowed them carefully away in the pocket of his jeans which had held the watch. She made him leave his name and address. He thought of refusing, of calling the whole thing off, even at this late stage. But he couldn't face the prospect of beginning this ordeal again from the start, in another place like this.

He turned away so quickly that she had to remind him to pick up his helmet and gauntlets when he had his hand on the handle of the door.

For Barry Hooper, it was the final humiliation.

Joanne Moss had watched the police car drive slowly up the unpaved track to the greenkeeper's shed, had known that the police must be interviewing Alan Fitch. Barry Hooper had ridden off on that new motorbike he was so proud of before the CID men came, so they had Alan to themselves. They were up there for a good half-hour; she was surprised how long they took with the normally taciturn Fitch. Joanne wouldn't have minded being a fly on the wall up there.

She had expected that the CID men would call in to see her before they left Camellia Park. She was left with a sensation of flat anticlimax when the police car drove slowly past the windows of the clubhouse and turned back along the road towards Oldford. She knew that the detectives had already spoken to Mrs Nayland and her daughter, and to Chris Pearson, the manager of the enterprise. Now they had interviewed Alan Fitch, who surely came below her in the loose hierarchy of Camellia Park. If you discounted Barry Hooper, the youngest and latest of the employees, who could surely have little to tell them, she was the only one of the staff who had not yet been interviewed about the death of Patrick Nayland.

Joanne knew it was ridiculous, but instead of being relieved, she felt a vague sense of disappointment, as if she had not been afforded her due status.

Half an hour after the police car had left, when she had tidied the clubhouse kitchen and made sure the food she needed for a busy Saturday lunchtime was ready in the

135

fridge, the phone rang. A rolling, unhurried, country voice. Detective Sergeant Hook, confirming the address of her flat. He sounded friendly, gave her the impression this was little more than routine, said he was sure she saw more of what went on at the little golf course than most, from her position at the hub of things in the club-house. They would like to talk with her in private, away from the distractions of the golf course. They would like to speak to her in her flat, that evening at six thirty.

Her status was restored. So was her appre-hension.

It was a few minutes later on that Friday afternoon that Detective Inspector Rushton, sitting in front of his computer, collating and cross-referencing the information accruing from the team assembled for the Nayland murder, discovered an important fact.

Facts, Superintendent Lambert always said, were the only reliable things. He was a regular Gradgrind about facts rather than guesswork, and the way you had to look for the significant ones. Well, this was a real belter of a fact. And he hadn't gone chasing about the countryside interviewing suspects to discover it, like that old dinosaur Lam-bert. This fact had come to Chris Rushton directly as a result of the application of modern technology.

Even Chris had thought he was merely observing routine when he had asked forensic to submit a sample of the dead man's plentifully spilled blood to the people who ran the National DNA Database, for comparison with anything they had recorded there. The database retains only the DNAs of those with criminal convictions, so it seemed a very long shot in the case of an ex-Army officer and respectable businessman like Patrick Nayland.

It was a long shot which scored a direct hit. The apparently highly respectable Mr Nayland had a conviction from eleven years earlier. He had been found guilty on a charge of Indecent Assault against a nineteen-year-old girl.

137

Ten

Joanne Moss had the tea tray ready when Lambert and Hook arrived at her flat on the dot of six thirty. Rather to her surprise, they accepted the offer; no doubt they had had a long day.

She left the door to her living room open whilst she boiled the kettle in the neat little kitchen. They looked round the room without disguising their interest. Perhaps that was part of the training, to develop a thick skin; perhaps nosiness was a built-in habit by now for these men who looked to her so experienced. She wondered if the place looked as bare to them as it did to her, if they were remarking the empty spaces from which she had stripped photographs and memorabilia during her hasty sweeping away of significant items yesterday.

She had dusted the surfaces, so that they could surely not realize that the now rather bare-looking room had been crowded with pictures and other trivia only a couple of days earlier. She congratulated herself again on the ruthlessness of her clearance. It was impossible that they could be aware of her expedition into Gloucester to get rid of the dustbin bag with its significant contents. All the same, she wished now that she had not left them alone in the room.

She took advantage of the final moment of privacy to check again on her own appearance by pushing the door to and looking into the mirror on the back of it. Her dark hair was perfectly in place, her make-up light but skilfully applied. Her deep brown eyes were clear now: the puffiness around them which she thought she had detected earlier in the day seemed to have disappeared. The white blouse and grey skirt she had selected after Hook's call to arrange this meeting still seemed appropriate; not at all gaudy, as if she was treating this death with unbecoming levity, but not too formal either, lest she should suggest that it meant more to her than was fitting.

With her confidence thus bolstered, she picked up the tray and moved boldly back into her sitting room. They did not speak as she poured the tea and offered them biscuits, but she was conscious of them studying her, weighing up her appearance in a manner more open than anything she had ever experienced.

Then Lambert said, 'You were the person who discovered the body. Will you describe that moment for us in detail, please?'

'I told your officers about it on Wednesday night, immediately after it happened.'

'Nevertheless, I should like you describe it again for us now, adding anything which you may have omitted in the excitement and shock of the discovery. Begin with the moment you left the restaurant, please.'

Was he implying she had deliberately tried to deceive the police at the time? She could deduce nothing from his demeanour. She said evenly, speaking like one in a dream, 'Things were getting very noisy in the restaurant. We were nearly at the end of the meal and most people had drunk a fair amount – we knew we had taxis arranged to take us home at the end of the evening. The noise level was very high: I remember thinking what a row we were all making when I was on the steps down to the basement. I went into the ladies' loo. I suppose I was in there for three or four minutes.'

'Was anyone else there at the same time?'

'No. I passed Michelle Nayland, Patrick's stepdaughter, at the top of the stairs, but no one else came down to the Ladies whilst I was there.'

She watched Hook making a brief note of the name, felt for a moment that she had betrayed the girl. Lambert said, 'Go on, please.'

'There isn't much else to tell. As I came out of the Ladies, I noticed the door into the gents' loo wasn't quite closed. Then I saw Patrick's foot – well, I didn't realize at first whose foot it was.' She felt herself reddening, as if she had almost given herself away. This was ridiculous. 'I could see enough through the gap in the door to realize that whoever was in there was lying flat. My first thought was that someone had collapsed, was in need of help. I called through the doorway, but there was no reply. I think I turned to go upstairs to get help next, but then I realized that the person in there might need immediate attention. So I pushed the door wide open.'

'And saw exactly what, Mrs Moss? The detail may be important.'

She looked him full in the face, heard herself saying almost aggressively, 'The detail I remember was the blood. It seemed to be everywhere, to be still running. It was the blood which seemed to dominate everything. I didn't even know who it was, for a moment. Then I looked at the face and saw that it was Patrick Nayland.'

'The PM report says that he was certainly dead at that moment. Did you realize that he was dead?'

'I'm not sure what I realized. I thought I was going to faint. I can remember having the absurd idea that I didn't want to fall into that pool of blood, get it all over the new dress I'd bought for the evening. I can't remember beginning to scream, can't remember anything else until everyone was around me. I think Chris Pearson spoke sharply to me to stop me screaming. I think he gave me a slap, but I'm not even sure of that. Anyway, that was the moment when I knew that this wasn't a nightmare, that I wasn't going to wake up and find everything back to normal.'

Lambert nodded slowly as Hook made more notes. Then he said an odd thing. 'You hadn't arranged to meet Mr Nayland down there?'

'No. Why on earth should I have done that?'

'I've no idea, Mrs Moss. We need to be clear about these things, that's all. We're still getting to know things about the murder victim and the people who were around him when he died. We don't know much yet about their various relationships with each other.'

'Relationships?' She repeated the word stupidly, as if this were something she had not considered until now.

Lambert said patiently, 'It is almost certain that it was their relationship, probably with Mr Nayland but possibly with someone else there on that evening, which caused someone to kill your employer.'

She tried not to be startled by that word 'employer'. An employee was what she was, after all, as far as these two were concerned, though she had long since ceased to regard herself as merely that. 'Yes. I suppose that must be so. You just don't like to contemplate such facts, when you know the people involved.'

'Since the subject has come up, I will ask you directly now. Do you know of any relationships which might have a bearing on this death? I need hardly tell you that you have a duty to be perfectly frank with us.'

She took her time, tried to give the appearance of giving due thought to a difficult question. She even furrowed her brow a little before she spoke: she was rather pleased with that little bit of acting. 'No, I can't. Patrick was a good employer, and most of us had reason to be grateful to him. Equally, I think most of us gave him good value for our wages as Camellia Park developed over the years.' She nodded with what she hoped was due modesty. 'I can't speak for any relationships in his private life, away from work, of course. You'd need to ask his family about that.'

Lambert's scrutiny of her face, his weighing of her every word, was disconcerting, but she thought she was doing rather well. He now made a sudden switch and said, 'You say that the door of the gents' cloakroom was slightly open when you came out of the Ladies, that this is what alerted you to the fact that something was wrong. Is it possible that it was already open when you came down the stairs three or four minutes earlier, before you went into the Ladies?'

She tried to look as if she had not thought of this possibility before. 'I – I really can't be certain, one way or the other. I suppose it's really quite likely that the door was slightly open then. I had eyes only for the door of the Ladies at that point. When I came out of there a few minutes later, I was more facing the door of the Gents and in less of a hurry, so the fact that the door wasn't quite shut must have been much more obvious.'

Lambert studied the well-groomed face for seconds that seemed to stretch endlessly. 'You realize the importance of this? If that door was shut when you went down to the basement, it almost certainly means that Mr Nayland was murdered behind it during the three or four minutes whilst you were in the Ladies. He may not even have cried out very loudly, if the first blow he received was the fatal one. If on the other hand he had been killed before you got there, it stretches the possible time of his death and gives us a larger range of suspects.'

'Yes. I see that. But it's only now that you point it out that I see it.' She wondered why she suddenly seemed only capable of monosyllables, made herself take a deep breath. 'Unfortunately, I can't be certain. At the time it didn't seem important.'

Lambert smiled, acknowledging a phrase he had heard a thousand times before. 'You said you saw Michelle Nayland coming back up the stairs as you went down.'

'Yes. That doesn't mean anything, though, does it? I just happen to remember her. The evening was pretty boisterous by that time, with a lot of laughter and shouting. There may have been other people around, without my noticing them.'

Lambert's slight frown conveyed how unlikely he thought that was. 'Are you quite sure that you didn't see anyone else, male or female, whilst you were down in the basement?'

She gave the matter due thought. 'No, I'm sure I didn't. No one came into the Ladies whilst I was in there, I can be definite about that. Michelle was the only one I saw on the way down. And I didn't go back up the stairs, did I? I found the body and screamed. The next thing I remember is everyone being around me, and me fighting for my breath.'

Joanne watched Hook making notes in his round, deliberate hand, wondered exactly what words he was writing, what was left for them to investigate with her. Then Lambert said quietly, 'How would you describe your own relationship with Patrick Nayland, Mrs Moss?'

145

She made herself take her time. She had known the question would come, in some form, though perhaps she had thought it wouldn't be as direct and calm as this. 'I've already told you the gist of it. He was a good employer; I think that I was a good employee, even if that sounds immodest.' How odd and formal that word 'employee' sounded! She could hardly believe that she was applying it to herself. Just for a second, a second which might have been disastrous, she found that she wanted to laugh at herself, at her grave delivery of these sentiments.

Then she reminded herself of how dangerous was this charade she was playing out and strove to put a little detail upon it. 'The catering at Camellia Park has developed from an original concept which was very modest into something more ambitious.' That sounded like a publicity brochure, she thought. She summoned up a smile and said, 'I'm the one who's developed it. My wages have gone up, but I think the club has had good value for what it's paid me.'

If Lambert had noticed her transferring his question from Patrick to the more impersonal matter of the club, he gave no sign of it. The grey eyes studied her for a moment before he said, 'Do you know of anyone else, within the club or outside it, who had reason to wish Mr Nayland dead?'

She kept her face serious and unrelaxed; it wouldn't do for him to see the lightening of the tension she felt with this more general question. 'No. I've thought about that since Wednesday night. I expect everyone who was there has been thinking about it, once they got over the first shock of the death. But I haven't come up with anything which could be a motive for murder. I don't know the family, of course.'

Lambert spoke almost as if she hadn't given him this carefully planned reply. 'You see, someone must have been very desperate or very disturbed, to kill him at that time and in that place.'

Joanne nodded slowly, digesting the thought. 'It was a complete surprise to all of us. But isn't that a good thing, from a murderer's point of view?'

'Possibly. But a killing in a more private, more anonymous place would have left a wider range of suspects.'

She nodded. 'I suppose so. It's not something I've ever had to think about before.' She gave a small, involuntary shudder. 'I'm a murder suspect, aren't I? I'll have to come to terms with that idea.'

'Only until such time as we make an arrest. Tell me what you can about the relationship between the victim and Mr Pearson.'

How abrupt he was! They didn't go in for small talk, these people. Even the tea hadn't

147

led to any introductory chatter. She wondered if this manner was natural to Lambert or part of a technique he adopted to throw people off balance. 'Chris Pearson? He'd been involved in the enterprise from the start, before the golf course even had a name. He was around for two or three years before I came on the scene.'

'It was his relationship with Patrick Nayland that I asked about.'

He was like a prosecuting counsel bringing her back to the point. 'They seemed to me to get on very well with each other. Chris is ambitious for Camellia Park, has lots of ideas about its development. It was he who saw the potential in the catering, as soon as the place had a clubhouse. I think it was Chris who brought me in. I was part-time at first. Chris asked me to take on the job full-time after about a year.'

'But it was Patrick Nayland who made the decisions?'

'In the sense that he controlled the purse-strings, yes. I don't doubt that Chris Pearson had discussed the matter with Patrick fully before he offered me full-time work. But it was characteristic of Patrick to let Chris make me the offer.'

'They got on well together, then, the two of them?' Lambert brought her patiently back to the question.

'Yes. Very well, as far as I'm aware. Of

course, Patrick was the one with the money, the one who took the ultimate decisions about everything.'

'And that led to tensions?'

How quick the man was to latch on to things. She wondered what he was asking other people about her. 'No, I'm not saying that they fell out over it. Chris knew what the situation was and accepted it. I just think that occasionally he must have felt a little frustrated, when he didn't see things moving as fast as he'd have liked them to.'

'For instance?'

'Well, Chris wanted to take in more land, to make the course an eighteen holer. A proper golf course, he called it. Patrick said it was a business enterprise. That he'd plough the profits back, in due course, but that the place must generate enough money to pay for its own expansion.'

'You seem very well informed, Mrs Moss.'

It sounded like a dig, but she refused to let it ruffle her. 'We're a small organization at Camellia Park. You get to know what's going on pretty quickly. And Chris Pearson talks to me from time to time.'

He looked at her sharply, as if he suspected some sort of liaison with Chris, but she returned his look without embarrassment. Then he said, 'What about the people who work on the course?'

'Alan Fitch is deeper than people think he

is. I don't see a lot of him, but he comes in from time to time. He's proud of what he does on the course, and I've no reason to think he had anything against Patrick Nayland. I know he was pleased to get extra staff. He was delighted when young Barry Hooper was made permanent.'

'And what do you make of Mr Hooper?'

She shrugged, feeling the moments of danger were past, almost enjoying playing her part now. 'He seems a nice enough lad. Thinks the sun shines out of Alan Fitch, who's rather a father-figure to him. I suspect he thinks we're all quite ancient, the permanent staff. As we are to Barry, of course. He told me he loves working in the open air, but once he's away from the course he's more interested in motorbikes than anything else. He's just got a new one: you know when he's coming and going by the noise it makes.' She smiled in recollection of the lean young black body, crouched earnestly low over the fuel tank of his bike.

It was Hook, looking up unexpectedly from his notes, who said, 'Do you know the model? I used to ride a fast machine myself, twenty years ago.'

She managed to stifle a smile at the thought of this burly, almost portly, figure as a tearaway boy racer. 'No. I'm afraid I'm not into motorbikes.'

Hook nodded. 'And how was he on the

150

night of the murder? Did he seem to be behaving normally?'

And she'd thought for a moment that they were going to be diverted into a little small talk! 'Barry? Well, he was rather on edge, particularly in the early part of the evening. I think he was a little overawed by the restaurant and the company. I don't think he'd been to anything like that before.' She wondered if that sounded a little patronizing. 'Well, I know he hadn't, because Barry chatted to me for a few minutes at Wednesday lunchtime, and he was quite apprehensive about the evening.'

'But not about Mr Nayland?'

'Not about his employer, no. I think he was just glad to be taken on to the permanent staff of Camellia Park. I remember seeing him talking to Michelle Nayland on Wednesday evening.' She wasn't going to say he was a little out of his class there, because she wasn't going to talk the lad down. Let them make their own discoveries.

'And did you notice anyone who was behaving out of character? Or any disputes?' Hook had his ball-pen poised over his notebook.

It almost tempted her into a little mischief. Instead, she said demurely, 'No. As I say, quite a lot of decent wine was drunk during the evening. People were letting their hair down, and there was a lot of boisterous fun, but I didn't see any serious arguments.'

They stood up to go then. Lambert looked closely at the sideboard, and then at the shelves from which she had swept things into the dustbin bag in her clear-out. For a moment, she fancied that he was going to run his fingers along the almost bare mantelpiece. Instead, he said, 'Keep thinking about that evening. However unpleasant the idea may be, one of the people at that table killed Patrick Nayland. Things may still come back to you. Sometimes quite small things can be significant, in the context of murder. I think you're quite a shrewd observer, so I'd appreciate anything you come up with.'

And with that last little piece of flattery, they were gone. Joanne Moss found that it was some time before she could bring herself to be still. She walked up and down the familiar room, then gathered and washed the tea things. She kept going over everything they had said, searching for the subtext beneath the questions, examining the replies she had given to those observant men.

When she finally sat down in the big winged chair and picked up the morning paper she had still not opened, she allowed herself a smile, which she then found she could not wipe away.

It seemed to have gone quite well.

Eleven

A hundred miles north of Camellia Park, in a village high in the Derbyshire Peak District, it was even colder on Saturday morning than in Gloucestershire.

There was a light dusting of snow on the upper slopes of the hills, and a hard frost in the valleys. The woman detective constable flapped her arms in defence against the cold, which hit her suddenly when she got out of the car. Just routine, they'd said, it just needs checking out. Go and see the first Mrs Patrick Nayland and make sure that she can't throw any light upon this death.

So no glory to be gained, then; just the possibility of a good rollicking and a career setback if you missed anything which might later emerge as significant. Wonderful! Just the assignment for a Saturday morning she had planned to spend in bed with her boyfriend! DC Ros Tebbit rang the bell of the detached stone house, blew into her cupped hands, and turned her back upon an east wind which was no doubt coming straight from Siberia.

It was a man who opened the door. Around fifty, which was ancient to Ros, but trim and fit for his age, she thought, with dark, well-trimmed hair and humorous brown eyes. He was not in a dressing gown, as Ros had half-expected, but fully dressed in casual clothes. When she apologized for calling so early, he laughed. 'After nine now, isn't it? Been up for hours. You aren't allowed a lie-in when you keep Labradors!' A belated barking from the rear of the house endorsed that view.

DC Tebbit explained that it was the lady of the house she needed to see, that it almost certainly wouldn't take very long. 'A routine enquiry, in connection with an investigation into a serious crime in Gloucestershire,' she explained, rolling the syllables out carefully, but trying to imply that she had much more serious local concerns to fill the rest of her day, that only her professionalism protected him from the yawn she felt was appropriate to this enterprise.

The former Mrs Nayland, now Mrs Calvert, took her into a large square room at the front of the house and shut the oak door, stilling the interchange between her husband and the dogs at the other end of this solid, comfortable residence. She had been told two days earlier of Patrick Nayland's death, and a little of the manner of it, so Ros was spared the ordeal of breaking the news.

In all truth, the first wife of the victim did not seem much affected by this death. She had kept an excellent figure, even if she was now slightly overweight; her face was lightly made up, even at this hour; her grey hair was attractively styled, without a trace of the tinting Ros would have expected. Her first words confirmed what her appearance suggested. 'I was shocked rather than grief-stricken when I heard about Pat. We haven't been in touch for years, but you don't expect a man to be struck down like that, do you?'

'Indeed you don't, Mrs Calvert. And that's really why I'm here. As a small part of a full-scale murder inquiry. No more than a cog in a very large machine, but a necessary cog, nevertheless.'

Mary Calvert smiled into the earnest face, which had lit up despite itself at the mention of the word murder, with its curious, slaughterhouse glamour. 'I'm afraid I won't be able to assist you much. I'd like to help – no one wants a murderer to get away with it – but I won't be able to tell you much.'

Just as she had feared, Ros thought. And she'd left a grumpy lover in bed for this. She said in a determinedly official manner, 'Can you think of anyone who had a grievance against Mr Nayland? Anyone who might have wanted him out of the way?'

'Only me, at one time! I'd cheerfully have seen him off, around the time of our divorce!

155

Except that I don't suppose I would have, would I, given the chance? We say these things, but not many of us mean it, or there'd be a lot more killings than there are. Ten years later, I can't think why I got so excited about things. The parting of our ways was a blessing in disguise, really.' She looked contentedly round at the well-furnished room, with its Persian carpet and its antique mahogany cabinets.

With diminishing hope, DC Tebbit said resolutely, 'It was a bitter divorce, then, at the time?'

'Most of them are, aren't they? Especially when the lawyers get busy on them. I'd given Pat the best years of my life, and all that stuff. Cast out as a lonely woman – Gordon didn't come upon the scene until a couple of years later. But I didn't kill the old sod, if that's what you've come to check on. He's long since ceased to matter to me, and I was at the theatre in Buxton on Tuesday night, with about a thousand witnesses.' She grinned at the younger woman, enjoying her gentle teasing.

Ros decided against reminding this middle-aged lady about the existence of contract killers. 'What I have to establish is,' she said portentously, 'whether you know of anyone who might have killed him on Wednesday night.' She saw the older woman beginning to shake her head, detected the beginning of a smile on her lips, and added desperately, 'Or of any trait of his personality, which you know about and we don't, which might have had a bearing on his death.'

'Not really.' Then, as she saw the disappointment on the unlined young face, she added cheerfully, 'Pat couldn't keep his trousers on, of course. Any pretty face turned him on. That didn't matter, it's natural enough, but as soon as Pat got any encouragement he was into bed with them.'

Being just the tiny cog she had described in the investigative machine, DC Ros Tebbit didn't realize it. But this was the first time any member of that team had heard anyone say anything derogatory about Patrick Nayland.

Barry Hooper had somehow expected that the police would interview him at his place of work. That's where they'd talked to Alan Fitch, after all. The wide-open spaces of Camellia Park, the anonymity of the greenkeeper's sheds, would have allowed him more confidence than he felt here.

They had simply knocked on the door of the house and been shown the way up the stairs to his tiny bedsit. A very tall Detective Superintendent and a slightly shorter, wider, Detective Sergeant: two large men who looked even larger, even more menacing, in the confines of this high, narrow room.

The three-storeyed house had been a good one in its late Victorian heyday. Now the once elegant rooms had been subdivided to maximize the letting potential, and you could hear the sounds of other residents through the thin hardboard walls. The district's steady decline had accelerated steeply since the horrifying murders of Fred and Rosemary West; the garden of remembrance which now occupied the site where they had perpetrated their appalling crimes was only two streets away.

The two men sat on the edge of Barry's bed, allowing him to sit facing them on the one comfortable chair the room allowed. They looked around the mean room, with its threadbare carpet, its wallpaper unchanged in twenty years, its scratched wardrobe and chest of drawers, its tiny scullery behind the inadequate curtain. There was nothing of Hooper himself visible in the place, not a photograph, not a picture, and Barry thought perhaps they were noting that. He said nervously, 'I've only been here for a few weeks. At least it's a place of my own.'

'When did you move in, exactly?' asked DS Hook. He shifted his position a little on the bed, and Barry thought for a horrifying moment that he was going to patrol the room and look into the drawers. But he merely produced a notebook and shifted his weight from his left buttock to his right.

It took Barry a moment to refocus on the question. 'I moved in here at the beginning of November. Once I'd got established in my job at Camellia Park.'

Hook looked hard into the too-mobile young black face. He said quietly, not unkindly, 'Pushing it a bit, weren't you? Your job wasn't made permanent until nearly the end of that month, was it?'

Barry hadn't expected them to know that. He couldn't think how they had discovered such detail. He didn't think about the employment records in the office at the golf course. He thought Alan Fitch must have told them, and for a moment suffered a searing shaft of disappointment at what seemed like treachery from the man who was his idol. 'No. But I'd been working steadily there for three months and the wage was coming in, with quite a bit of overtime at the weekends – I helped out in the clubhouse when they were busy. I suppose I just hoped I'd be made permanent.'

'Like it there, do you?'

'I love it. Like working out in the open air. Like seeing the results of what we do in the months afterwards. Like going back to grass we've sown and trees we've planted and seeing them come on.' His enthusiasm was almost childlike. He stopped suddenly, as if feeling that he had betrayed himself with his eagerness, as if he was waiting for them to

159

mock him for it, as the lads he saw in the evenings had done.

But Hook just nodded and smiled, as if as a countryman he fully appreciated such ardour for the outdoor life. 'Bit of a change from what you've done before, the work at Camellia Park.'

'Yes.' They seemed to know everything about him, this pair.

'Changed your companions as well, have you, Barry?'

'Yes.'

'Because you were keeping bad company a year or two ago, weren't you?'

'Yes.' He suddenly lifted both of his hands together and ran the slim fingers through his wiry black hair, in a gesture that was pure nerves. It appeared to free his tongue. 'That's a long way behind me now, Mr Hook. Two, perhaps three years. I don't see those boys now.'

'Two of them are inside, so you wouldn't see them, would you? Given up thieving now, have you?'

'It was never proved, Mr Hook. Not against me.' This was as bad as he had thought it could be in his worst imaginings.

'I think it was, Barry. You were found guilty. You were lucky that the care home manager spoke up for you. And the man who ran the hostel said you'd been led astray by others. That you weren't a ringleader. But

160

we're used to reading between the lines when we look at police records, you see. We know that you were lucky to get off with a few hours of community service.'

'I was, yes.' Barry Hooper wondered why he was agreeing with the police, why he was allowing himself to be led gently into all kinds of admissions by this burly man with the old-fashioned sweater and the soft Herefordshire burr. He said inconsequentially, 'I couldn't hold a job down, in those days.'

'No. "Unreliable", they thought, at the supermarket; and then at the foundry; and then at the glass factory. Interesting word, "unreliable". It has a multitude of meanings, when employers use it.'

'Yes.'

'Often means you can't get in on time in the mornings. Can mean more serious things, sometimes. Like thieving.'

'I wasn't a thief. Not after that first time. I'd learnt.'

'Glad to hear it. Sometimes, if it's petty thieving, firms sack a bloke because it's easier than taking him to court.'

'I wasn't sacked for thieving. I – I didn't have much luck, in those days.' He realized what a desperate whinge that sounded. 'It's true what they said, though. I was just not reliable.'

'Wonder why that was, Barry. Young lad like you were then, making his way in the

161

world. And not unintelligent, according to the care home manager. There doesn't seem to be any reason why you shouldn't have been perfectly reliable.'

'But I wasn't, was I? Perhaps I hadn't—'

'Given up the drugs now, have you, Barry?'

It was like a blow in the face. He didn't see how they could know, and yet they did. He didn't know that an experienced man like Hook could read the symptoms at a glance, then feed in speculation as if it were an established fact.

Barry put his hands together between his thighs, gazed hard down at the knees of his jeans. He dared not look up at his tormentor, in case his eyes strayed to the drawer near the top of the dresser. 'I've given them up, yes. It was only pot, you know, never more than a few spliffs. But that was what made me unreliable.' He stared at the hole in the carpet beyond his feet, wondering if that had sounded like a lie to them. He had lost all sense of judgement now.

Hook studied the abject figure for a moment, then gave the briefest of nods to Lambert. It was the Superintendent who said, 'Anyway, you seem to be holding the job down at Camellia Park. Everyone there seems quite pleased with you, in fact.'

Barry forced himself to look up into the long, lined face, into the grey eyes which seemed to look effortlessly into his very soul.

Was this the hard-cop/soft-cop routine he had heard his friends talk about? Yet Hook had not seemed harsh; Barry could not work out how he had revealed so much about himself to that soft-voiced, avuncular figure. Relieved now to be able to speak without reservation, he said, 'I love the work on the golf course. Love working with Mr Fitch.' Just in time, he stopped himself from going on about the birds and the wild flowers and what he had learned about them from his mentor.

'How did you get on with Patrick Nayland, Barry?'

'I hardly knew him, did I? I used to see him sometimes, when I was coming in to work or leaving. But I scarcely said more than "Good morning" to him. It was Mr Pearson who interviewed me, when I was appointed. He had Mr Fitch with him, though.' He added that as if he did not want to denigrate the status of the Head Greenkeeper.

'Mr Nayland must have been pleased with your work, though, to make you a full-time employee.'

'I suppose so. I expect it was Mr Fitch who spoke up for me. We get on very well together. He says I'm a quick learner.' It was impossible to detect a blush on the black cheeks, but Barry Hooper gave every other sign of a pleasurable embarrassment.

'And now the man who paid your wages

has been brutally murdered, at the end of an evening where he had been the host to all of you.'

'Yes.'

'And have you any idea who might have done this dreadful thing, Barry?'

'No.' There was more fear than he could have thought possible in the explosive monosyllable.

'I expect that at some time during the evening you'd been down to the basement where Mr Nayland died, hadn't you?'

'Yes. Everyone had.'

'I see. Watching the others, were you?'

'No. I just mean that the meal took a long time, so I expect everyone went down to the washroom at some time during the evening.' Amidst his anxiety, he was stupidly pleased that he'd come up with that word 'washroom'. It wasn't a word he'd ever used in his life before, but he'd remembered the delicious Michelle Nayland using it to him on that night.

'It wasn't you who found the body. So how long before the discovery was it that you were down there?'

'I couldn't say.' Barry Hooper stared resolutely at the fraying threads of the carpet between his feet.

'You can do better than that, Barry. Ten minutes? Twenty? Half an hour?'

He shook his head, like a bull tormented

by the matador's darts. 'I can't be sure. A long time. Perhaps an hour.' He knew immediately that he'd overplayed his hand, but he couldn't take it back now. He wondered what the others had said, whether anyone had observed his comings and goings on the night. He didn't think so, but you couldn't be sure, not with so many pairs of eyes to take into account.

A long time seemed to pass, but he would not lift his eyes from the carpet. You could see a bit of the floorboards at one point; he'd never realized that before. The words seemed to come from a long way away when Lambert said, 'Who found the body, Barry?'

He looked up then, startled. 'Mrs Moss. She screamed the place down and we all went down there. But you must know that.'

'We do indeed. It's just that you seemed so vague about your own movements that I wondered how much you remembered about the murder.'

'I remember that. And I know it was a long time before Mrs Moss screamed that I was down there. I just wasn't sure of exactly how long.'

'An hour, you said.'

'That's what I think it was.' Barry felt as he had done years ago at school, when he had been detected in a lie and could do nothing but go on obstinately repeating it to the teacher, even when the facts had exposed it.

'All right. Who else went down there, in the time between your visit and the discovery of the body?'

'I don't know. Everyone, I should think. Pretty well everyone, anyway.'

'What were you doing when you heard Mrs Moss screaming?'

He must be careful here. Everyone should remember what was happening then, shouldn't they? 'I was talking to Alan – to Mr Fitch. He'd just come back upstairs from the washrooms.'

It was out before he could stop it. The man he would least have wanted to incriminate. He felt like Judas. And he hadn't even thirty pieces of silver for his pains: he had just been trying to save his own skin. There was a long pause, as if they wanted him to appreciate what he had done, before Lambert said, 'How long before the screams was this?'

'Quite a while, really. It must have been, because we were talking for quite a while. He was warning me to keep off the port, that it was lethal stuff for a young man. He was telling me some tale about when they'd docked in Portugal, years ago, and he'd had a skinful of port.' He tried desperately to extricate Alan from what he'd done to him. It wasn't true: the tale about the port had been during one of their lunch-time talks in the greenkeeper's shed, weeks ago. He must remember to tell Alan what he'd said, or

166

things would only get worse, with these two worrying at it like dogs with a bone. He was conscious of Lambert waiting, whilst Hook made a careful note of what he'd said.

Then the Superintendent said quietly, 'Do you remember anyone else going down to the basement in the period immediately before the body was found?'

'Yes. Michelle Nayland. And Mrs Nayland.' He flayed around like a novice on ice, desperately trying to save his friend.

'And can you remember the order in which they went down there?'

'No. I'm not sure how long it was before the screams. Probably they went later than Mr Fitch.' He felt that he was probably contradicting himself now. 'I'd drunk a lot. And I didn't think any of this was going to be important at the time.' Belatedly, he came up with the excuse that everyone had offered.

'And yet you're sure that a full hour elapsed between your own trip to the basement and the discovery of Mr Nayland's body.'

'A long time, I said. I'm sure it was a long time.' He looked up into the long, lined face, desperate and wide-eyed, pleading to be believed.

'Who do you think killed Mr Nayland?'

'I don't know. Not Mr Fitch.'

Lambert nodded very slowly. 'I see. Mr Fitch built a bonfire at Camellia Park on the day after the murder, didn't he?'

'I don't know.' Then, as he realized how ridiculous this denial sounded, Barry said, 'Yes, I remember now, he did.'

'And what did he burn?'

'I don't know.'

'You weren't there?'

'No.' Then another belated attempt to retrieve things. 'Well, not when he started the fire I wasn't. I helped him later on. We were burning brambles that we'd cut down on the course. That and other rubbish. We have to get rid of things every so often, so we have a bonfire.' He wondered if he was now saying too much, even though he knew that he wasn't really saying anything. Nothing that was useful to these inquisitive CID men, that is. When they didn't react, he added inconsequentially, 'It was a good day for a bonfire, Thursday.'

'So why weren't you there when the fire was lit?'

It sounded like an accusation. 'We were told we needn't come in at the usual time on that morning, after what had happened the night before. But Alan was in at the usual time.' Again he felt he was letting down the man he least wanted to implicate, so he said limply, 'I expect he couldn't sleep.'

'I expect you're right. If you think about anything you haven't told us yet, get in touch immediately. You never know, your recall of things might improve.'

It sounded like a threat, but all he could think of was that they were going at last. He was on his feet too quickly, standing by the door to open it for them. The tall one, the Superintendent, looked at him for a few seconds without speaking before he left. The Sergeant, who had grilled him at the beginning and then kept silent, said as he turned in the doorway, 'Honesty is much the best policy for you, Barry. This is murder, and you're out of your depth here.'

Absurdly, he found himself thanking the burly man for that thought. That was almost admitting some sort of guilt, he told himself angrily, as he sat where Hook had sat on the bed and considered what he had said to the CID men.

At least they hadn't searched the place. Probably they weren't allowed to do that, probably they needed a search warrant. But he knew that he'd have been powerless to stop them, if they started opening drawers and cupboards.

Barry Hooper walked over to the scratched old dresser, slid open the second drawer down, moved the white vest and blue socks to one side, watching his slim black hand as if it belonged to someone else. The two white cocaine rocks were there, as he had known they would be.

He tried to firm up his resolve to kick the habit.

169

Twelve

It was after the inquest on Monday morning that Chris Pearson buttonholed Liza Nayland.

He had watched her carefully during the solemnities of the coroner's court. She had given the brief evidence of identification in a clear, controlled voice, then listened, grave-faced but attentive, to the rest of the proceedings. She had cast her eyes down during the forensic evidence about the knife-wounds and the blood, but had given a little sigh of relief when the inevitable verdict of Murder by Person or Persons Unknown was brought in ten minutes later.

Mrs Nayland accepted the coroner's sympathy, nodded her understanding of his regret that the body could not yet be released for burial or cremation. She was dignified, but in control of herself, Chris judged. Not too upset to talk business. And what he had to say was very urgent.

Black suited her: with her tallness, her dark blonde hair and her deep blue eyes, she looked very elegant beneath the brim of the black hat she had donned for the inquest. Chris Pearson had never seen her in a hat before; it seemed to distance her a little further from him. He felt a little inhibited as he approached the widow, as if he were speaking to her after a funeral rather than outside the modern brick building where the coroner's court operated.

'I'm sorry to bother you at a time like this, but I'd like a few words about what happens now at Camellia Park. If you can spare the time and feel up to it, that is.' He felt as formal as if he were back on the parade square, marching up to the CO to declare the parade ready for inspection, observing the ceremonial and the constricted language of Army life. But that was all right, he told himself: Liza Nayland had been an Army wife, in her time. She must understand these things.

And she did. She didn't even seem surprised by his request. She gave him a small smile and said, 'Of course. I expect everyone at the golf course is wondering just what is going to happen. Life goes on, and the sooner we can clarify things, the better it will be for all concerned, I'm sure. Would you like to come back to the house now?'

'But wouldn't that be inconvenient for you? I expect your daughter will be going back home with you...' His words tailed away as he realized that he was behaving again as if this were a funeral, with family mourners to be accommodated and the rituals of internment to be observed.

Liza said, 'Michelle is going straight back to her school. She wasn't really needed at the inquest, but I think she felt she had to be here to support me. I'm going to drive home now; if you follow behind me, we'll have a talk at the house. I've been thinking myself that there are things we need to sort out.'

The two of them stood for a moment together, watching the small crowd who had attended the inquest melt away along the pavement. Apart from reporters, and one or two curious members of the public attracted by the sensational nature of this crime, they were mostly the people who had been at Soutters Restaurant on that fatal evening. Chris wondered if Liza Nayland had realized that the person who had murdered her husband was almost certainly among these innocent-looking citizens.

He noticed that stolid Detective Sergeant Hook, standing unobtrusively at the edge of the gathering, quietly observing the bearing of everyone who had been at that dinner. Watching to see whether the murderer would give himself away, Chris supposed. He decided that DS Hook was a man who was easy to underestimate, and stored that thought away for future guidance.

Liza Nayland had got rid of her coat and

hat by the time he had parked his car and entered the big, detached house. 'Whisky?' She poured each of them a generous measure, filled her glass to the brim with water, pushed the jug towards him, and sat opposite him in the easy chair by the fireplace. Only her outer garments had been black for the coroner's court. Underneath them, she was wearing an attractive light-blue dress. She took a sip of her whisky and said, 'What was it you wanted to talk about, Chris?'

It was friendly enough, but he had hoped she would lead the way into the discussion. He realized now that he didn't know this alert-looking woman as well as he had thought he did. He had only met her socially before, and always found her pleasant enough. He had no idea what weight she carried as a businesswoman. He found himself saying, 'It's a bit awkward, really. Coming so soon after Patrick's death.'

'That was a shock to all of us – perhaps to me most of all. But I realize that you and other people who worked for him must be wondering what happens next. That's natural enough.'

This preliminary fencing was only making him more nervous. Chris Pearson wasn't used to being nervous, and it threw him off balance. He hadn't put as much water with his whisky as his hostess, and he now took a stiff pull at it, downing half of it in one go, feeling the fire spread into his chest. He said, 'I don't know how much you know about the way Patrick ran Camellia Park.'

'I know that he gave you a pretty free hand.'

'He did. All the decisions were his, of course, which is only right – he who pays the piper calls the tune, and all that.' He laughed nervously, found he was despising himself for the cliché. 'But he discussed everything with me, and on the vast majority of occasions we were agreed about what we should do. And Pat seemed to be happy about the way I put our decisions into action.'

'He was. I know that much at least about the enterprise. And perhaps know a little more than you think about what went on.'

His heart sank at that, but when he looked at Liza Nayland, she didn't seem to be taunting him. He plunged on. 'I'm sure you do. But I need to know what you plan for Camellia Park. The staff have already been asking about it.' That was a small lie, but certainly warranted, in the situation.

'I intend to go on providing the money to develop the course and the clubhouse at Camellia Park. I've no idea yet how much money Pat has left me; we hadn't got round to talking about that and it didn't seem necessary.' Her voice almost broke on the last phrase. She took a determined sip of her whisky and a few seconds to recover herself.

174

'Pat had other irons in the fire, as I'm sure you gathered, and some of them are in the early stages of development, where they may need capital. But I'm confident there'll be the money to press ahead with developments at Camellia Park. It was one of Pat's pet projects, and it will remain one of mine.'

'That's good to hear.'

'Please relay that to the staff, if you think it will help them. Uncertainty isn't good for any workforce.'

'Thank you.' He was probing, trying to find out just how much she knew. 'And the place is already making a healthy profit. I'm quite certain that further developments could be self-financed.' He tried not to sound too sycophantic as he said, 'And I'm sure you and I will be able to work very well together.'

'I'm sure of that as well. I'm not going to pretend that it will all be plain sailing. I don't know anything like as much as Pat did about the detail of the course. As I say, it was his pet project. He'd walked every blade of grass, since the days when he bought the land as farmer's fields. And he was a golfer, which must help when it comes to decisions. I don't even play the game.'

Chris Pearson smiled. He was certain now that she didn't know. 'I play. And I'm pretty familiar with the place myself, by now.'

'Of course you are. And we'll need your

175

knowledge, more than ever in the months to come. I don't propose to be as "hands-on" as Pat was. I'll depend on you, Chris. I know you won't let me down.'

'I won't. I take it that there is to be no change in policy, then.' This was the key moment. He dropped the thought in as casually as he could, with the air of merely confirming what they had been saying.

'No change in policy. But I realize that in effect I'm asking you to take on extra responsibilities. I wouldn't expect you to do that without proper recognition.'

It was his opportunity, and he took it. 'As a matter of fact, Pat had been talking in similar terms. It was something which had been understood between us from the start, but never written down. We didn't need written contracts: we got on too well for that.' When he dared to look at her, he fancied that the clear blue eyes were regarding him keenly. He backed off a little and added apologetically, 'But this is hardly the moment to talk about these things.'

'On the contrary, the sooner the situation is sorted out, the better it will be for everyone concerned in the organization. What did you have in mind?'

'I'm not talking about money. Or not primarily about money. I'm confident that what I have in mind would eventually be to my financial advantage, but that's because I

176

have faith in the future of Camellia Park.' He picked his way carefully through the phrases he had rehearsed on the previous night.

'You want to be more than just Chief Executive.'

He grinned, seeing an opportunity to lighten the atmosphere. 'That's a rather grandiose title for a plant which at present has four full-time workers. But yes, Pat and I had always had an understanding that at a certain stage I would become a partner in the enterprise. I would put all the energy I had into the place in its early days, knock it into some sort of going concern, give it a future. My reward for taking a lower wage in the early stages was to be a partnership.' He did not dare to look at her. He fixed his eyes on the vase of chrysanthemums in the fire-place and said, 'A few days before his death, we had agreed that the time to implement these plans had arrived. That the place was now sufficiently developed for the idea of a partnership to be feasible.'

There was a long pause. He wondered as it stretched if he had overplayed his hand. But her words when they came were like music to him. 'I think that's feasible. I said I hadn't Pat's knowledge of the detail of Camellia Park and how it works. But I do know how hard you've worked and how highly Pat rated you. I think it's in my interests as well as yours to keep you around. And the best way to do that is to give you a role in the place which goes beyond mere wages. I've no objection in principle to your notion of a partnership. In fact, I welcome the idea.'

How cool and businesslike she was, for a woman widowed less than a week ago. He could envisage working well with her, in the months to come. He said, 'I can't buy myself in, I'm afraid. But I'm not looking for an equal partnership, or anything approaching it. I'll go on working for the same wage as before. It's just that I'd like to have a real stake in the future of Camellia Park, and a share of the profits in due course, when the situation warrants it.'

She said, 'This isn't the time to talk detail, Chris. Let's just accept the idea in principle, and get the accountants to look at the books. We can do our hard negotiating about the detail in due course.'

She leaned across and gave him a refill of whisky. Chris noticed for the first time that his own glass was empty and hers still three-quarters full; he must have been even more nervous than he'd realized. He said, 'Thank you. I hadn't thought it would be so difficult for me to talk about these things. I think I found it easier undertaking special assignments in the Army than this.'

Liza Nayland didn't know exactly what he'd done in the Army; he'd never mention-ed it before, and now didn't seem the time to follow it up. She said, 'Pat used to say things like that, when things got complicated. But I don't suppose he meant it.'

'I don't suppose he did. They're a long way behind us now, those Army days.' Chris stood up and offered his hand. It seemed the right thing to do, a clinching of a satisfactory business deal. He drove out of the wide drive of the big house with a cheerful wave to the woman who stood upon the step, scarcely daring to believe what he had achieved from the encounter.

His elation lasted until late in the afternoon, when he received the news that the CID wanted to speak to him again about the murder of Patrick Nayland.

John Lambert held the unofficial conference with DI Rushton and DS Hook as much to clarify his own thinking as in the hope of any fresh information or insights. He felt confused about what he had anticipated would be a straightforward case. He didn't want to call the whole of the murder team in and thus suspend the work of investigation, but three heads were definitely better than one when you wanted to elucidate the position.

He began by narrowing the field. 'There were sixteen people in the restaurant at the time when Nayland was killed. Does any one of us think that any of the spouses or partners who were attending the meal at

Soutters ranks as a probable for this?'

Hook, who had seen most of the people involved said, 'There is just the one spouse I would except from that. Mrs Nayland. She and her daughter, Michelle, are certainly in the frame. Apart from them, I think only the four people who work at the golf course are serious suspects.'

Lambert looked at Rushton, who nodded and said, 'All the others have been formally interviewed, as have Fred and Paula Soutter, the owners of the restaurant, and the skivvy who was helping Fred Soutter in the kitchen that night. None of them has given us any reason to think they stuck that knife into Nayland. Unfortunately, none of them seems to have seen anything helpful, either.'

Hook said gloomily, 'It doesn't help that at that stage of the evening most people had drunk quite a lot. They weren't at their most observant and their recollections are not completely reliable.'

Lambert nodded. 'I'm more concerned that those recollections seem highly selective. We should have learned more from them than we have about the victim. If they're not actually lying, then some of them at least are withholding things from us. And if they're reticent about the victim, it makes me think they're not being completely honest about the other suspects, either.'

Rushton said, 'So far, we've learned more

about the victim from other sources than from the people who lived with him and worked with him. We've turned up that conviction for Indecent Assault. And the only interesting thing his ex-wife up in Derbyshire said about Patrick Nayland is that he couldn't keep his hands off the women around him. I don't suppose for a moment that the leopard has changed his spots.'

Policemen are not puritans: they see far too much of the seamier side of life for that. But Chris Rushton's lips pursed in distaste as he spoke of the dead man's lechery; the distaste, perhaps, of a man whose own marriage had failed and who did not find it easy to open up new relationships with women.

Lambert suppressed the unworthy thought that he wished there were more criminals with DI Rushton's puritan ethic; men who stepped out of their trousers at every opportunity invariably complicated murder investigations. The old saw was that sex or money lay somewhere behind every serious crime; in his experience, sex was much the more complex of the two. You knew where you were with money, you could measure it in figures, judge whether these were sums which people might think it worth killing for. You couldn't get inside a man's head to measure the effect upon him of a glimpse of thigh or a fierce sexual coupling.

Hook said, 'The date of the conviction for Indecent Assault was well before his second marriage. It's possible Liza Nayland isn't aware of it, even now. It's the kind of thing most men would want to hide, if they could.'

'And it may be that people are holding back because of not wishing to speak ill of the dead. All the same, I'm sure some of them at least must know more about Nayland than they've been prepared to tell us. Chris Pearson, for instance, has worked with him as his right-hand man since the idea of a golf course was first mooted.'

Hook looked down at his notes. 'Pearson actually told us that he knew Nayland "as well as any man outside his family". But he didn't tell us anything about that family; it's odd that he should claim to know nothing at all about that, and everything there was to know about the business side of things.'

Rushton said, 'I'm still waiting for the full details of Pearson's Army career. We know that he was decorated in the Falklands and that he spent the bulk of his service with the Royal Artillery. But apparently he transferred for the last few years of his Army service, and Army records so far haven't come up with any details.'

Lambert said, 'We'll have further words with Mr Pearson, when we get a fuller picture. He struck me as the coolest of all the people we've seen, the one who had come to terms immediately with this death, who in interview gave us exactly what he intended to give and no more.'

There was silence. The other two men in the room were thinking how neatly that description fitted the murderer in a case like this, but conscious also that Lambert would not welcome speculation, would insist on assembling facts. With that in mind, Rushton went for the statistically most likely candidate. 'What about the widow? Even if Nayland had concealed a court case from many years ago, she can hardly have been unaware of his eye for the ladies.'

It was a curiously old-fashioned phrase from much the youngest man in the room. Lambert said, 'Nayland might have turned over a new leaf, of course, with a second and happier marriage. It's been known.' No one contradicted him. But no one endorsed that view either. There was too much experience of human nature in the room for that.

Hook said, 'Liza Nayland certainly gave the impression in our interview that it was a happy marriage and that she had no problems of that sort. Either he'd changed his ways, or she was unaware of any transgressions.'

'Or she knew about them and wasn't letting on that she knew to you,' said Rushton with a cynical smile. He wasn't letting go of a prime suspect that easily.

Lambert said, 'If she did know of a woman or women her husband had recently been involved with, then she lied to us about it. She told us specifically that she knew he wasn't having any affairs.'

'They say the wife is always the last to know,' said Rushton stubbornly.

Lambert nodded slowly. 'And that could be true in this case. Liza Nayland seemed confident that her husband had no sexual liaisons. But such ignorance is convenient for her: it removes her most obvious motive for murder, because she couldn't then have killed in a fit of sexual jealousy.'

Rushton said, 'She's still the one who's gained most from this death. In a monetary sense, I mean. I know you'll say that women can get divorced and do very well out of it nowadays, but this way she gets the lot.'

Lambert wondered just how much Chris Rushton himself had left after his divorce. The Inspector was living in a tiny, aseptic flat now, with limited access to the small daughter he had doted upon in the years of her infancy. He said, 'What did you think of Mrs Nayland, Bert?'

'I think she was genuinely grieving for his death. That doesn't mean she didn't kill him, of course. Many murderers are immediately upset by what they've done. I'm not sure whether she was concealing things about her husband or not. But I'm sure she wasn't telling us the whole truth and nothing but the truth. I thought she was very cagey about the relationship between her daughter and Patrick Nayland.'

'Nothing unnatural in that. Not many families care to air their differences in public. She admitted the two didn't get on at first, but she said they were happy enough together at the time of this death.'

Hook checked his notebook again. 'She said, "Michelle had realized that my happiness was bound up with Patrick, and had accepted the situation." It's hardly a glowing testimonial. And she instanced that they'd had a happy meal together, only a few days before the man's death. If you have to pick out a particular meal where things went well, it strikes me that it was the exception rather than the rule.'

Lambert sighed. 'We can put rather more pressure on Liza Nayland, now that we're a little further away from the murder and we know a little more about her husband. What about her daughter?'

'An intelligent and attractive young woman. Just the type that young, divorced detective inspectors should be pursuing.' Hook kept his face impeccably straight as he looked down at his notebook.

Rushton felt that he was blushing, despite the fact that he should have been well used to shafts from this duo by now. 'She's much too young for me.'

'Eight years or so? Probably needs an experienced man like you to keep her out of mischief, Chris.'

'And she may be a murderess. I think we should stick to the point.'

Lambert controlled the wish to smile and nodded earnestly. 'Attractive young women have been known to stick knives into people before now. What struck me is that her recall of what went on at Soutters last Wednesday night was very precise – until it came to the moments that might be of use to us. Then she became as vague as the rest of them; that makes me wonder if it was a convenient vagueness.'

Hook said, 'She was very definite in insisting that she was Nayland's stepdaughter, not his daughter, despite adopting his name. She said, "I gave Patrick a hard time, at first, and I'm sure he thought I was a right little cow." But she claimed they were getting on "perfectly well" by the time of his death. But she was back at work within thirty-six hours of the man's death and she wasn't grief-stricken: she said, "I'm not going to simulate a misery I don't feel." She thought Nayland must have been killed by someone he'd offended in his business dealings.'

Lambert nodded. 'Which would conveniently strike Michelle and her mother off the list of suspects, of course. There's a surprise!

186

But we need to see the delightful Miss Nayland again, to press her harder about one or two things. There's some discrepancy in the times when she was at the scene of the murder, as well as this query about her relationship with the dead man.'

'We'll put a good word in for you, when we see her, Chris,' said Hook. 'Tell her you're sound in mind and body – well, body, anyway.'

'What have you turned up among the employees?' said Rushton grimly, his eyes firmly fixed on his computer screen.

Lambert smiled. 'Pearson we've already discussed. Joanne Moss, the Catering Manager at Camellia Park, is the woman who discovered the body. The others agree that they went down there and found her in near-hysterics with the corpse. No one has said anything yet to clear her of the murder, but equally no one has even suggested the idea that Joanne Moss killed him.'

Rushton said, 'When I spoke to her on Wednesday night, Joanne Moss was still too upset to be coherent. How was she when you spoke to her on Friday night? Did you find her account of how she came to be down in the basement with a dead man in her arms convincing?'

'As far as it went, yes. She says she was in the ladies' loo for three or four minutes. It's probable but not certain that the door of the

Gents was slightly open when she went down there, without her noticing it. In which case, Nayland might have been lying dead during the time she was in there and even perhaps for some time before that. She noticed that the door was slightly ajar and then saw his foot there as she came out of the Ladies. The configuration of the doors means that you are indeed much more likely to notice a gap in the doorway of the Gents on your way out of the Ladies than on your way in there.'

Rushton nodded slowly, measuring the statement from Joanne Moss, which he had turned up on his computer screen, against his memory of the geography of the basement at Soutters. 'She could, of course, have arranged to meet him down there, knifed him, and then screamed her head off.'

Lambert agreed. 'She could have done just that. It's something we must bear in mind. For what it's worth, she denies any suggestion that she had arranged to meet Nayland down there, and we haven't found anyone else yet who supports such a theory.'

Hook had rather liked the competent and personable Mrs Moss; she had given them tea and home-made biscuits after a long hard day. He said, 'But if she killed him, why not simply walk back upstairs and let someone else find the body? There's no suggestion that she was caught red-handed: it was

188

her screams which brought people to the scene.'

Rushton was reluctant to let her go as a suspect. 'She would have had to account for the blood on her clothes, if she'd come back up to the restaurant. The hysterics might have been genuine. They might be the only part of her story that is genuine.' But he didn't sound convinced of that.

Lambert sighed, 'That leaves the two blokes who work on the course. Alan Fitch and his sidekick, Barry Hooper. One of the problems I have with this case is that none of the people involved has struck me as a likely murderer in interview. Often we have the problem that we have several likely candidates; in this case there isn't one of them that I'd be glad to arrest and lock away. This chap Fitch has seen violence in the past, and in my judgement he would certainly be capable of killing someone, if he felt strongly enough about it. But that's very different from saying I think he's the man who killed Nayland in Soutters on Wednesday night.'

Hook said, 'He's got a past all right. He says he learned how to look after himself when he was seeing the world with the Merchant Navy, but that's usually a euphemism for being handy with your fists, and sometimes with worse weaponry than that. He's got a conviction for causing an affray, which could easily have been for GBH. On the other hand, that's a long time ago now, back in his Merchant Navy days, and he has a clean record since then. And he enjoys his work on the golf course and enjoys being the one in charge of things. I can't see what he's going to gain from this death.'

'I agree with that,' said Lambert. 'And yet his manner didn't quite reinforce it. He was very reticent about Nayland, so much so that I got the impression that he didn't like the man, didn't even regret his death much. He was at the golf course before anyone else on the morning after the murder, and he lit a bonfire. No reason why he shouldn't have done that: there was rubbish to dispose of. Barry Hooper confirmed that. But Fitch seemed very defensive about it, and very nervous when we had a look at the remains of the bonfire. But if he had been burning anything incriminating, he'd done it very effectively: there was nothing but a circle of black earth left for us to see.'

Rushton said, 'What about this black boy, Barry Hooper?' and flashed the appropriate file up on his monitor screen. 'Chequered background, hasn't he? Conviction a few years ago for thieving. Probably on drugs.'

'Nothing to suggest this level of violence though. And it's three years and more since he was last in trouble. And he loves his job at the golf course. So why get rid of the bloke who employs you?' Hook, who had pressed

190

Hooper so hard during interview, felt the need to stand up for him now.

Lambert smiled despite himself at Hook's earnestness. 'Hooper was jumpy when we interviewed him. Perhaps that's only to be expected, when he's been in trouble with the police before. I felt that he was concealing something, but I couldn't think what it might be – unless we consider the obvious possibility that he'd killed Nayland. But like Bert, I couldn't for the life of me see why Barry Hooper would want to kill the man who paid his wages, who had only recently decided to make him permanent in the first job in his life that he really enjoys.'

Hook said, 'I thought he was immediately cagey about that fire which Fitch had lit. He wasn't there at the time. As you say, Alan Fitch had come in before anyone else was around and immediately lit that bonfire; that makes you wonder if he'd come in whilst it was quiet with that specific purpose in mind. Hooper made it seem more suspicious, because he too seemed to think that there was more in it than met the eye.'

Lambert said, 'Young Mr Hooper might be useful to us when we know a little more. He isn't a natural liar. Bert verbally roughed him up a bit at the beginning of our meeting and he was putty in our hands after that.'

Rushton looked at the rubicund Sergeant in surprise; Bert didn't have a reputation for being hard on lads like Barry Hooper. When accusations of institutional racism were hurled at the police, DI Rushton always cited Bert Hook as an example of how ridiculous the notion was.

At that moment, there was a beep from the desk behind him as an email arrived in his inbox. 'Probably won't be anything useful, but better check it out,' he said.

His face lit up with a modest pleasure as he read the message. Technology coming up with the goods again, when John Lambert thought he could do everything by his old-fashioned methods. In all truth, this wasn't a lot. It wasn't going to lead to an immediate arrest, but it was an addition to their knowledge in this baffling case; he was glad it had come in whilst Lambert was in the CID section.

'Details I've been waiting for of Christopher Pearson's Army record,' DI Rushton explained. 'Decorated in the Falklands, as we already knew. Served the bulk of his time as a warrant officer with the Royal Artillery. But there's one interesting thing we didn't know. He spent the last three years of his service with the SAS.'

'Now why on earth would a man wish to conceal something like that from us?' said Superintendent Lambert thoughtfully.

Thirteen

For a young man of such slight build, Barry Hooper was surprisingly strong. Alan Fitch noticed that fact once again on the raw afternoon of Monday the eighteenth of December, as they lugged railway sleepers off the tractor at the side of the ninth tee at Camellia Park.

He was proud of the strength of his own stocky physique, developed on the ships in his youth and preserved with no sign of diminution into middle age. The speed of movement left you, but the strength stayed, so long as you continued to use it regularly. But he was surprised how Barry kept up with him until they were both breathing heavily with satisfaction as they had the final baulk of timber in place at last.

They had extended and elevated this teeing ground. Now they were putting in five steps at the side of it, to enable golfers to ascend easily and avoid damage to the turf on the side of the tee. Inevitably, there would be some who would ignore their diligently constructed steps, who would slip and leave ugly slide-marks in the carefully laid grass. If such transgressors went arse over tit in their descent from the tee, that would give Alan Fitch a certain kick.

He tapped the end of their final sleeper the last quarter-inch into place with the sledge-hammer, checked the spirit level on the top step, and said approvingly, 'Good job, that, young Barry. Be here when I've gone – perhaps when you've gone, if you don't slow down on that motorbike.'

'We'd like a few words with you, please. On your own.' Lambert, speaking quietly from behind the pair, felt a reprehensible sense of power as the two of them started like guilty things upon a fearful summons. But it seemed unlikely that either of these men was familiar with *Hamlet*.

Alan Fitch recovered quickly. He dismissed the image of vultures which had sprung into his mind when he had turned to find the two dark-suited men standing motionless on the higher ground above him. He said, 'We'd best go back to the sheds, then. Barry, you stay here and carry on with that path. It'll need a few more barrowfuls of aggregate before we can finish it off. You do that now, whilst I have a word with these gentlemen, and we'll do the final levelling tomorrow.'

He led the CID men away to his den, as he had come to regard the room at the end of the long concrete shed where they kept their tractor and mowers and other course equipment. He had preferred the old wooden shed in which he had been based when he started here, with its intimate smells of oil and grass and metal, but when safety regulations required a more modern building, he had adapted surprisingly quickly to his own section at the end of it.

Within a month, Alan was pleased with its solid wall which cut him off from the oil and the chemicals, with its modern shower and washing facilities, its new kettle and crockery which Joanne Moss had sent up for him from the clubhouse. With a few ornaments like the ship in a bottle contrived by one of his messmates from the Navy days, the animals carved painstakingly from bone by some anonymous Victorian sailor, the black and white picture of a teenage Alan Fitch with arms folded in his football team, he had put his own stamp upon the place. The fact that these were the things his wife would not allow him to display in their small, neat home only made this place more of his own den, as did the fact that few people other than Barry Hooper ever ventured in here.

He offered the two large, observant men who had followed him into that den a cup of tea, but they refused, politely but briskly, with the air of people who had more important things upon their minds. They invited him to sit down in his own place, and he did so, perching awkwardly on the edge of the battered armchair, then easing himself equally awkwardly back into it, as he tried to simulate relaxation.

Alan Fitch was a man of action, a highly able man in the strictly defined sphere where he operated, a man who derived confidence from that competence. Ten years and more ago, his aptitude had manifested itself in the multifarious operations needed to sail a modern cargo ship; now he had mastered the very different processes involved in maintaining the fairways and greens of a golf course. But when he was denied action, when he was removed from the areas where he thrived, he was more nervous than men who dealt habitually with words. Alan's closest relationship outside his home was with Barry Hooper, and that had grown naturally out of the work they did together, out of the actions which the older man could demonstrate and teach to his acolyte. He could not keep his strong hands still now as he sat opposite his two visitors. Even to have made them tea, to have sought out tea bags, beakers, milk and sugar, would have been a release for him, a release which was now denied by these men who studied him so closely.

There was no real preamble. Lambert said abruptly, 'You didn't like Patrick Nayland, did you, Mr Fitch?'

They knew, then. He accepted it immediately, never thought they might be bluffing. They had known about his conviction for causing an affray, known that it might have been a much more serious charge. Yet he couldn't just admit it, not with the man lying dead and these people hungry for an arrest. 'He paid my wages. Gave me the job here. Made me Head Greenkeeper, with an Assistant.' He pronounced the titles carefully, as if the formality could give weight to his argument.

'But you didn't like him. He knew things about you, didn't he?'

They knew everything, then. He must concentrate, in this world of words where he was least at home. Channel all his energies into convincing them he hadn't twisted that knife in Nayland's guts. 'He knew things, yes. I couldn't help that. But he threw them at me, reminded me about them. I didn't see him much, avoided him when I saw him about the clubhouse and the course. But he owns the place. I couldn't avoid him if he came looking for me.'

'What did he know, Mr Fitch?' Lambert's voice was gentle, understanding, even sympathetic.

Alan was dimly aware that perhaps they had not known everything, that perhaps he had already given away more than he needed to. But he knew he must concentrate on the killing, must summon all his resources to cover up what had happened in the basement of that restaurant. 'He knew I'd killed a man, didn't he? In a fight. I was attacked, was only defending myself. But he said it should have been manslaughter at least. That if it hadn't been in Aden, I'd never have got away without a charge.' He had looked down at the old rug on the dusty floor through all this, concentrating on the words, the treacherous words which could give him away. Now he looked up and said, 'But you know about all this, don't you?'

'Patrick Nayland was in Aden at that time. In the Army.' Lambert was thinking aloud, but he uttered the phrases as if they were statements, clothing speculation as fact.

'He was in Aden all right. I'm not sure whether the Army was still operating there or not. But Nayland was there. He knew some of the people who were involved. Knew the man who was killed, he said.' Fitch shook his head confusedly, like a cow dismissing troublesome flies.

Lambert fancied that Patrick Nayland might have done a little bluffing too, might have pretended he knew more than he did about the incident: Fitch was an easy man to deceive. None of that mattered now. What mattered was its effect on this powerful man who sat so nervously before them. Had Nayland's knowledge been a powerful enough factor to trigger his murder? The Superintendent said quietly, 'Did he threaten you? Threaten to reveal what he knew to others?'

'No. No, he taunted me. Whenever he felt like it. Talked about it as a great joke.'

That confirmed the view that Nayland had picked up gossip rather than concrete evidence. It was easy to convince Fitch that you knew more than you did. 'You could have got another job, Mr Fitch.'

'Not one like this. I like the work I do here. I'm good at it. I've developed this place from scratch, and it's going to get better and better.' Alan Fitch had spoken spontaneously for the first time, and his pride and his stubbornness rang in the words.

'So you know more about the murder victim than you were prepared to tell us when we saw you on Friday. Well, we know more about him ourselves now. He had an eye for the ladies, we're told.'

'Nothing to do with me, that.'

'No? But you knew about it and didn't tell us. And that when we'd told you that we needed to learn as much as we could about the dead man.'

Alan hadn't thought this was going to come up. He was bewildered by this turn in the conversation. He said uncertainly, 'Mrs Moss has told you all about it, I expect.'

Lambert stored away this gem for future use, his face betraying not a flicker of excitement. 'Put it about a bit, your former employee, didn't he?'

'I wanted to warn her. She should have seen it for herself.'

Joanne Moss was going to have some interesting questions to answer. Lambert divined suddenly that this stocky figure with the tattoos on his powerful arms felt protective about the Catering Manager, a self-possessed lady who had hardly seemed in need of such a defender. He said, 'Do you think Patrick Nayland exploited his position as owner to get women?'

Alan Fitch shook his head in bewilderment. He wasn't familiar with the idea. He said doggedly, 'We've all met men like him. Couldn't keep his hands off women. Couldn't be trusted.'

Lambert nodded slowly, as if he was wondering whether to follow up this line of questioning. Then he said suddenly, 'What were you wearing last Wednesday night at Soutters restaurant, Mr Fitch?'

Alan felt as if he had received a blow between the eyes, even fancied he could feel a physical pain in his forehead as he tried to adjust his brain to this new line of attack. It was the one he had feared. He told himself that he had expected this, that he had been prepared for it. Yet he still felt like a fighter struggling to regain his balance after a heavy blow. 'I was wearing my best suit. The one I wear for weddings and funerals. I don't have much use for suits.'

'And?'

'What else? Well, a white shirt and a blue tie, I think. And black shoes. Does it matter?'

'It may do, Mr Fitch. You could produce these garments if we went to your house with you, could you?'

Alan tried to keep the rising panic out of his voice as he said, 'I expect I could do that, yes.'

His widening eyes had been drawn to Lambert's calm face, like a rabbit watching the weasel which is eyeing its throat. But it was Hook, looking up from his notes, who now said quietly, 'And your wife would be able to confirm that these were the garments you wore last Wednesday night, would she?'

She wouldn't. And he hadn't briefed her what to say. He could picture her staring un-comprehendingly at the hanger which had once supported his best suit and now held only the jacket, giving him away, then telling them that she had not washed the shirt he had worn, had not seen it since that fatal night. It was too powerful an image for him to cope with. He said dully, 'I don't want Mary brought into this.'

Hook said gently, 'I don't expect you do. Be much better if this information came from you, wouldn't it? The real information, I mean.'

The soft Herefordshire tones sounded wonderfully persuasive in Alan Fitch's ears. He knew he must resist, but he could not see how to do it. His broad shoulders rose and fell helplessly, but he said nothing.

Lambert, quiet but inexorable, said, 'What exactly did you burn last Thursday morning, Mr Fitch?'

Alan wanted to deny them, but he could not find the words to do it. And when the words would not come, the will melted away. He said hopelessly, 'I burned the shirt and the trousers I had worn the night before.'

'And why did you think it necessary to do that?'

They knew, of course. This was just a formality, a tying up of loose ends. He heard a long, heart-deep sigh, and for an instant did not realize that it had come from him. He said, 'They had blood upon them. Nayland's blood.' Alan had wondered if he should have burned the black shoes too, instead of just wiping away the blood. They were nearly new, his only black pair. He waited a moment for them to speak. When they did not, he added the ritual of denial, 'I didn't kill him.'

'Then don't you think you'd better explain yourself? Explain how you came to have a murder victim's blood upon your clothes. Explain how you came to destroy what seems like vital evidence.'

'You won't believe me. That's why I—'

'Try me.'

Alan Fitch tried to think, to organize his thoughts, to put what he knew he had to say as convincingly as possible. It was no good; his head seemed to be spinning, his voice coming from far away as he said, 'I found him down there. He was lying on his side. I went and got hold of him, turned him on to his back.'

There was a pause, agonizing to Alan Fitch, before Lambert took up the questioning again. 'You were trying to save him?'

He should have said yes, and tried to make it convincing. But he heard himself saying, 'I wanted to make sure he was dead.'

'You admit you wanted him dead?'

'I just said that, didn't I?'

'And why were you happy to see him dead, Mr Fitch?'

He hated this careful, polite 'Mister'. It was as though they were taunting him, getting ready to take him in and lock him away. He faltered out, 'I told you, he was two-timing Mrs Moss. She's a good woman.'

'And worth killing for?'

Perhaps they were trapping him. It seemed as if they were querying his motive. And he knew that it sounded silly: he should never have tried it. He'd feared his other reason would sound even sillier. But he had no other thoughts left in him. He said, 'He kept threatening to tell Barry about me. About me killing a man, all those years ago.'

The two CID men glanced at each other. It was Hook who said to the downcast head, 'That would have been bad for you, would it, Alan? Barry Hooper's important to you, isn't he?'

'That lad looks up to me. Looks to me for guidance. He's – well, he's like...' He could not bring himself to pronounce the word.

'Like a son to you,' Hook completed the sentence quietly.

Alan Fitch looked up, saw that they were not mocking him, and nodded. 'I've never had a son of my own, you see. Always wanted one.'

Hook said, 'I can understand that. Did you kill Patrick Nayland, Alan?'

'No. But I'm glad he's dead. He was no good, that man.'

'We'll need you to say all this again, then sign a statement for us. I want you to consider whether you want to change anything before you do that.'

He said he understood that. He couldn't believe that they weren't marching him away between them with the handcuffs on him. He went to the door, watched the police car rock its way slowly down the unpaved track, then speed up as it reached the tarmac road by the clubhouse.

Alan Fitch wasn't much of a drinking man,

these days. But he went and got out the half-bottle of brandy he kept in the medicine cupboard and gave himself a stiff measure before he left the sanctuary of his den. He did not take long over it, but threw his head back and downed it quickly, feeling the relief as the power of the liquor flooded his torso.

Somehow, he did not want Barry Hooper to come into his den and quiz him about his encounter with the CID. He went out, felt his head swim for a minute with the impact of the cool, fresh air, and walked determinedly through the early winter twilight towards the spot where he had left his workforce. The man he had spoken of as a substitute son was emptying a barrow of stones and sand between the shuttering of the path they had laid out together.

'I hope you've not been slacking, young Barry!' he called out sternly to the slim young back.

Fourteen

Alan Fitch was totally unaware of it, but he had opened up a new line of CID enquiries on the Catering Manager at Camellia Park, Joanne Moss. It was whilst conducting a routine check on the morning of Tuesday the nineteenth of December that Rushton came up with another interesting fact.

Employment files are not most people's ideas of riveting reading, but they are always of interest to the police in a murder investigation. The details of the backgrounds of the workers at the course, preserved from their original applications for their posts, had already thrown up areas of questioning for John Lambert for the initial interviews.

Salary sheets are usually less interesting and less revealing. They reflect the hierarchy in an organization, but little beyond that. Perhaps only someone as painstaking over detail as Detective Inspector Rushton would have taken the trouble to peruse the returns from Camellia Park so carefully. But Chris believed that no stone should be left unturned. That was one of his favourite phrases, one of the ways in which he bored those he directed; it was also one of his strengths.

This was such an occasion. The salaries paid at Camellia Park had been handled by Patrick Nayland himself. Nothing very unusual in that: lots of proprietors of small businesses liked to keep the details of what their employees earned to themselves. DI Rushton looked first at the monthly returns, then at the annual figures which were submitted to the accountant. There was no doubt about it, something was wrong here. Chris Pearson, as overall manager of the enterprise, the man responsible for the whole of the development and the staff who operated to his orders, received a salary of thirty-five thousand.

Joanne Moss, who had begun as a part-time employee and then become full-time, as the modest catering in the small clubhouse expanded, was no doubt very efficient, but in a small, self-contained job. Catering Manager was a rather grandiose title for what she provided at the course.

Yet she was paid five thousand pounds more than anyone else at Camellia Park.

Liza Nayland chose to come into the station at Oldford, when Hook rang to say that they needed to speak to her again. He wondered why she did not wish them to go to the big detached house. She said her cleaner was there on Tuesdays and they would have more privacy at the station, but there were many rooms in that comfortable house where they could have isolated themselves easily enough for this exchange.

The widow did not seem to be nervous. She looked round the interview room, with its windowless green walls, its high central light, its table fixed to the floor and its spartan upright chairs. 'Not designed to make people feel at home, this, is it?' she said. The smile seemed confident beneath the firm nose and the intelligent blue eyes.

'You could say that,' responded Lambert, with a grimmer smile. 'We wouldn't want a room designed to put people at their ease. We get some strange folk in here. There are times when you are quite pleased that the table is fastened to the floor.'

'I promise not to throw anything at you.'

'And we promise not to lock you in a cell. Unless of course you compel us to do that by what you have to tell us.' His tone was light, but the smile did not extend to those grey, observant eyes; eyes which seemed to Liza to be already estimating her motives. 'We've now spoken to everyone who was at Soutters Restaurant last Wednesday night. As a result of what we have heard, there are things we need to follow up. With other people, as well as with you.'

Liza nodded. 'DS Hook told me as much

when he rang me at home.'

Lambert said, 'You have not been cautioned, of course, so this is not strictly necessary. But I'd like to record what you have to say, in case it conflicts with anyone else's view of things. Would you have any objection to that?'

She wondered why she heard a threat in the words, found herself wanting to refuse. But she said with a nervous laugh, 'There's no way I can refuse without it seeming suspicious, is there? Of course you must record this, if you think it will be useful. Though I can't imagine what I shall be able to add to what I've already told you.'

He didn't reassure her, as she had expected him to do. This dreary room must mitigate against the social graces, she thought. He merely nodded to Hook, who reached across and pressed a button on the machine to her left. She tried not to watch the cassette turning silently, not to think of her every word being recorded for future dissection by these men whose business it was to see the worst in people.

Lambert said, 'We now have the findings from forensic. We know from your previous statements that first Mrs Moss and then you were in contact with the body. There is also evidence on the clothing of contact with other people. I apologize if this is distressing, but we need you to think back again to the minutes before your husband's body was discovered. Can you recall who went down to the basement after your husband had left the table?'

'You say someone else touched Pat before Mrs Moss found him. Who was that?'

'I'm not at liberty to reveal that to you, Mrs Nayland.' Sometimes the stiff, official phrases were the best ones.

'You think this person killed him, don't you?'

'Not necessarily. We shall be interested to know why the person or persons concealed their contacts with him. There may be innocent explanations.' His tone made that seem unlikely.

'I'm afraid I can't remember any more about the time immediately before Pat was killed than I told you last time. I was busy talking to other people – it was Pat's party, and I was playing the hostess, if you like. I still don't remember Pat leaving us, so obviously I haven't any clear memory of the period after he had gone or who might have followed him down to the basement.' She paused, trying to estimate how far these two believed her. 'Surely, if you've found evidence of other people's presence from Pat's clothing, you must know now who killed him?'

It was a nice try at innocence, but it brought her only a grim smile from Lambert. 'We know that both you and Mrs Moss had held Mr Nayland's body, and as you would expect, there is evidence of that, upon his clothing as well as yours. We could take that as evidence that one of you held that knife, if we did not accept your stories.'

'Which of course you do!' She gave another nervous, involuntary laugh, but it drew no reassurance from Lambert. 'But I see what you mean. People who were perfectly innocent could have touched the body.'

'Or they could have been in contact with your husband much earlier in the evening, when he was alive and unthreatened.'

She thought about that. 'That is certainly possible. Patrick moved among his guests before we sat down for the meal, and even moved around between courses to make sure everyone was enjoying the evening.'

'People have not been honest with us, Mrs Nayland.'

She nodded slowly. 'One person is certainly lying to you; we all have to accept that. Have you any idea yet who it is?'

He smiled a little at her naivety, fairly sure this time that it was at least partly assumed. 'More than one person has lied to us, Mrs Nayland.'

She wondered how a simple statement could sound so menacing. 'Really? I can't think why that would be.' She wished she hadn't spoken at all, when she heard the words sounding so trite in the small, windowless room.

'People conceal the truth. It amounts to the same thing as lying.' Lambert was suddenly weary of the multiple deceits of the case. 'People have their own reasons for withholding information, not always connected directly with the death. But it all helps to protect a murderer, in the end.'

She digested it slowly, being determined not to speak, not to incriminate herself any further. Yet the next second she heard herself saying, 'I can see that. It can't help you when people want to preserve their own secrets. I've tried to be as honest as I could with you, but others—'

'Have you, Mrs Nayland? Have you really been as honest as it is possible to be with us?'

She heard the strain in his voice, realized suddenly that this calm, authoritative man had to cope with his own tensions, with the frustrations caused by the people he had to question about a high-profile killing. The newspapers were beginning to dwell upon police bafflement in this case, to question the progress of what should have been a straightforward investigation. She said with dignity, 'I'm sure that I haven't held anything back from you, that I've been as frank as it's possible to be—'

'You've been frank about your husband's character, have you, Mrs Nayland? Told us everything that you know about him?'

She felt herself flushing as the anger rose within her. 'I've answered everything you've asked me. Told you everything it was relevant for you to know.' She stopped suddenly, betrayed by her own phrase.

'So you decide what it is appropriate for us to know, do you? Not us, who have the duty of finding a violent killer, who have a picture of things which you can never have, because we are talking to all the people involved? At present we are trying to piece together the true version of events last Wednesday evening from the snippets which people like you accord to us!'

Bert Hook had never seen Lambert so near to losing it with a quiet, apparently co-operative witness. He said quietly, 'Mrs Nayland, you must see this from our point of view. Sometimes it seems as if everyone we speak to is trying to confuse things rather than illuminate them. We know that one person is fighting against the truth, has a clear interest in setting us upon false tracks. But sometimes it seems as if everyone is conniving to help him or her, as if everyone is part of a conspiracy to prevent us discovering who killed Patrick.'

She said dully, 'I'm sorry if it seems like that. I'm sure there is no conspiracy. I'm sure most of us don't mean to be unhelpful.'

Lambert controlled his irritation, recovering the composure which had temporarily deserted him. He let the silence build between them. Silence standing like heat: he remembered that Larkin comparison. It was certainly hot in this airless room, despite the cold in the world outside. Eventually he said, 'What sort of a reputation with women would you say your late husband had?' It was clumsy: he had been avoiding DI Rushton's 'ladies' man' phrase, but he was pretty sure he had produced something more orotund.

Liza Nayland said, 'Pat had a bit of a reputation, I know. But that was all in the past.'

'You're sure of that?'

'Are you trying to be gratuitously insulting?'

'I'm trying to get at the truth, Mrs Nayland. A moment's reflection will tell you that this line of questioning is relevant.'

She breathed deeply, trying to retain control, to reveal only as much of herself and her emotions as she had to. 'You mean that if Patrick was playing around, I might have killed him in a fit of jealousy.'

'I meant that if anyone was jealous of what he was doing, that person might have killed him in a fit of murderous violence. It happens, and this death has the marks of a killing like that.'

She made herself speak evenly, to sound as

if she was a woman who would never have lost control of herself like that. 'Pat had a certain reputation as a Lothario, in the past. When he proposed marriage to me, I was shocked, because I had heard that he played the field, that he wouldn't be serious enough to venture upon a second marriage. I speak in the past tense, because that's where this side of his character was left. We had occasional spats in our marriage, as most successful marriages do. But we did not have any problems with either of us pursuing other sexual partners.'

None that you are aware of, thought Lambert automatically. But he could not offer that reservation to Liza Nayland without being pointlessly discourteous. He went as far as he could, saying stiffly, 'Other people have spoken of a certain reputation attaching to your husband. You will understand that we needed to ask you about it.'

'And now you have. And now you have my assurance that this is a line of enquiry which won't lead anywhere.'

He doubted that. But he thought she meant what she said. They said the wife was always the last to know, and sometimes it was true. He said, 'Forgive me, but I have to ask this. Are you aware that your husband had a conviction for Indecent Assault?'

She could have hit him, for bringing this up now. Instead, she looked into the grey eyes and said, 'I was aware, yes. But thank you for reminding me of it, six days after Pat's death. I don't wish to discuss the rights and wrongs of the accusations, though I have my own opinions on them. It's a long time in the past, part of an unhappy world Pat had left far behind him.'

Redeemed by a good woman, thought Lambert. The old story. Or, much more often, the old illusion. Many women thought they could reclaim a reprobate by tender loving care, and much more often than not they were wrong. He said, 'You admitted last time we spoke that your daughter had experienced certain difficulties in adjusting to life with her stepfather.'

'Yes. I also said I thought they were normal difficulties, which should not be exaggerated.'

'Would your daughter support your view that her stepfather was no longer interested in women other than you?'

How insolent the man was in his persistence! She reminded herself that this was part of his job, forced herself to be coldly polite. 'Of course she would! Any difficulties Michelle had with Pat were nothing to do with that, I'm sure. If you want my view, their clashes were more concerned with her deficiencies than with Pat's.' She hoped desperately that Michelle would support her on this, if they spoke to her again. Surely she owed that much loyalty at least to Pat.

'What will happen now to Camellia Park?'

It was one of those bewildering switches by which he often caught people off guard. Liza took her time, then decided with relief that she could see no tripwires in this line of questioning. 'Essentially, it will go on as before. We haven't agreed the details, but I have asked Chris Pearson to take up a partnership in the enterprise.'

'That's generous of you.'

If she took the implication that it might be precipitate, with Pearson still a suspect in a murder investigation, she did not show it. 'Chris deserves it. He's worked very hard at that golf course, right from the time before it opened. And it's not entirely unselfish you know: if Chris decided his future lay somewhere else, I'd be in a hole. No one knows the ins and outs of all aspects of the development as well as Chris Pearson.'

'Who controls the pay structure at Camellia Park?'

It was abrupt again, without the greasing of the wheels she was used to in more normal conversations. She was beginning to realize that this man's very brusqueness was a tool, not a social deficiency. 'Pat did, when he was alive. He always kept finance in his own hands, whatever he delegated to others. But Chris will take it over now, I imagine, though it's one of the things we shall no doubt confer upon. Both of us will want to know how well the place is doing financially: that will determine future plans for development. And salaries are a big issue in that equation.'

'Would Mr Pearson have known about the wage structure whilst your husband was alive?'

She thought carefully, anxious now to convince him that she was holding nothing back. 'I think probably not. Pat would share everything else, and I know he rated Chris highly, but it was something of a fetish with him to be secretive about what he paid people. He said he'd had to endure people knowing exactly what he earned when he was on military pay scales, and he hadn't liked it. So people who worked in his enterprises were going to enjoy privacy in that. Pat used to say that knowledge about salaries only led to petty jealousies, so it was better that everyone only knew about his or her own wage.'

'I think he was probably right about that. Your husband and Mr Pearson were both ex-military men, weren't they?'

'Yes. They'd both served many years in the Army. I think that was a common bond between them. They seemed to get on well from the start. People forget that everyone thought it was quite a risky enterprise, starting a golf course from scratch. And of course

218

Pat had to lay out quite a lot of money before there was anything coming back from the course. He put most of his officer's gratuity into it. There was an interval of fifteen months between the time when he bought the land and the moment when the first green fees started coming in. I can remember that April morning very well.'

'Did you know that Mr Pearson used to be in the SAS?'

'No.' She tried not to resent the fact that he had dragged her rudely away from her reminiscences of happier times. 'Is it important?'

'I've no idea. Probably not. It seems rather odd that he doesn't seem to have told anyone about it, but I gather that secrecy is encouraged by the SAS.'

Suddenly, Lambert stood up, looking very tall in this small, claustrophobic setting. 'If you have any further thoughts, Mrs Nayland, whether in connection with the issues we've raised today or anything else in this case, please get in touch with the CID section here immediately.'

DS Hook ushered her out to her car. Liza Nayland sat silently for a moment before she started the engine, scarcely believing how much the exchange had taken out of her, how searching it had been.

She was surprised to see her hands trembling on the steering wheel as she drove home.

Fifteen

Barry Hooper was nervous. The CID men had been back to see Alan Fitch again and they must have given him a real grilling. He couldn't get the full story out of his boss, but he could see that they'd upset him. It wasn't easy to disturb Alan, but those buggers had done it.

And if they'd been back to Alan Fitch, they were sure to come back also to him. Yet they didn't. All through the long length of Tuesday morning, he waited for them to come, but there was no sign of the police Mondeo making its cautious way up the unpaved track to confront him in the greenkeeper's shed.

Alan Fitch clearly wanted to be alone with his thoughts after the previous afternoon's confrontation with the CID. He had given Barry a job on his own this morning, repairing the damage caused by subsidence at the back of the ninth tee. The young man went about it methodically, peeling the turf back carefully and adding soil to level the ground beneath, making sure that the grass when he rolled it back into place was just slightly proud of the ground around it, to allow a little for settling. Alan had shown him how to do work like this, and Barry wanted to show his mentor that he could do a perfect job without supervision or guidance.

Yet it took Barry Hooper longer than it should have done, because for once he could not give his mind fully to the work. All the time, as he sliced beneath the turf and peeled it carefully back, he watched the entrance to the club, expecting to see that police car turning carefully between the high brick pillars into Camellia Park.

When he met up with Alan Fitch for lunch in the room they knew so well at the end of the shed, few words were exchanged. Each man was preoccupied with his own concerns, and the part of the day which Barry normally most enjoyed was tense and joyless. After a few minutes, he could stand it no longer. He muttered some excuse to Fitch and roared away on the Ducati, feeling some of the tension stripped away from him as the icy wind howled around his face on the way into Gloucester.

He knew what he wanted when he walked into his familiar room, where the police had talked to him three days earlier. But he made himself a cup of coffee first, pretending to unwind, simulating the actions he would have taken in a more innocent context. He wished yet again that he had not done what he had done last Wednesday night at Soutters, tortured himself anew with the picture of how serene his life might have been now if he had only acted differently then.

The shabby wallpaper, with its almost indiscernible twenty-year-old pattern, and the torn curtain which concealed the tiny scullery were comforting to him by their very familiarity. At this time of day, most people who lived in this rabbit warren of a house were out, and no sounds of his neighbours came to him through the thin dividing walls. He should have enjoyed the privacy, but today he found himself longing for the reassurance of other, human noises around him.

Having delayed the action as long as he could, he walked as he had always planned to do to the scratched dresser and opened the second drawer down. The last bit of cocaine, the rock he had cut in half, lay like an accusation beneath the white vest and the blue socks. He had meant to save it, to make his supply last longer this time. But he needed it now, not at some time in a future he could not predict.

When all this was over, he would definitely give up the habit.

For a few minutes, he could not dismiss the thought that he might not be at liberty when all this was over. Then he felt the lightness in his head as he went out to the Ducati. Better go carefully, on the way back to the golf course. It would be ironic if the police picked him up just for speeding, after what he'd done last Wednesday night.

Unlike Liza Nayland, Chris Pearson was anxious to be interviewed in his own home. Bert Hook had no objection to that. A drive through the Gloucestershire lanes, even on the nineteenth of December, with the temperature low and the trees leafless, had its own charms after the pressures of the station.

The near-white sun was already low, but the winter sky had that crisp blueness which seems to be deepened and accentuated by the long English twilight. The pasture fields rose between walls and hedges towards the long ridge of the Malverns on their left, a landscape which had not changed much in several hundred years. The gaunt skeletons of oak and chestnut stood like sentinels over ancient farms, as if protecting them against the changes which besieged the life around them.

It was an illusion, Bert Hook knew – the country now employed a twentieth of the people who had made their living from it a century earlier, and television aerials and discs rose above the old farmhouses and cottages – but an agreeable illusion, nonetheless. And the lanes were pleasantly free of traffic: they met only one other car on their journey to Pearson's village.

Pearson had the wide oak door of the long thatched house open as they went up the path. He said, 'The wife's out for the afternoon in Cheltenham at a meeting of the Fine Arts Society. We won't be disturbed.'

Hook wondered if the unnecessary detail, like his readiness to receive them, betrayed nervousness in a man who he would have thought was rarely troubled by nerves. Pearson took them into the neat dining room with the prints of the Middle East on the walls, where they had spoken five days earlier.

Lambert waited unhurriedly until they were all sitting down and Hook had his notebook at the ready, watching how Pearson's fingers drummed briefly upon the table, how he stilled them and withdrew his hands from sight below the table top, as if he feared their movements might betray him. Then he said, 'We now know rather more about the murder victim. It seems that some people, including you, withheld information about him at our first meetings.'

It was a challenging start, and it looked for a moment as though Pearson would show his annoyance at it. But he controlled himself and said, 'I told you what I knew about Patrick. I answered all your questions.'

Lambert gave him a bleak smile. 'When you know nothing about a dead man, as we did then, it is not easy to know the right questions to ask. I said "withheld information". I did not accuse you of a direct lie.'

'Patrick was a good friend to me. You can't expect me to blacken his reputation, especially after he died like that.'

'A fair point, in normal circumstances. But you do not need reminding that these are hardly that. Is it true that Mr Nayland was a womanizer?'

Chris looked up into the calm face with the grey eyes which studied him so closely. He had not expected so direct a question; he had become used to the cautious, respectful reactions of the people Pat Nayland had employed at Camellia Park. 'Yes. Pat wasn't good at resisting anything in a skirt – or in trousers, if it was female and attractive. Is this relevant?'

'It may be. I don't need to explain why.'

Chris nodded slowly, taking his time, taking care to disguise his relief at this line of questioning. They didn't know the important thing he had concealed, just as Liza Nayland hadn't known when he spoke to her yesterday after the inquest. 'Yes. I can see that now. I apologize for not mentioning this aspect of Pat's character to you last Thursday. I can only say that it would have seemed disloyal, on the day after he had been

225

murdered. Pat was a good friend to me.'

'Mrs Nayland didn't seem to us to be aware of her husband's predilection for other women. Do you think she was?'

He gave it thought, happy to stay on this theme, which could surely not harm him. 'No, I don't think she was. But I didn't see her often, you know. She very rarely came to the golf course.'

'But if she had, she would have seen things which distressed her?'

It was almost a statement, rather than a question. He was quick, this man. Chris wondered how much more they'd discovered which they weren't revealing to him yet. They'd talked to every one of the staff at Camellia Park, he knew that. He'd better be as frank as he could, in this area where he was not threatened. 'Pat flirted with every pretty woman. Nothing wrong with that. But if he got the slightest encouragement, he went further.'

'Are you aware that many years ago he had a conviction for Indecent Assault?'

'No. But it doesn't really surprise me. And the leopard hadn't changed his spots. I sometimes thought that the modern laws about sexual harassment would catch him out, but he got away with it.'

For a man who'd claimed to be anxious to respect a dead friend, he was now being almost too frank. But that was what they had asked him to be, after all. Lambert said, 'And who in particular attracted his favours?'

Chris Pearson smiled ruefully. Behind the smile, his brain was working quickly. He was pretty certain now that they knew the important name. He couldn't afford to conceal it; on the contrary, he could only see that it was in his interests to reveal it and divert suspicion. 'I told you, Pat wasn't very discriminating, or even very cautious. He was prepared to put it about wherever the opportunity offered. But I think he had a long-term affair going with Joanne Moss.'

'How long ago did this begin?'

'I couldn't be precise about that. I knew Pat would make a pass at her, as he did at most attractive women, but I didn't know he'd had a favourable response. Joanne at least was very discreet about it, particularly in the early days. And she was only working part-time at first, and they no doubt met away from the course. It's been rather more obvious in the last couple of years, to me at least. But Joanne has never spoken about it to me, and I've never raised it with her. For all I know, she still thinks no one but the two of them knew about it.'

'And did he confine his extramarital attentions to his mistress?'

It seemed a strange way of phrasing the question. But they were trained to be accurate, to exclude any possibility of confusion, he supposed. 'No. I told you, he was unable to resist a pretty face or a female curve. He was always flirting with the more attractive women golfers on the course, testing the ground for more serious approaches. Pat was discreet when Joanne was around, but I doubt if he was capable of being faithful to any woman.'

'You said last time we spoke that you were very close to him. Did he discuss his affairs with you?'

This had gone far enough. He had given them every impression of being open and helpful. He didn't want to emerge now as a man who betrayed confidences. 'Professionally close, I should have said. We developed the course together, and discussed every aspect of that project together. But he was, after all, my employer, and both of us knew it. We didn't discuss his women. Had Pat asked my opinion on his behaviour with women, I should have given it, but he didn't.'

'You clearly know more than anyone left alive about the running of Camellia Park. Mrs Nayland acknowledged that.'

Chris said stiffly, like a man who is suspicious of praise, 'I believe that is true. It was and is my job, after all.'

'You are no doubt familiar with the pay-sheets, then.'

It had been slipped quietly under his guard, like a stiletto slid silently into the ribs. He said, 'No. That is one thing Pat kept to himself.'

'Even though you were familiar with all aspects of the development.'

His own phrases were being thrown back into his face; but there was no ring of irony in Lambert's voice, just a careful, persistent curiosity. Chris summoned a smile and said, 'That was the one aspect that Pat kept to himself. He said if people were content with what he paid them, there was no need for them to know what anyone else earned.'

'And you accepted that?'

There was no need for him to admit to how much it had irritated him. They could not have found that out from anyone else, because he had never revealed his annoyance to others; that would have meant a loss of face. 'I accepted it happily enough. It was a harmless foible, probably not unusual among the owners of small businesses, for all I know. I was happy enough with what I earned myself, and there had always been an understanding between us that there would be a partnership for me, in the medium term.' He had carried that off rather well, he thought.

'An understanding between two ex-military men?'

'I hadn't thought of it that way. But I think

I mentioned when we spoke last week that our military background probably contributed to a happy working relationship.'

'You did indeed. However, you didn't tell us that you spent the last three of your Army years in the SAS.'

'Didn't I? Well, I suppose I—'

'Royal Artillery, you said. No mention of the SAS.'

Chris knew that this adversary who kept so still was watching him as intently as ever. It was unnerving, but he could think of no way of stopping it. 'We weren't encouraged to talk about the work we did in the Special Air Service. Most of the members are recruited from Parachute Regiment volunteers. I was approached after my service in the Falklands. We are supposed to remain anonymous.' A little of his pride had seeped into the explanation, but there surely couldn't be anything wrong with that.

'Trained in combat procedures, aren't you, in the SAS?'

He saw the way this was going. 'Part of the initial training course involves learning the most effective methods of killing people. The premise is that you should be able to defend yourself and your mission if you get into desperate situations.'

'You would know how to kill a man with a knife.'

'If necessary, yes. If I were in a one-to-one

230

situation or worse, and I felt my own life was threatened.' Chris outlined the conditions carefully, for he could see where this was going now.

'You would know exactly where to stab a man, if you wished to kill him quickly.'

'Yes.' He felt the need to make some amelioration of the stark admission. 'A man may also be killed as Pat Nayland was killed, with a random blow which strikes lucky and hits a ventricle.'

'You know that this is what happened?'

Chris Pearson smiled. 'I can guess at it. I have, as you have just said, a certain amount of knowledge about how people may be killed.'

'Indeed. And you are right about the ventricle, though it remains to be seen whether it was luck or expert knowledge which rendered the wound fatal. Do you know who administered that blow?' Lambert was quiet, unsmiling, intense.

Chris forced himself to take the time to formulate his response. 'I don't know who killed Pat. You seemed to be implying that because I had been trained in certain forms of combat, I must have killed him. I was trying to point out that there were other possibilities, that's all.'

It was Hook, looking up from his notes, who said, 'We don't like luck, Mr Pearson. We like to proceed on probabilities. We find them more reliable as indicators. It is bound to arouse our interest when we find that someone has knowledge which could have helped him in a particular situation.'

'The fact that I was in the SAS does not mean that I killed Pat. It's ridiculous to suggest it.'

'Not so ridiculous, Mr Pearson.' Lambert was sober but insistent. 'Of course your service in the SAS does not mean that you murdered a man. But the fact that you chose to conceal that service is bound to arouse our interest.'

'I told you: SAS personnel are not expected to boast about their work.'

'Was Mr Nayland wearing a watch on the night of his death?'

The switch of ground was so sudden that it seemed discourteous. Chris tried to assess the question as his mind reeled, to see what hazards it might hold for him. He said, 'I can't remember. Is it important?'

'You said on the day after his death that you checked the carotid artery to make sure that he was dead. That you detached Mrs Nayland, who was holding the corpse, as gently as you could. You don't recall whether he was wearing a watch?'

They made it sound as if he was hiding something, as if it was absurd to suggest that he could have been so unobservant. But he genuinely could not remember, and nor could he see where this was leading. 'No. I had too much on my mind with the man lying dead and blood all over the place to notice whether—'

'Do you recall whether Mr Nayland was wearing a watch earlier in the evening?'

'No. Is it important?'

'Did he habitually wear a watch?'

'Yes. Most people do.'

'A good watch?'

'I expect so. Pat normally bought good stuff. Whereas as far as I'm concerned, modern electronics mean that even a cheap watch—'

'If you have any further thoughts on the matter, please let us know. Have you decided who killed your employer?'

He'd already denied that he knew who had struck that fatal knife-blow. Now the repetition of the question made it sound as if he must know, as if he must be concealing some vital information. That was the penalty, he supposed, for holding back his knowledge of Pat's womanizing, of his own SAS training. But they still hadn't unearthed the thing he felt was really important for him to conceal.

That gave him confidence. He managed to keep calm, even to conjure up a smile at the absurdity of the notion that he should be protecting a murderer. 'If I knew who'd killed Pat, you'd be the first one to hear from me, Superintendent. I don't think this was a family killing. Beyond that, I've no idea.'

'And why are you so certain that this wasn't down to Liza Nayland or her daughter?'

They picked him up on everything. He had thought he was just being courteous in eliminating the two women, but he realized now that it was because he couldn't afford to have Liza as the killer, or his partnership would be in jeopardy. He hardly knew Michelle Nayland and had hardly considered implicating her as a suspect. He said, 'I'm not sure it wasn't one of those two. It's just a gut feeling, if you like.'

Lambert looked so sceptical that Chris thought he was going to say he didn't like it. Instead, he rose and said, 'New information is coming in each day, Mr Pearson. I remind you again that it's your duty to contribute to the sum of that knowledge with anything that occurs to you about this death.'

Chris Pearson watched them drive away. He went into the living room at the back of the house and made for his familiar armchair. Then he changed his mind and went back into the little-used dining room where he had talked to the CID men. It felt as if he would have been soiling the living room, as if his wife might have picked up something of his deceptions, if he had thought through this latest exchange in the room where they lived out so much of their life together.

He didn't usually drink until the evenings, and that sparingly, nowadays. He'd given up alcohol completely during those SAS years, and never reacquired the taste for it. But at four fifteen in the afternoon, he now poured himself a stiff whisky and sat down to evaluate the meeting. That bit at the end about more facts coming in each day had sounded like a warning. They'd tried to shake him about the SAS and the fact that he had concealed Pat's philandering, and they'd even succeeded, to an extent.

But the main point was that they still didn't know the essential thing. Didn't even suspect it, apparently.

Sixteen

Barry Hooper got more and more nervous as the early winter night dropped down and the effects of the coke wore off. It was only a small fix, and it didn't seem to be as effective as usual. He could feel his confidence ebbing away and his anxiety returning, as he waited through the long afternoon for the policemen who never came.

He was home early; there wasn't much he could do at the course once the light went. Alan Fitch spent the odd hour maintaining the course machinery in the coldness of the big, high shed, but Barry hadn't the expertise to do that, and on this day the older man was too preoccupied with his own thoughts to offer him any instruction.

Back in the familiar room in Gloucester, Barry made himself beans on toast and watched the local news on the little portable television set, whose picture came and went with the intermittent efficiency of its portable aerial. The announcer said that the police still hadn't made an arrest in the Newent murder case. The man who'd interviewed him, Superintendent John Lambert, was apparently something of a local celebrity: the newsreader listed some of the killers he'd arrested in the past. Barry waited for him to appear on the television, but he was apparently too busy with the case. The Chief Constable, very smart in his dark blue uniform, appeared and said that several lines of enquiry were being pursued.

Barry wasn't experienced enough to realize that this was policespeak for they hadn't a clue and weren't near an arrest, as a more streetwise contemporary of his told him confidently later in the evening.

He washed the dishes, dried them and put them back in the cupboard in his tidy way. You had to keep things neat in such a small living space, or it would be a pigsty in no time. He found himself putting out the cereals and the bowl ready for morning. But it was scarcely seven o'clock and the evening stretched like a dead whale before him, grey and unpromising. He tried to read the book he had bought at the car boot sale on Sunday, but he couldn't get into it. He tried to watch television, but he wasn't one for the soaps, and he certainly wasn't going to watch *The Bill* at eight o'clock; coppers, real or fictional, were the last things he wanted to see.

Not long after eight o'clock, Barry Hooper was doing what he now recognized had been inevitable from the moment he got into his room. He was zipping up his leathers and preparing to go out into the winter night.

He couldn't really spare the money, but he needed the stuff. He couldn't see how he was going to get through the night, let alone the rest of the week, without a fix. He would give up, as he had promised himself he would. He knew he could do it. But that would be after this murder hunt was over, and he was still at large. He didn't allow himself to say 'if'.

He slapped the saddle of the Ducati when he went out to it, as though greeting a faithful horse. He drove through the narrow Gloucester streets with elaborate care; no way the pigs were going to get him for speeding or dangerous riding. They had a thing against bikers, the pigs. Picked you out and went for you, the way they didn't do with car drivers. You were one down with the pigs to start with, if you rode a bike. Especially if it was a Ducati; the sods were jealous of bikes like that. He could work up quite a thing against the fuzz, once he had his leathers on and the tribalism of the bikers kicked in.

He opened up when he got to the dual carriageway to Cheltenham, accelerating fast up to eighty, enjoying the startled looks from drivers, as he surged past them almost before they realized he was behind them.

238

He clenched his knees tight against the machine, trying to foster the image of rider and machine as a blended unit, moving with effortless power and control amongst the cumbersome vehicles around him. He was king when he was on the Ducati, supreme in skill, speed and power over all those lesser mortals, the anonymous subjects of the world he ruled.

He parked in the alley behind the pub which his pal had shown him when they first went there. It was better than the car park, where you could get hemmed in by thoughtless parkers of Fiestas and Sierras and rubbish like that. When you were a biker, you never knew when you might want to be away quickly.

The man he wanted wasn't there yet. He bought himself a half of lager and told himself to be patient. Within ten minutes, he had been joined by two of the others. He didn't know either of them very well, and hadn't particularly liked what he'd seen. But he was glad of company of any kind. It would have been a nervous wait alone, wondering whether you stuck out like a sore thumb in the place, whether even the barman was noting your presence and wondering about it.

The man he had been waiting for came in at just after nine. He was short, with hands thrust deep into the pockets of his black anorak. His dark eyes looked even blacker, even more deep-set, in a face that had not seen a razor for several days. He bought himself a whisky, poured water into it from the jug the barman slid towards him, and stood at the other end of the bar, where he could take in the whole scene. He let his glance stray slowly round the occupants of the low, smoke-filled room, registering nothing more when he noticed one of his customers than when he looked at complete strangers.

Barry Hooper knew that he must wait, that he mustn't try to take the initiative. Eventually the man looked at him for a moment, gave him an almost imperceptible nod, then turned to the barman and said, 'Must take a leak.' He turned and walked unhurriedly out of the bar.

But when he reached the door of the toilet, he passed it without checking his step and passed out into the yard and the cold night air behind the pub, not worrying about whether Barry was following him. The sudden darkness was extreme after the brightness within. Barry caught a glimpse of white breath from the man as the brief shaft of light from the door briefly fell upon him. Then the automatic spring shut the door abruptly behind him and he was plunged into an icy darkness. He almost walked blindly into the man. He caught an anoraked arm, felt himself shaken off with a low-throated curse.

'Sorry!' he said automatically. 'Couldn't see you in the dark with your black clothes and—'

'You're a fine one to talk, black boy!' The words came contemptuously at him, close to his ear. 'Nigger black, they used to call it, you know. Nobody would ever find *you* in the night, if you weren't so bloody clumsy.'

It was nigger brown actually, the colour. For an absurd moment, Barry wanted to correct him. Instead, he said hoarsely, 'You got coke?'

'I got pot, black boy. Good enough for the likes of you. Do you twenty spliffs at a good price.'

For a moment, he was tempted. It was all he could afford, really. Then he thought of those calm CID men and the grilling he would face from them, sooner or later. 'I want coke. Only coke will do.' It was not until he heard his own voice rising that he realized quite how much on edge he was.

'Easy, black man, easy. I got coke. It costs though, coke. Good rocks like I got don't come cheap.'

'How much?' He knew he was too eager, that he was playing into the pusher's hands. But how did you simulate apathy in a situation like this?

The man chuckled coarsely, as if he read

his client's mind and saw the futility of his resistance. 'Eighty quid a gramme. Do you ten good snorts, a gramme of this will. More, if you cut it with glucose.'

'I haven't got eighty quid.'

'Then why are we wasting time on this fucking freezer of a night? I got bigger fishes than you to fry, you black bast—'

'Look, I'll have a quarter of a gramme for twenty. And you know I'll be back for more, at the weekend. I'm a regular customer, it's worth cutting me a bit of rope and—'

'Take your hands off me, black man!' The voice was so close to his ear that he could feel the bristles of the man's beard on his cheek; in his eagerness to buy, he had not realized that he had taken hold of the dealer's arm again. 'You don't get a quarter of a gramme for twenty, moron. A quarter's thirty. It's cheaper if you buy in bulk, but tossers like you don't understand that!'

Barry Hooper understood it well enough, but he was in no position to go for quantity. He'd cash the cheque he'd got in Oxford for the watch as soon as he could. In the meantime, he must take what he could get; he needed a fix, and quickly. He felt into the pocket of his jeans beneath the leathers and pulled out the notes. 'Thirty,' he said gruffly. 'Give me the quarter!'

'All in good time, black boy!'

Barry heard the contempt coming at him

through the darkness, and hated the man in black, and himself, and this dark place away from normal humanity, and the world of drugs, and the whole business of bartering. The man flashed on a tiny torch, checked the two ten pound notes and the two fives unhurriedly, as if he was still unsure whether to go ahead with the transaction. Barry caught a glint of the white of his eyes, but the black pupils remained invisible still.

Then the foil with the coke within it was pressed into his palm, and the voice in his ear muttered, 'Don't come back for less than a gramme next time, black boy. If I didn't have other and better customers, it wouldn't be worth my while bloody dealing. Now get going, and on your way back through the bar, send out the blonde girl in the blue anorak. We'll see if she's got more than a measly thirty fucking quid to offer!'

Barry turned and fumbled in the darkness for the handle of the door. It was at that moment that the dustbin fell with a startling clatter on to the flags, and a new voice rang out, overriding the curses of the man in black as it shouted that he was under arrest on suspicion of dealing in Class A drugs, that he was not obliged to say anything, but anything he did say...

The rest was lost in a confusion of shouting and action, as Barry found the handle of the door and wrenched it open. The voice concluded the words of arrest and yelled at him to stop. But he was away through the bar, sighting as he fled the pale-faced blonde girl his dealer had told him to send out, pulling up the zip of his leather jacket as he fled through the illuminated car park of the pub to the alley where he had left the bike.

The Ducati started first time, as he had known it would. He slid the helmet and goggles on with practised ease and zipped the leathers tight up beneath his chin. He revved the engine, hearing its smooth roar echoing along the brick walls around him. Confidence rose in him with that noise. He'd be all right now: a Ducati 620 was more than a match for anything the police could throw at him.

It was not until he had nosed the machine out of the alley and on to the narrow street behind the pub that he saw the police car. He should have known the two men arresting the dealer would not be alone.

The engine started and the dazzling lights flashed in his face as he was accelerating gently down the street. The window eased down and a voice shouted to him to stop. The car was facing him. It moved to block his path as he rode towards it, turning sideways across the dimly lit street. The gap left for him seemed to narrow in slow motion as he moved towards it. There was a thin film of drizzle now. His brain said inconsequentially, even in the midst of this crisis, that he had thought it too cold for rain.

It was a good thing he knew just what the Ducati could do; a good thing he controlled its power so expertly. He gave the engine a little more juice, felt the bike leap like a live thing beneath him, twisted the handlebars just enough to the left, and was through the gap and away.

He had to mount the pavement briefly to do it, and he felt the beginning of a skid on his rear wheel as it hit a steel grating in the gutter. But he corrected that instantly, almost contemptuously, and he was away. Away towards Gloucester, oblivion and safety.

He heard the police car switch on its siren, caught the flash of its blue warning light on the damp tarmac in front of him as he leant low over the handlebars, flattening himself against the machine until he became almost part of it. He wasn't worried about the police car. He could leave it behind quite easily, if he kept his head. And he would do that: he knew everything the Ducati could do, and it wouldn't let him down. Bikes could always outdistance cars, when there was traffic about. This was a situation where Barry Hooper was in control. Goodnight, pigs!

He threaded his way expertly through the outer streets of Cheltenham, overtaking a couple of tardy cars and a van, and back on to the A40 to Gloucester. The wailing of the police siren was already fainter when he reached the dual carriageway beneath the neon lights. He opened the throttle, moved swiftly and smoothly up to seventy, eighty, ninety. He checked his mirror to make sure the road was empty behind him and opened up to the ton, exulting in the surge of power, giving a V-sign to the white-faced, startled woman behind the wheel of a Nissan, which he passed as if it were standing still.

He'd lost the cops now. They must be a good mile and more behind him. He'd do the ton along here until he came to the first roundabout outside Gloucester, give himself even more of a start on them. Then he'd move at a sedate pace through the Gloucester streets he knew so well to his own pad, leaving them baffled behind him. He could just see their faces, just visualize their dismay as they had to report their failure.

He had reckoned without police radios.

He passed the first roundabout all right, leaning low to the ground to take it at speed as he saw that he could pass in front of the car coming from the right. There was another two miles of dual carriageway on the Gloucester by-pass then, where he opened up and put another half-mile between himself and any pursuit.

It was at the third roundabout, the one

where he planned to turn into the area near the Gloucester docks and thence home, that he met problems. He had already indicated a left turn and was slowing to make it when he saw another police car, poised by the round-about, with its emergency lights flashing to warn other motorists of its presence.

Barry reacted quickly, ignoring the signal he had given, crouching until his knee almost touched the ground to take the bend of the roundabout, denying his left-hand signal and moving on towards Ross-on-Wye. He caught the blare of a car's horn behind him, the driver outraged at his refusing to turn left as he had indicated. Then, as that sound died, he heard the louder and more insistent note of the police Rover's siren.

There was traffic on this road, two lines of it. He could not at first make much headway, for motorists were switching lanes, according to whether they wanted to continue along the A40 to Ross or swing right on to the B road for Newent and Hereford. Barry realized he had to make a decision himself about which route to take; the police siren remained a constant distance behind him, insistent in his ears now that this slower speed was forced upon him.

The lights for the right turn on to the Newent road changed from red through amber to green when he was two hundred yards short of them, shining bright through the darkness and the thin mist of drizzle as he approached. That decided him. He chose the familiar road, and swung right on to the B4221.

His brain was working well in this pressure situation. He was pleased about that: when he was safely home and had the time, he would even be proud of himself. This road was the one he took every day to Camellia Park: he knew it like the back of his hand and was confident he could outwit the fuzz in their Rover 75. It was a fast car, but no match for a Ducati on this twisty road. Goodnight, pigs!

The B4221 skirted the village of Highnam, a notorious trap for speeding motorists, where Barry meticulously observed the thirty limit every morning on his way to the golf course. Now he roared over the mini-roundabout and flashed past the gates of the course, where he normally turned carefully left. The speed camera flashed white and brilliant in his face, blinding him for a second, taking him dangerously towards the hedge at the speed he was travelling. He righted the bike just in time, with practised, unhurried skill, which gave him extra confidence.

He opened up to sixty, feeling the closeness of the road to his body as he leant low, perilously low, first one way and then the other, on the Z-bend, as he moved beneath overarching trees and out between open fields. He was driving near the limit, on damp surfaces; he had better be careful. But that was why he had chosen this route: he could outwit any car on this road.

He heard the police siren switch on behind him as the big Rover left the village of Highnam.

It was nearer than he had expected: they were good, these blokes. But not good enough. There was a small white car ahead of him. Its rear lights seemed to leap towards him as he caught up with it quickly, reminding him how fast he was going. But he did not shut the throttle. He swept past the car at the end of a straight stretch of road, ignoring the glow against the hedge ahead which told him that some invisible vehicle was approaching from the opposite direction. He was conscious of the double white lines, unnaturally white, unnaturally near to him beneath his wheels.

Then everything disappeared in the blinding headlights of the lorry which hurtled towards him. He twisted the throttle more open still, roared straight at the high, blinding lights, heard the head-splitting blare which he realized only later was the lorry's urgent horn. Then he twisted his handlebars, missing the wing of the pantechnicon by a margin so small that the wind from its front wing almost had him over. He saw the huge letters of the firm on its side as he turned into the skid which was trying to take him out of control and roared on. The Rover 75 wouldn't get past the car as he had done: it would have to wait for the right stretch of road. So goodnight, pigs!

He was proud that he had opened the throttle even wider back there, when his instinct and everyone else's would have been to brake, dazzled like a helpless rabbit in the lights of the lorry. If he had done, he'd have been hit, and that would have been the end of it. Only his speed had got him through that narrowing, fleetingly visible gap. They were a good team, Barry Hooper and the Ducati. He had always known that, and they were proving it tonight.

And he knew now what he was going to do. This road led to the M50. That is why it carried the heavy goods vehicles which would not normally use a B road: the canny, experienced drivers knew it was a short cut to the motorway. He would turn on to the motorway when he reached it. If he could put enough distance between him and the Rover by then, they wouldn't know whether he had turned north or south.

But Barry knew where he was going. He would turn north towards Birmingham, opening up the Ducati to the ton, to a hundred and twenty or thirty if necessary. He had never ridden as fast as that before, but the machine would do it, when he called upon it. When he was sure he had shaken them off, he'd turn off, probably at the Tewkesbury exit. Then he would make his way home at leisure on the minor roads, enjoying his triumph, letting the coolness of the night air bring him slowly down from his high.

Thank God for the Ducati. He had forgotten now why he was being pursued, why the chase had begun. He was conscious only of the chase itself, of the exultation, of the absolute necessity of escaping the hunters. He heard the siren again behind him. They'd got past the van, then. There hadn't been much going the other way, after the monster which had nearly hit him.

Barry Hooper felt the coldness of fear for the first time about his heart.

He was approaching Newent now, the place where they had gone to the restaurant last Wednesday night, the place where it had all started to go wrong. It seemed unbelievable that it was only six nights ago. But this road by-passed the old market town and there would be a long stretch of straight road after he had zoomed past the turning for Newent. A car threatened to pull out in front of him, then realized just in time how fast the single headlamp was approaching, and pulled up with a jerk. Thank God for that.

He was on the straight stretch now. He

opened up the bike to the ton, glorying in the smoothness of the rising whine of the engine, loving the swiftness of the acceleration between his thighs, even in this moment of crisis. Then he remembered. Just round the bend, where the old road at the other end of Newent ran at right angles across this road, there were traffic lights.

He would go through them, even if they were at red. He made the decision as he ran beneath trees and slowed for the bend. He had no alternative. If he respected the red of the lights and halted, the big Rover would be up beside him, the coppers tumbling out to grab him. He could hear the siren again. He could not understand how they had managed to stay so close. They were good, those guys.

The lights were green. They came at him as if they had life and movement of their own, reminding him again how fast he was going. He was through them like the wind, raising his right fist for a second in brief, unwitnessed triumph, willing the lights to turn to red before the police car reached them. The pigs had an advantage, with their sirens and their flashing lights: other traffic would give way to them. It wasn't fair really. But he still had the Ducati to balance that.

As he left Newent behind and moved on to a winding stretch of road where the double central lines forbade overtaking, he heard the siren behind him again. They were through the lights.

He was three miles now from the motorway, on a road which had a maximum speed of fifty for the first mile and forty after that. They would know which way he had turned at the motorway, unless he could put more ground between him and them.

The road was blessedly free of traffic, and he took the willing machine up to eighty, then ninety, roaring on the wrong side on the bends, trusting that if he saw no oncoming glow of light, there would be no oncoming vehicle. At the bottom of a short, steep hill, a road turned away at forty-five degrees towards the Forest of Dean, and a vehicle of some kind was beginning to ease out across his path, to turn whence he had come.

He willed it to stop, then blasted his own horn in a long, insistent warning to get back. It was an old car, and it kept moving. He had to cancel his plans to go in front of it at the last minute, as it kept moving at a snail's pace across the road. He twisted the handlebars left, shot through the narrow space which miraculously opened on his own side of the road, behind the car, and fought to retain control of a bike which was moving too fast to turn at this speed.

There was nothing coming the other way, and he used every foot of the road as he fought the skid, first one way, then the other, using all of his strength as well as all of his skill to regain control of the Ducati. 'Pushed you too far there, babe! Won't do it again, so don't you worry!' Barry patted the machine's flank as if it were a mettlesome horse, then realized that the peal of laughter which rent the darkness above was coming from him.

Relief, that was. He'd been lucky there, might as well admit it. But if he hadn't been skilful as well as lucky, he wouldn't have made it, would he? He roared jubilantly over the hill with the old stone church hall on his left and down the steep, short slope beyond it. Almost there now! Goodnight, pigs!

A sign on his left said forty miles an hour. That was a laugh, when he was doing over eighty! But it was less than a mile to the motorway now, and he must surely be far enough ahead for him to confuse his pursuers about the route he would take. He'd keep a low profile for weeks of riding after this, just in case they circulated a description of the Ducati. Better safe than sorry!

As he flew past the dark shape of the post office in Gorsley on his right, he heard the siren again behind him. They could surely not be as close as that awful wailing through the damp night air said they were?

He was tempted to change his plans and speed south down the motorway, past Ross-on-Wye and into Wales. It was an easy, natural turn to the left, and he would scarcely need to slacken his speed. But they might have alerted other police in Ross. That would be the way they were expecting him to turn.

He sped on over the motorway bridge, holding his speed for as long as he dared. It was a tight turn on to the northern carriageway of the M50: this entry had only been built as a temporary one, twenty years and more ago, but it remained unaltered, because the planned permanent access had never been built. That was all right, because Barry Hooper knew it well, knew that he must turn through almost 180 degrees in forty yards.

He would probably have managed it all right, if the siren hadn't sounded again as he began to slow. It was cruelly close, probably beside the little primary school, scarcely two hundred yards behind him.

If a huge van hadn't been turning off the motorway to take the short cut along the B road, he might still have got away with it.

As it was, Barry slowed just too late, thrust at the brakes in belated panic, felt the tyres of his faithful machine sliding beyond control beneath him, felt the wet tarmac tearing through his immaculate leathers to the flesh beneath, saw the side of the massive van coming at him like a concrete wall.

The bike went on, sliding sixty yards down the hard shoulder of the motorway with a

255

rending of tortured metal. The rider hit the base of the van with a sickening sound, then disappeared beneath it.

The police Rover 75 parked carefully: there was no longer any need for haste.

The driver left his roof light flashing; its intermittent, garish blue light gave a hellish illumination to the scene around the stationary pantechnicon. Its driver, climbing stiffly from his warm cab, clad bizarrely in a string vest, said in an odd voice, 'I didn't have a chance.'

The police traffic control men nodded, radioed for an ambulance, moved cautiously to the side of the huge vehicle. A boot, ripped off in the impact, lay pathetically beneath the rear wheel of the van. Whatever else was left of Barry Hooper lay invisible beneath it.

Goodnight, pigs.

Seventeen

The police Mondeo which Barry Hooper had waited so anxiously to see on the previous day drove into Camellia Park on the morning of Wednesday, the twentieth of December. But it did not drive up to the groundsmen's office, where Hooper had watched so anxiously for its arrival. It turned instead into the car park beside the clubhouse. The tall figure of John Lambert levered itself stiffly from the passenger seat and followed Bert Hook round the back of the low modern building, glancing for a moment at the wintry sky as he moved.

Joanne Moss had laid out the pies, the bacon and the various forms of bread her clients preferred. She was as meticulous and neat and well prepared as ever. 'It's mostly fast food, I know,' she said apologetically, 'but it's what they want and enjoy. There won't be many of them, in weather like this, but they like something hot, and they don't want to wait too long for it!' Her nervous little laugh said that she knew they were not here to discuss the culinary merits of her offerings.

Joanne knew they must know a lot more now than when they had talked to her on Friday night. They'd talked to all the others now, some of them more than once. They must have found out a lot more about Patrick. Things she hadn't wanted them to find out, probably. She steeled herself for that, telling herself that this was no more than she had expected, all along.

The next half hour could well be the most important of her life. She told herself not to be melodramatic, but she could not rid herself of that idea. Well, she was up to it, anyway. She hadn't killed Pat, had she? Cling on to that idea, Joanne, and go for it.

The Chief Superintendent seemed in no hurry to start. He studied her without embarrassment, even when they were all sitting down, as if estimating her state of mind, her preparedness for this interview. Perhaps that was part of his technique. Joanne determined to play it cool, to stay as calm as this man heavy with experience seemed to be, as he looked so hard into her face.

'Tell us again about your discovery of the body.'

It was like a blow to her face, the way Lambert went straight in without the slightest attempt at preliminaries. Joanne swallowed hard, forced herself to take her time over this. The question couldn't harm her: she held on to that thought as she said slowly, 'There was a lot of noise going on in the restaurant as I went down to the basement. I met Michelle Nayland coming back up the stairs, but no one else came down to the Ladies during the three or four minutes whilst I was in there. I don't know whether anyone was in the Gents at that time, murdering Patrick.'

She looked up at that point, into impassive, attentive faces. 'I noticed the door of the gents' cloakroom was slightly open as I emerged from the Ladies and saw Patrick's foot through the gap. The door was probably already open when I came down the stairs, but if it was I didn't notice it. I found the body, saw the big pool of blood around it. The next thing I remember is Chris Pearson slapping me to stop me screaming.'

It was delivered as if she had memorized it, as if she was anxious to get through it without making a mistake, without contradicting any detail she had given them before. It sounded a little odd, like a careful childish recitation in this nightmarish framework, but there was nothing unnatural in that. Anyone who had discovered a corpse in this gory context would have been over the scene many times, running the events through like a loop on a videotape.

Lambert said, 'It is almost five days since

we last spoke to you. Have you recalled any-thing else about that night which now seems to you significant?'

'No.' The denial came a little too quickly, but she had more things to think about than timing.

'And you're sure you didn't see anyone else but Michelle Nayland, from the moment you left the restaurant until you discovered the body?'

It was an opportunity to divert suspicion from herself, to bring others into the equation; even to help Michelle, perhaps. Put someone in the frame: that was what the police called it, wasn't it? But there was no need for that, if you weren't guilty. Stick to what you'd said all along: anything else would only arouse suspicion. 'I can't be certain that Michelle was the only one. What I said is that she's the only person I can *recall* seeing; I had no idea at the time that it was going to be important. And of course I had no idea who was in the gents' cloakroom when I went down there, or who might have gone in there whilst I was in the Ladies.'

Lambert nodded slowly, seeming to digest things, to check them against the sum of his knowledge, without once taking his grey eyes off her face. It was most unnerving. Eventually he said quietly, 'Is there anything you would wish to add to what you told us on Friday night, Mrs Moss?'

260

'No. I've just told you all I—'

'About your relationship with the deceased, for instance?'

'No.' It was coming, then. She told herself that she had always known it must, that she must let them make the running, if she was not to give away more than they already knew.

'What is your salary for the work you do here?' He looked round the neat kitchen with its stainless-steel implements, its industrial microwave, its fast food ready for the modest lunchtime demands, as if minimizing the work she did.

Joanne found herself saying, 'My salary is my own business. It is no concern of anyone, except myself and the person who chooses to pay it to me.'

'In a normal situation, yes. In a murder inquiry, emphatically no.'

She had known this must come out. She went through the ritual of resistance. 'I'm paid a generous salary. I'm good at what I do.'

'No doubt. Good enough to warrant more money than anyone else on the staff? Five thousand more than Mr Pearson, who runs the whole enterprise?'

'Perhaps not. But I support myself, Chief Superintendent Lambert. It was not my decision to raise my earnings. You cannot blame me for taking whatever salary was offered to me.'

'Patrick Nayland seems to have been a shrewd businessman, well aware of the rates necessary to recruit efficient staff. Can you account for the fact that you are paid twice as much as any other member of staff?'

'No. It wasn't my decision. I admit I was surprised to get such a rise in salary when I became full-time, but—'

'You were having an affair with Patrick Nayland, weren't you, Mrs Moss?'

'That's my business.' She snapped it out primly, trying to buy herself time to think. She hadn't expected it to come out like this, to hear Lambert's blunt, almost contemptuous challenge ringing in her ears as she tried to marshal her resistance.

'And our business too, Mrs Moss. You must see that, in the circumstances.'

She shook her head dumbly, unable to discover the words for further defiance.

'And the fact that you chose to conceal this relationship, when specifically asked to declare any such allegiances at our first meeting, is now of great interest to us.'

They had declared the affair as fact now, when she had never admitted to it. They must be very sure of their ground. 'Who told you about this?'

'You would not expect us to reveal that.' A grim smile. Triumph, she thought. But not complacency. They hadn't got her for the murder of Patrick, only for having an affair with him. She said defiantly, 'There's no law against it. I'm a free woman.'

Lambert did not point out that Patrick Nayland had not been a free man. He wasn't getting into that. He said patiently, 'We're investigating a murder. It could be said that you've obstructed the police in the course of their enquiries. I'm not particularly interested in pursuing that line, at the moment. I'm interested in the reasons why you chose to conceal information which may have a vital bearing on this death.'

'It doesn't. And it's natural I shouldn't want my affairs blazoned all over the newspapers, with a grieving widow and her daughter around.' That had come out spontaneously, and Joanne thought it sounded better than the stuff she had carefully prepared.

Lambert ignored her. 'How long ago did this affair start?'

'It's been serious for two years.' That was precise enough. She could be even more exact if she wanted to be, but that would show how deeply the passion had bitten.

'Did Mrs Nayland know about it?'

'No one knew, as far as we were aware.' Except Alan Fitch: she made that reservation to herself, but saw no reason to tell them of it. 'I'm not proud of taking away a woman's husband.'

Except that you hadn't taken him away, had you? thought Lambert. There was a saying that the wife always won out in the end, if she wanted to. And the cool, well-organized Liza Nayland was still very much around.

Lambert said, 'Other people did know, Mrs Moss. They always do, if an affair lasts very long, however discreet you think your behaviour is. In the light of that, I ask you again: how sure are you that Mrs Nayland was completely ignorant of the situation?'

'She didn't know. Pat was sure of that.'

'Because if she did know, it would make her a candidate for this murder, wouldn't it?'

He was watching her closely, studying her reaction, she supposed. She was amazed to find that she was quite enjoying the situation. 'It would, wouldn't it? I hadn't thought of that. If Pat had—'

'So how sure are you that Mrs Nayland didn't know about the situation?'

She took her time, as if digesting a new idea. She raised a ringless hand to move the strand of dark hair which had strayed towards her eye. 'Pat said he was sure she didn't know. I've hardly met the woman, for reasons which I trust are obvious. All I can say is that she's never been in to confront me.'

'This looks very like a crime where passion was involved. Where a man was killed in an impulsive fit of rage or jealousy.'

She was conscious of Lambert studying her closely, even of the possibility that he might be setting a trap for her. But they didn't do that, did they, these people? Not when they were facing someone who was completely innocent? Joanne had again that strange, unexpected feeling of excitement, of playing a game for high stakes which was still a game. 'Yes, I can see that. If you stick a knife repeatedly into someone, it's likely to be on impulse rather than pre-planned, isn't it? And of course there's—' She stopped abruptly, her hand flying in horror to her mouth, as if to still the indiscretion on her lips.

'There's what, Mrs Moss?'

Her voice was low now, scarcely more than a whisper. 'Not what, Superintendent. Who. I was thinking of what I've already told you. That the only person I saw immediately before I found Pat's body was Michelle Nayland.'

'And a daughter who feels that her mother has been wronged might well have killed on her behalf? It's a possibility we have considered, Mrs Moss. Until we know for certain what has happened, we have to consider every scenario.' He was calmness personified. She wished he would take his eyes off her face, if only for a moment. He did not even seem to need to blink.

'Who told you that I was Pat's mistress?'

She wanted to know that; wanted to know who, under pressure like this, had known about her and blown the gaff to these two. Somehow, she knew that it would have been to these two, not to one of the lesser lights in the team who had been taking statements from all and sundry around the place. Had someone been trying to implicate her, to plant the suggestion that the mistress might have killed, if she wasn't having things her own way?

Not many people cared for that old-fashioned noun 'mistress' nowadays. Lambert smiled at her, looking as hard as ever into her face, trying to work out exactly what was going on behind the smooth brow beneath that glossy dark hair. 'You wouldn't expect me to reveal our sources of information. Have you decided yet who you think killed Patrick Nayland?'

It was one of his sudden switches, endeavouring to catch her off guard, to lead her into some indiscretion. She wasn't going to be caught out like that. She said boldly, 'No. But I don't have to pretend I'm indifferent any longer, do I? I was in love with Pat. I want you to get the bastard who killed him, and put him away for a long time. If I get there first, he'll wish he'd been arrested, I can tell you!' Her voice rose in a sudden fury on the last sentence.

Lambert did not rise to the suggestion, did

not even warn her against taking the law into her own hands. He said dryly, 'So the sudden rise in your salary no doubt dates from the time when you established a serious relationship with Mr Nayland.'

Another of his switches, away from the emotion of her feelings about Pat's death to the area she thought he'd finished with. She said limply, 'My salary was sharply increased when this job warranted a full-time Catering Manager. But I suppose that was about the time when I became Pat's mistress, yes.'

'A salary which was comfortably higher than that earned by the General Manager of the whole enterprise,' he reminded her again.

Damn the man, she thought. He made it sound like prostitution, as if she were being paid for her services in places other than this neat, well-equipped kitchen. But probably he was trying to rile her: people revealed much more of themselves when they were annoyed. She made herself smile as she said, 'I can't help it if Pat wanted to pay me more. All right, I recognize that he was paying well above the rate for the job, but he wanted to do it. He said we were going to be married eventually, so the money was staying in the family firm, really!'

'You were planning marriage?'

He had raised his eyebrows as if that surprised him, the insulting sod. But the important thing was not to let him rattle you. 'It was on the agenda, yes. I was leaving it to Pat to decide when was the right moment for it to happen.'

He looked at her quizzically at that, as if he had not known women in her situation to be as patient as that. But he couldn't know what had passed between them in the privacy of her flat, could not know the softly spoken discussions they had had in bed after sex, could he? Never would know now, with Pat dead. And in this matter at least, no one else could stick their oar in. He could know only what she chose to tell him. She said, 'I didn't wish to hurt Liza Nayland or her daughter any more than was strictly necessary. I've been through a divorce myself, don't forget.'

Lambert nodded two or three times, pausing as if to evaluate what she had said. Then he said quietly, 'So you were and are quite convinced that Mr Nayland was serious in his intentions towards you.'

She felt herself reddening, tried to keep the anger out of her voice as she said to him, 'Of course he was serious! Do you think I wouldn't have known in an instant if there was anything phoney about the plans we were making together?'

He was not at all embarrassed. In an ordinary conversation, a man would have been rushing to apologize for the suggestion he had made, to rescue himself from a gaffe before it became a social disaster. But this was no ordinary conversation, and she should have adjusted to that by now. He raised an eyebrow at her reaction, then said, 'We only know Patrick Nayland through other people's impressions of him. We have had to build up a picture in the last week from what the people who lived with him and worked with him have told us. He has not emerged to us as a man who went in for lasting sexual relationships, as a man who would give up his marriage for an affair. You are giving us a different picture: we have to weigh your view against other people's recollections of a man who cannot speak for himself.'

So other people had been yapping, had been mouthing off about things they knew nothing about. She wondered who. But she mustn't be diverted into that now. She must give all her attention to this man with the long, lined face and the dutiful dolt at his side, who watched her and made an occasional note. 'I was closer to Pat than anyone. My view should count for more than these others you have spoken to. And I can assure you, he was very serious about me!'

'He was a reformed character, then.' For the first time, and then only for an instant, he took his eyes off her and looked at Hook beside him, as if the two were mentally

269

comparing notes.

She wanted to flay his visage with her nails, to tear away the smugness with which he seemed to be treating everything she said. But she controlled herself, trying not to reveal the effort that cost her. 'I'm not a fool, Superintendent. I knew Pat had a certain reputation for the way he treated women. I was cautious at first, even fended him off. But he convinced me that he was serious. And I am not an adolescent girl. As a divorcee, you get lots of offers from men who spot a bit of spare, who think you must be desperate for sex. You have to learn to look after yourself. I have acquired a certain judgement in these things.'

It was a good argument. Convincing even, except to policemen who had learned to be cynical about such protestations. Love, even infatuation, could soon unbalance judgement. 'So you are quite certain that once Mr Nayland had begun a serious affair with you, he made no other sexual advances.'

She let herself go now. 'Of course I'm sure of it! Do you think that if Pat had put his hand up anyone else's skirt, I'd still have been there for him? What kind of woman do you think I am?'

Lambert was not at all put out. He smiled at her and said, 'We are still finding that out, Mrs Moss. Because, as I have to remind you, you concealed a considerable amount about yourself at our first meeting. We now find you are a spirited woman, with the kind of reactions you have just declared. A woman who might even have killed a man, if he had been telling her less than the truth about his intentions.'

It was stated so calmly that it took a moment for her to realize that he was giving her a motive for Pat's murder. She told herself that it was natural enough, that she had expected this from the start. She had not expected it to be so baldly and calmly stated. She tried not to show how shaken she was feeling as she said, 'I suppose it's logical for you to examine such possibilities. I can only tell you again that I had every confidence in Pat, in his intentions, in our future together.'

She felt her breathing uneven, shaking her whole body. She expected that he might press her further on this, but he merely nodded two or three times. It was Hook who said, 'You clearly knew much more about Patrick Nayland and his plans than you were prepared to reveal at our first meeting with you. What can you now tell us about his relationship with his General Manager?'

She looked into the weatherbeaten countryman's face, found the blue eyes watching her as keenly as his chief's had before him. She was trying to determine what her tactics should be now, with the transference of attention from her to others, but she found it

271

difficult to think as clearly as she wished to under the intense scrutiny of these two pairs of unembarrassed, acutely interested eyes. 'Chris Pearson? Pat trusted him. They got on well together. Surely other people must have told you this?' She waited for a comment, for some snippet which would offer guidance to her, but they gave her none. 'They didn't have many disagreements.'

'But they had some.' Hook made it a statement, leading her on, implying that she had started on something here.

She couldn't think how he had contrived that; perhaps he was rather more than the dutiful dullard she had decided upon. 'Occasionally they disagreed, yes. Usually it was when Chris wanted to push ahead too fast. Pat said it was easy to have grandiose plans, when you weren't spending your own money.'

'Mr Pearson wanted to stretch the course from nine holes to eighteen, didn't he?'

They knew about that then. She wondered who had told them, how much else they knew about the personalities involved, how people had spoken to this inquisitive pair about her.

Then she remembered with a shock that she had told them herself. It was a reminder of how very careful she needed to be now. 'Yes. Pat planned to expand too, but Chris was more impatient. Pat said he wanted to

272

see a healthy profit from the nine-hole set-up before he moved on to eighteen. That the project must generate its own income for expansion.' She brought out that phrase from the past and could almost hear Pat saying it.

'And this was one of their major sources of disagreement?'

'Yes. As a matter of fact, I heard them having a bit of a row on the day before Pat died. I imagine that it was about that.'

'But you aren't certain.' Hook's tones were as slow and measured as earlier; he gave no sign of his excitement, no clue that they had heard nothing of this dispute until this moment.

'No. I heard raised voices in the office whilst I was working in here. I remember it clearly because Chris was shouting at Pat. I don't think I'd ever heard that before.'

'But you don't know what they were arguing about.'

'No. The dispute went on for about ten minutes, I suppose, and they both looked pretty heated after it was over. But neither of them spoke to me about it afterwards. Pat would no doubt have told me in due course, but I didn't see him alone again before he was killed at Soutters.' She hadn't meant to say all that, but it was out before she could stop herself, and she had delivered the words without breaking down.

'Did anyone else have a reason to want Mr Nayland out of the way?'

It was a curious phrase, that, 'out of the way'. She had a feeling Lambert would have been more direct. But Hook was just as searching, in his gentler way. 'No. Well, Alan Fitch didn't like him. But that's different from wanting him dead, isn't it?'

'Indeed it is. But we have to be interested, nevertheless.'

'Well, he doesn't say much, Alan. Not to anyone, unless it's to Barry Hooper. But he did tell me to be careful, a couple of weeks ago. He said the leopard didn't change his spots. He was talking about Pat.'

It was the very phrase about Nayland that had come from a very different source, DI Rushton. It had been repeated by Chris Pearson, who had known Nayland as well as anyone. They wondered as they drove away from Camellia Park whether Joanne Moss had eventually come to a bitter acceptance of that view.

Eighteen

Eleanor Hook and Christine Lambert were agreed. Their husbands were not going to wriggle out of the treat, just because they were a week into a murder case.

The women had booked the seats for the performance of *Die Fledermaus* at the Malvern Theatre months ago. December the twentieth was Bert Hook's birthday, and this was just the right sort of entertainment for the period before Christmas: lighthearted, not too demanding, and yet with enough good tunes and splendid singing to keep everyone interested. The men needn't dress up; they could even wear sweaters if they must. But they must take their wives to the theatre and celebrate Bert's birthday with an outing.

The evening beguiled but did not distract either of the CID men. The operetta was about a celebration, for a start. This was a more elaborate and extended celebration than the one at Soutters Restaurant which had ended so dramatically exactly a week earlier, but nevertheless for the CID men events on stage held overtones of that memorable night.

Die Fledermaus has a comic jailer to get the evening off to a good start, a non-singing part which might have been calculated to go down well with policemen, who tend to think they know a thing or two about such people. And the core of the plot involves a masked ball, with all sorts of deceptions going on. It is half a joyous romp, half a satirical swipe at a corrupt society: just the sort of mixture to appeal to seasoned, cynical detectives.

John Lambert found himself wondering about the motives for deceit, about the mechanics of duplicity, about the seeming willingness to be gulled of those who swallowed the deceptions. Over their interval drinks, he and Bert compared notes about the morning interview with Joanne Moss, about how much they could accept of what she had said to them that day.

Eventually, Eleanor Hook overheard their muttered conference and brought it to an abrupt end. She encouraged her husband to talk about sopranos, which he did with a surprisingly comprehensive knowledge, and about the advantages of the Viennese lilt to Strauss in his operettas. Christine Lambert listened and was filled with admiration. 'On the timetable at Barnardo's was it, Bert, opera singing?'

276

Hook grinned. 'If you listened to anything but pop groups, you were highly suspect then. It wasn't much better when I was a young policeman in the section house. They thought you were probably gay if you listen-ed to classical CDs! It wasn't until Pavarotti and the three tenors and Nessun Dorma at the World Cup that coppers were allowed to like opera singing.'

He proceeded to discuss different versions of the Czardas in *Die Fledermaus*, totally unconscious of the contrast between his village-bobby exterior and the erudition he was exhibiting. John Lambert knew that this disparity between appearance and reality, between Hook's stolid exterior and the active, imaginative brain beneath it, had stood them in good stead again today, when he was pretty sure that Joanne Moss had underestimated Hook.

During the second half of the operetta, the extravagant costumes and the luscious music of the ball on stage, not to mention the multiple intrigues and resolutions of the plot, should have taken up his full concen-tration. Instead, Lambert found his mind constantly straying to what they had to do in the days to come, to the people they still had to confront with new knowledge, to the conflict they had heard about between the dead man and his General Manager, Chris Pearson.

In retrospect, Lambert thought that it was probably at that beguiling moment when the entire company joined in the waltz from *Die Fledermaus* that the identity of the murderer of Patrick Nayland came to him.

Thirty-six hours after he had been eased out from beneath the pantechnicon, Barry Hooper was fit to be interviewed by detectives. Modern medicine has its disadvantages as well as its blessings.

The delicate black hands looked curiously fragile as they lay without movement on the very white hospital sheets, like the hands of someone who worked all day at a desk rather than on the various tasks of golf-course maintenance. The dark brown eyes in the too-revealing young face filled with fear when he saw who his visitors were. 'I panicked. I knew I was going too fast, but I couldn't seem to do anything else.' He addressed his remarks automatically to Bert Hook, whom he remembered from their first meeting as the more sympathetic of the two, a man who had ridden motorcycles himself in his youth.

'It's a good bike, the Ducati 620,' said Hook. 'But dangerous, in the wrong hands.'

'Is it a write-off?' Even now, when he knew he must watch his every word, Barry couldn't resist the query about his beloved machine.

'It's been taken into a garage and examined with a view to charges by our forensic people. I hear it's repairable.' Despite himself, Hook found himself smiling at the pathetic relief on the slim black face. 'But you won't be riding anything for quite some time, lad.'

Barry had memorized all the ward sister had told him about his condition. 'I've got a broken leg and a broken collar bone, and a couple of cracked ribs. They thought at first that my pelvis might be smashed, but it's only severe bruising. I was really very lucky. I might be out in a week or ten days, with luck.' He listed his injuries carefully, almost proudly, managing that peculiar male feat of sounding as if his survival reflected some sort of credit upon himself. He looked at the drip above his head, at the multiple medical equipment around his bed, as if he could scarcely believe his luck.

'You'll need to be able to move about and fend for yourself before you're fit to leave,' said Hook automatically. He thought of the tiny shabby room in that rabbit-warren of a house in Gloucester, of the difficulties of being an invalid in an anonymous, uncaring, squalid place like that.

'Alan Fitch and his wife came in to see me last night. They say I can go there until I'm able to look after myself.' Hooper announced it with a proud wonderment. Bert, who remembered the first time when someone had invited the young Hook into their home, understood perfectly that delighted response to a kindness which seemed almost miraculous.

He didn't remind the man in the bed that such a convalescence would be dependent on neither of the men being behind bars by then.

Lambert thought the preliminaries due to an injured man had gone far enough. He said caustically, 'You're in trouble, Mr Hooper, apart from your injuries.'

The dark young face clouded. 'I was speeding, I know that. Taking risks I shouldn't have done, and—'

'You were in possession of a Class A drug at the time. A drug which a Drugs Squad officer had witnessed you purchasing in Cheltenham.'

Barry told himself he should have known they'd come up with that. Suffering from the shock following his smash and the pain of his injuries yesterday, he hadn't even thought about what had happened to his motorcycle leathers. The police must have taken them away and gone through the pockets.

He struggled to adjust to the idea that these men were here to pursue a crime. Everyone had been so kind to him since he had come round in hospital that it was difficult for him to adjust to the idea of the law coming after him. Could they arrest him, whilst he was lying in bed, unable to move? Would they charge him with what he had done? He said feebly, 'I wasn't dealing. It was just a small quantity, for my own use.'

'But crack cocaine is a Class A drug. We're not talking about pot here, are we?'

'No. I'm going to give it up. I was well on the way to kicking the habit, but then we had all the stress.'

He couldn't bring himself to define the stress. It was left to Lambert to say, 'The stress of Mr Nayland's murder? Now why should you find that stressful, Mr Hooper? Horrible yes, shocking yes, but once you'd got over the initial impact of seeing a man struck down like that, why should you find it so stressful?' The word seemed to become more menacing each time he repeated it.

'I don't know. He'd just given me a full-time job. I've never seen a man dead before. Never knew there could be so much blood when someone was stabbed like that.' He was floundering, and he knew it.

Lambert studied him for a few seconds, which seemed to Barry to stretch towards minutes. 'You were under stress all right, Mr Hooper. But not for the reasons you state. Did you kill Patrick Nayland?'

The question was there, boldly, nakedly asked. More nakedly than Barry had ever imagined it put, even in his worst nightmares. His face contorted for a moment in pain; he cried out with the sudden agony of it. He must have moved his shoulder, must have squirmed under the gaze of this calm torturer who had never raised a hand to threaten him. He gasped as he tried to ease the pain, but Lambert did not move a muscle, did not alter a line in his long, observant face. It was Hook who poured a glass of water and held it to the young man's lips.

Barry saw a nurse look in for a moment at the door of the room, hoped that she would intervene, would tell these men in their grey suits that her patient had had enough, that they must come back another time if they wanted to continue this. His heart sank as she turned away, apparently satisfied that he was in good hands. He said, 'I didn't kill Mr Nayland. I'd never have done anything like—'

'Not even in the pursuit of theft, Mr Hooper? Not even when he resisted and panic took over?'

'I don't know what you mean. I never—'

'Perhaps before you tell us any more lies you should know certain things, Mr Hooper. Such as that a Rolex watch was handed over to the Oxford police on Monday as suspected stolen property. A watch which I could produce for your identification, were it not safely bagged away, ready to be produced as

282

an exhibit in a murder trial. A trial in which you should prepare yourself to be a leading witness.'

'But what has this to do with—'

'With you, Mr Hooper? Perhaps I should tell you that the pawnbroker who fulfilled his duty by taking this watch to the police gave a detailed description of the person who presented the watch to the lady in his shop. When he understood that we were engaged in a murder inquiry, he also gave us your address. Perhaps you shouldn't have settled for such a derisory amount in payment. The proprietor had stopped the cheque his assistant wrote out for you by the time he spoke to the police in Oxford.'

Barry knew the Rolex had been worth more, that he should have held out for something nearer to its true value. All he had done by accepting less was to arouse suspicion. 'I won it. Won it on a bet.'

Lambert smiled at his naivety. 'From a man in a pub, no doubt, whom you haven't seen before or since. Let's stop all this nonsense, Mr Hooper. The watch has been identified by Mrs Nayland as belonging to her husband. He was wearing it on the night of his death. It was taken from his wrist by someone who killed him in the pursuit of theft.'

'No!' The word rang like the cry of a trapped animal around the quiet room, with its crowded array of medical equipment. It was a noise full of fear and anguish: its echo seemed to bounce back from the smooth magnolia walls long after the monosyllable had been uttered. Barry Hooper hoped again that it might bring the nurse to his rescue, that he might be released from this torture, even if only temporarily.

But there was no caring female face, no comforting flash of blue uniform in the doorway. He said, 'All right, I took the watch. But I didn't kill Mr Nayland.' Even now, in this crisis, he couldn't bring himself to leave out the dead man's title, to deny him in death the respect he had always shown to him in life.

'You'll need to convince us of that. Having lied to us about practically everything so far.' Lambert looked towards the door of the room, checking that they weren't going to be interrupted yet by the medics. 'You told us when we first talked to you on Saturday that you'd given up drugs and given up thieving. Wrong on both counts, weren't you? So we'd better have a new version of your visit to the basement at Soutters Restaurant on the night of the murder, and what you saw then. And this time make it an accurate account, and don't leave anything out. Our patience is exhausted, Mr Hooper.'

Barry believed that. He tried to force his brain to concentrate on the one essential task of convincing them that he hadn't killed Nayland. He felt as he had done years ago at school, when he was trapped in a situation where he had lied so much that no one was going to believe him about anything. Other boys had had parents to speak up for them, but it had always felt as if there had been no one for him from the care home.

Fat lot of use it would be telling this unyielding, ancient copper stuff like that. And he couldn't remember now exactly what he'd told them the first time. No doubt the burly one, who'd seemed sympathetic at first, had it all down in that notebook of his. No doubt he was waiting to pick him up and accuse him again of lying as soon as his new tale didn't tally. Barry looked down at his fingers, pathetically thin against the stark white sheet, and said, 'I didn't tell it right the first time. I got it wrong last Saturday, when you came to the house.'

'In more ways than one, Mr Hooper. We'd better have it right this time.'

No one ever called Barry 'Mister'. This Superintendent Lambert was doing it all the time, and it was unnerving. He wondered if it was something coppers had to do when they were going to charge you with murder. He'd better make it good, this time. No use trying to protect Alan Fitch, or anyone else except himself. He closed his eyes and said, 'I left the meal and went down to the washroom much later than I told you on Friday. Alan Fitch had just come back into the restaurant. Mrs Nayland came back in, just before I went down, as far as I can remember.'

'How long before?'

'A couple of minutes, I think. And Alan just before that.' He was conscious of the two big men, staring hard at him, looking as if they didn't believe a word he was saying. As if they weren't going to believe the next few sentences, which were the most important of his life. 'I met Michelle Nayland in the doorway as I went out.' He paused, wanting to be interrupted, to be given another question before he had to deliver the next part. But just when he most wanted them to speak, they said nothing. 'I went into the gents' washroom. Mr Nayland was lying dead on the floor. His eyes were open, and there was a big pool of blood.'

Lambert neither nodded nor shook his head. He just continued to study the injured man, until Barry felt he must cry out with the tension of it. He swallowed hard and looked longingly at the glass and the jug of water beside him. But to ask for a drink suddenly seemed like a confession of guilt. He said throatily, 'Mr Nayland was lying on his back, with his right arm flung out. His sleeve was up and the Rolex was very obvious on his wrist, as if it was asking to be taken. I slid it off and put it into my pocket.'

It suddenly seemed banal, such a stupid thing to have done that it could not possibly be the truth. He wanted to embroider his action, to add a series of details which would convince them. But he could think of nothing, and his voice would go no further. Now, when it was too late for him, DS Hook filled up the glass of water with elaborate care and passed it to him. His fingers trembled so much that he had to raise both hands to get it to his mouth. He tilted it slowly, until the liquid ran into his throat, then channelled cold into his chest and out into his body, as if he were a man dying of thirst in a desert.

Lambert's words seemed to come from a long way away as he said like a prosecuting counsel, 'I put it to you that you struck your employer down to get that watch. That this was murder in the pursuit of theft.'

'No.' He could only manage the monosyllable, when he wanted more.

'If it happened like that, you might get away with manslaughter, with a good brief. You could say you never meant to kill him.'

'No.' Barry summoned an immense effort. 'It was as I said. It happened just like I said.'

Now, when it was too late for him, a nurse, plump and motherly, came into the room and studied the exhausted face and the limp submission of the slim, shattered body beneath the sheets. 'I'm afraid that's enough for today. Whatever he's done, the lad's exhausted. He was in a bad smash, you know.'

Lambert rose immediately. 'Thank you. I think we have all we need, for the present.' He smiled at the nurse and left without another glance at the man in the bed.

His last words rang in Barry Hooper's brain long after he had gone.

Nineteen

The man was waiting to see the Chief Super-intendent when he got into the station at Oldford. A man in an impeccable dark-blue suit, a white shirt and a silk tie. Lambert glimpsed him as he went through to CID.

It wasn't until he reached his office that he learned that the man was any concern of his. 'Tell him we're up to our necks in a murder inquiry. Get him to talk to someone else,' he said wearily.

'He says it might have a connection with the case. And it's confidential: he refused to speak to me about it.' DI Rushton tried not very successfully to conceal the pique he felt at that.

'I'll see him right away, then. And I'll send him away with a flea in his ear if he's just prying for information. But he doesn't look like a journo.'

Indeed he didn't. The man was probably in his late thirties. His dark suit fitted perfectly and there was the scent of an aftershave which had a subtlety not often experienced in police stations. His hair was expensively cut and he looked ready to preside at a board meeting.

'Dermot Rawlinson,' he said, holding out an immaculately manicured hand to Lambert. 'Marketing Director of European Fairways Limited.' He smiled affably, obviously expecting the name either to be recognized or to impress, or better still both. When neither Lambert nor Hook reacted to it, he pulled from his briefcase a glossy brochure with an impressive colour picture of a course in Portugal on its cover. His sales background was apparent in the proud flourish with which he produced it. 'The company owns twenty-seven courses in six European countries,' he explained modestly.

Lambert took the brochure and put it on his desk without a glance. 'You said this might be connected with a serious crime investigation, Mr Rawlinson. If it isn't, I'm afraid—'

'It may be. You'll have to decide that. All I can tell you is that the death of Patrick Nayland has come at a very awkward time for us.'

Lambert looked down at the brochure on his desk. 'Was your company in some kind of business negotiation with Mr Nayland?'

'Yes. Well, we were further than that, actually. We had reached an agreement with him. We are going to take over the golf course at Camellia Park. We shall upgrade it, spend money on it, and make it one of the best courses in this area. Extend it to eighteen holes, for a start. Open up a gym and a health centre. We believe the place has great potential, with a sizeable investment.'

He was in danger of slipping into a sales spiel again. Lambert said hastily, 'You had signed an agreement with Mr Nayland?'

The smooth face fell again as its owner came reluctantly back to reality. 'No, not quite. We had shaken hands on a verbal agreement. Mr Nayland was ready to sign the formal contract as soon as our lawyers had drawn it up. I need to press ahead now, despite the unfortunate timing of Mr Nayland's death.'

'And I need to know how many other people knew about this verbal agreement you had made with a man who is no longer around to implement it.'

'Mr Lambert, I have to tell you that in some circumstances, a verbal agreement can be as legally binding as—'

'And I have to tell you that I'm conducting a murder investigation. All I'm interested in is finding out who killed Patrick Nayland. In the light of that, I need to know how many other people knew about this understanding you had arrived at with a man who cannot implement it.' He was suddenly weary of this expensively tailored man and the world of takeovers and high finance that

291

he represented.

Rawlinson looked for a moment as if he was going to take offence. But if he was to get what he wanted out of this exchange, it must remain affable. He said smoothly, 'No one except Mr Nayland had been consulted by us. But he was the sole owner of the company, the only man whose agreement we needed to secure.'

'And when did you arrive at this "verbal agreement" with Patrick Nayland?' Lambert quoted Rawlinson's phrase back at him as if it were an outrageous, suspect thing.

'Two days before his death. He was quite definite that he wanted to—'

'And who else at Camellia Park knew about it?'

'That I cannot tell you. Mr Nayland was quite insistent that he was the sole owner, that he didn't need anyone else's agreement to dispose of this asset.'

'What would happen to the existing staff at Camellia Park?'

An urbane smile descended like a mask over the practised features of the man in the Savile Row suit. 'It's far too early to talk about that. We shall need to do our own survey of the entire plant and—'

'So there is no guarantee that they will keep their jobs?'

Dermot Rawlinson looked pained that an outside party should concern himself with such sordid matters. 'It is normally our policy to install our own operating staff, when we take over a concern which is to be developed. People who share the company ethos, who know the way that we operate our complexes, who recognize the ways in which we maximize the potential of an enterprise.'

Lambert suddenly hated this bland smoothie who was introducing new complications into his life. 'So you're saying the existing staff would need to fear for their jobs.'

Rawlinson shrugged his immaculate shoulders. 'Nothing is certain in the modern industrial world, Superintendent. There would be ample notice of any redundancies.'

Lambert sighed, controlling himself with difficulty, telling himself that this new factor wasn't really this odious man's fault; not directly. He said heavily, 'You have just given me a reason why four people who worked at that little golf course might have wished to kill its owner.'

'Oh come, that's surely rather melo-dramatic, Mr Lambert. What I need to know is whom we should be talking to now, to implement the agreement we made with the unfortunate Mr Nayland. Life must go on, you know.'

'I understand that Mrs Nayland will be inheriting the bulk of her husband's estate. You might wish to know that she is planning to offer the former Chief Executive at Camellia Park a partnership in the company. I imagine that may make the furtherance of your plans much more difficult.'

It gave him a lot of satisfaction to see the smugness drain out of those self-satisfied features. It wasn't until Rawlinson had gone that he turned his attention back to quite how urgent a motive Chris Pearson had acquired to dispose of his employer.

Tomorrow was the last day of term. At the end of the penultimate school day, the children trailed happily homewards, to hours of hackneyed Christmas songs and decking trees with tinsel. In the deserted school, Michelle Nayland waited patiently for the CID men.

Hook had suggested that they came to see her at home, but she knew she couldn't do this with her mother anywhere in the offing. She would move out, eventually. But her departure wasn't as urgent, as absolutely necessary, as it had been before last Wednesday. She would go in a few months, she thought. For the present, she would stay and support her widowed mother through the grief which wracked her, however mistaken that grief might be.

She attempted to prepare her lessons for the last day of term as she waited. She tried not to watch the groups of children straggling down the drive, the boys indulging in noisy horseplay, the girls in confidences about the day they had passed and the night to come. She was near enough in age to the older girls to imagine the kind of things that were being said. After the last day of school tomorrow, they had the mixed delights of the Christmas season and family festivities to come.

It was not until she saw the police car coming up the drive that Michelle realized what she had really been looking for.

She took the Superintendent and his Sergeant through to the school library, now closed for the day, where she knew they would not be disturbed. They were noncommittal in the face of her faltering small talk as they followed her. She shut the door and sat down behind the desk where she had often done a stint as librarian, issuing books, guidance and encouragement to children in the school.

These men needed none of these. They studied her coldly for a moment, watching her hands clasping each other on the desk. Michelle wanted to fold her arms, but the body-language analysts said that was a gesture of keeping people at arm's length, so to speak, that it denoted a lack of co-operation. And these two were certain to be experts in body-language. She resented their calm assessment before they had even asked her a question.

Then Lambert said, 'We had better begin with a warning, Miss Nayland. We know that you held information back from us when we met last Friday. We are fairly certain, indeed, that you told us deliberate lies on that occasion. I should therefore warn you that in a murder investigation any further deceit will be regarded very seriously, and could even lead to criminal charges.'

His opening tone was gravely neutral, but Michelle was sure she detected a certain relish in the last sentence. She said, 'I'm sure any deception was unintended. After all, I have nothing to hide.'

She thought they would challenge her on that. She wanted them to do just that, to show their hand and tell her exactly how much they had learned from the others. Instead, Hook flicked his notebook open and said suddenly, 'I think we'll have your account of your visit to the basement of Soutters Restaurant again. In detail, this time, with anything significant which you may have omitted on Friday.'

'I'll tell you everything I can remember. I went down there well before the murder – well, I suppose I should say well before the body was discovered. Twenty minutes at least before that, I should say. I went to the Ladies, was in there for no more than two or three minutes, and came back up the stairs and into the restaurant. I think Patrick was still at the table when I returned, but I couldn't be certain of that: things were pretty boisterous by that time.'

Hook nodded slowly. 'That is more or less what you told us on Friday. Did you see anyone else whilst you were down there?'

'No. There was no one in the ladies' loo. There may of course have been someone behind the closed door of the Gents, but I haven't got X-ray eyes.' She was sorry she'd said that, as soon as it was out. Flippancy would only antagonize them.

Lambert studied her for a moment, then said without preamble, 'Either you are lying or other parties are. Since at least two people have reported seeing you coming up the stairs just before the murder was discovered, it seems highly probable that it is you.'

She swallowed hard, finding her tongue suddenly very dry against the roof of her mouth. 'I may have made a mistake, I suppose. None of us thought at the time that the order of events was important. Except your murderer, I suppose.'

'And we have to ask ourselves why you lied to us, Miss Nayland.' Lambert carried on as if she had never spoken. 'We have to ask ourselves whether the people who saw you in the basement and on the stairs were witnessing a murderer leaving the scene of her crime.'

'They weren't.'

'You must try to convince us of that. In the circumstances, I'm sure you will agree that that is only fair.' He allowed himself the ghost of a smile, enjoying cornering this cool young adversary.

Michelle made herself take her time, nodding slowly as she digested what he had said and decided there was no alternative. 'All right, it's true what you say. What others have told you. I was down there only shortly before the corpse was discovered. I saw the young black boy, Barry Hooper. A couple of minutes later, Joanne Moss had found Patrick's body and was screaming hysterically.'

'So why tell us otherwise?'

She made herself pause, telling herself that she had known this was going to come out today, that however long she took over her replies they couldn't hold it against her, whatever they thought. Only the actual words she used, not how long she took, would be recorded by the fat one in his damned notebook. 'I wanted to put myself as far away as possible from the killing. I thought it was bound to come out eventually that I didn't like the victim, that if I said I'd been down there just before he'd died, you'd be bound to conclude that I'd put the knife into him.' It sounded thin to her as she said it, but it was the best she could do.

'We don't work like that, Miss Nayland. And you're far too intelligent not to realize that anyone you saw down there immediately before the murder was discovered has to be a leading suspect. So why did you withhold that information?'

'Because I wanted whoever had done it to get away with it! Because as far as I was concerned, he'd executed a cruel bastard, not committed a murder!' This time the words came leaping out of her spontaneously. Her relief that she was being honest at last startled her even as it flooded through her. Her anger was like a drug; perhaps this was a drug, adrenaline, she thought, her elation widening her eyes and making the blood sing in her ears.

It was Lambert who paused now, wondering if he had his killer sitting before him in the unlikely setting of a school library, watching her excitement seep away as he studied her and did not speak. 'You told us on Friday that your stepfather was kind to you. That you'd got over the initial difficulties of a new man replacing your own father in the household. That he was sympathetic to your problems when you were training to be a teacher.'

She listened to her own breathing, hearing it slow as he deflated her with her own words. 'All right, that was a load of balls! I hated Patrick Nayland. Nothing was going to alter that.'

'Your mother thinks he was a good man. That he had your best interests at heart.'

She had no need to conceal her contempt for him now; she was glad to hear it flaring in her words as she said, 'My mother saw what she wanted to see. Nayland was a randy goat who didn't trouble to control his urges! He shoved his hand up any skirt that offered, and quite a few that didn't.'

'Including yours?'

She had expected him to contest her wildness. Instead he had gone quietly to the heart of the matter. She had never intended to give them this, to present them with a red-hot motive as well as wounding the one person she wanted to protect, her mother. But she said, just as quietly now as Lambert, 'Including mine, Superintendent. Not withholding the truth now, am I?'

'You're telling us that Patrick Nayland made a sexual assault on you?'

'I'm giving you more than that. I'm telling you that he tried to rape me!'

'When was this?'

She'd never expected them to be so calm, to accept her astonishing revelations without argument. It dawned upon her dimly that these men probably heard startling things like this all the time. 'A fortnight before he was killed.'

'We need some details, please.'

300

Lambert spoke softly, even sympathetically. She wanted to deny him, to scream at him that her word was enough, that she could not relive that day. But she had lied to them, lied more or less throughout her first meeting with them last Friday. So now they would need convincing; women sometimes did make wild allegations about rape, didn't they? She said dully, 'I said he tried. He didn't succeed.'

'We need a little more. I'm sorry.' Lambert was apologetic but insistent. She wondered if he had daughters himself.

Michelle nodded. Now that she was embarked upon it, it didn't seem such a terrible thing to have to talk about it. The important thing was to convince them what a sod Nayland had been. 'It was after I had come home from school. Mum was out. Patrick wasn't normally there at that time, but he was on that day. Afterwards I thought he might have been waiting for me. I didn't suspect anything, at first. He sat me down and gave me a stiff gin and tonic, said I needed to relax after the trials of the school day. Ironically enough, that was quite true: I'd had a difficult day; it was mild but wet, and the kids couldn't go out much at lunchtime. That always gets them overexcited in the afternoon.'

'But you gave him no encouragement.'

It was a statement, not a question, and that

emboldened her. 'No. But at first, I'd no idea what he intended. I knew that he couldn't be trusted with women, but I never thought he'd try anything on with me. I even thought he was trying to be pleasant, to build the bridges between us that my mother was always on about.' She shuddered even now at the thought of that early evening moment, in the quiet house with the winter darkness around it.

'But it wasn't like that.' This was Hook, as sympathetic as his chief, offering nothing more than the prompt she needed to continue a difficult tale. It was almost as if they were apologetic on behalf of their sex.

Michelle said, 'He put his hand on my shoulder, said what an attractive woman I was now, how he'd enjoyed watching me turn from an adolescent into a desirable young lady. Then he put his nose in my hair, said how beddable I smelt. I tried to move away, said something about this not being the sort of thing I wanted to hear from a stepfather. He said he wanted to be much more than that, that he could introduce me to the joys life had to offer to a woman like me. That was his phrase: I can hear him saying it, even now.' A trembling took her over unexpectedly, running, slight but insistent, through all her limbs.

Hook said, 'You must have realized what he was up to by this time. What did you do about it?'

'I told him not to be so silly. I couldn't believe it was happening to me. But it was. He grabbed me with both hands when I tried to move away from him. Said I was a tease, that I'd led him on, that I knew very well what I was doing.' She stopped in horror, remembering how she had lied to these men, how important it was to her now to convince them. 'I didn't, though! Lead him on, I mean.'

Hook gave her a tiny smile of encouragement, a smile which said he believed her. 'No. It's what nearly all men claim, in cases of assault and rape.'

Michelle was more grateful to that stolid man for that than she could ever have imagined. 'He said it was time to stop play-acting, that this was for real. He pressed me against the back of the sofa, then almost had me on the floor when I fought him. He said that there was no way out of this, that I wanted it really, that I'd be grateful to him afterwards, that I'd come back for more and beg for it.' She spoke with mounting revulsion, as if piling up the details of a bad dream. It had become just that, in the days since Nayland's death.

Lambert had heard enough. 'But he wasn't successful: you said at the outset that he attempted to rape you.'

'Yes. I wasn't quite the sitting duck he'd

fondly imagined. I kneed him in the groin. Hard. He called me a vindictive bitch and said I'd better keep my mouth shut about this, because no one would believe me. I screamed something at him and ran out of the house. I didn't come back until the next day.'

'Who else knows about this?'

'No one.'

'You didn't tell anyone? Not even your mother?'

'Least of all my mother. She's the one person who might not have believed me. She thought the sun shone out of Patrick. Oh, I'd have told her all right, in due course, but I was going to pick my moment. I told the bastard that, two days after it had happened. I'm afraid I was rather enjoying watching him suffer, letting him wonder just when I was going to blow the gaff to Mum.'

'Didn't you think of going to the police?'

'I'd no evidence, had I? If he'd actually succeeded, there'd have been semen and wounds. I didn't even have a scratch to show.'

Lambert decided that he believed her story. But he asked the question any lawyer would have put. 'You realize that we only have your word for this?'

Michelle wanted to fly at him. Instead, she held on to her emotions, telling herself that she had always known that they would say something like this, that it was part of their job to do it. She said coolly, 'It happened all right. Why should I make it up?'

'There could be all sorts of reasons. For a start, it's almost the worst possible thing you could say about a man you didn't like. An effective way to blacken the memory of a dead man who can't speak for himself.'

'That's what Mum would say! But she'll believe me, when other things have come out, as they're surely bound to do now.'

'And you say you haven't told anyone else?'

'No. I didn't want it getting back to Mum from anyone else, did I? I wanted to choose my moment to break it to her.'

'You realize you've given yourself an excellent motive for killing Patrick Nayland?'

She had feared this suggestion, when she rehearsed this interview before they came. But now that it was here, she found that she could take it in her stride. 'I realize that perfectly well. Why do you think I concealed all this, when we talked last week?'

'I don't know. We spend a lot of our time trying to convince people that the truth is much the best policy in murder investigations. Did you kill Patrick Nayland?'

'No. I felt like killing him, in the days after the rape attempt. I won't pretend I'm not delighted that someone did it for me!'

'And who was that someone?'

She was taken aback by the sudden

suggestion that she might know the killer, delivered as it was in this calm, matter-of-fact manner. 'I don't know. I'd tell you if I did.' She knew that did not sound convincing, that it more or less contradicted what she had said in anger earlier, so she added, 'I don't approve of murder. But I'm certain the man who killed him will turn out to have had good reason.'

Lambert gave her no reaction to this. Instead, he studied her for a few seconds and said, 'Let's see if you can help us now, then. You say that you saw Barry Hooper immediately before the murder was discovered. Who else went down there in the period immediately before Mrs Moss discovered the body?'

She shook her head. 'I can't be certain. I think the greenkeeper from the course – Alan Fitch, isn't it? – went down there a minute or two before I did, but I couldn't be certain.'

'And your mother?'

'You surely can't think she killed Patrick? I told you, she thought the sun shone out of him. She'd never—'

'And if she discovered he was two-timing her? More than two-timing her? This looks very much like a crime of passion, doesn't it?'

'It wasn't my mother.' Michelle's lips set in a stubborn line. 'She didn't go down to the basement in the period you've been talking about. The first time she saw the body was after Joanne Moss had found it, when Mum held Patrick in her arms and Chris Pearson had to detach her from him.'

'And Chris Pearson?'

'I think he came back into the restaurant a little while before I went down the stairs to the basement. I couldn't say how long.' She was conscious of the electric silence her words had created. 'I didn't mention that before because I can't be absolutely certain of it. The same as with Mr Fitch. I wouldn't like anyone to be accused of murder because I report something which isn't much more than an impression.'

'No one will be, don't worry about that,' said Lambert grimly. 'You can imagine just what a defence lawyer would make of your vague impressions.'

'Yes. I'm just trying to be as honest as I can. I'm sorry I tried to deceive you at our first meeting.'

Neither of them commented on that. They left her with the instruction that she should go on thinking about that night at Soutters, that some significant fact might yet surface from her subconscious.

They had listened to her so carefully, been in the main so sympathetic, that she was almost sorry when they had gone. She had a curious sense of deflation in the hour which followed. She wondered how their discussions with other people were going.

They still didn't seem to have found out about her meeting with Joanne Moss. She felt sure that lady would keep quiet about what she'd told her over lunch in the pub.

Twenty

Chris Pearson was feeling rather pleased with himself. Liza Nayland had rung to tell him the partnership plans were going ahead. He should have a draft from the company lawyers within two or three days, and then she and he could hammer out the details together. She was sure they would have no difficulty in reaching an amicable solution, one which would suit both of them.

It had been a very friendly conversation and it left him feeling that his ambitions were after all to be realized. He decided to spend the morning of Friday, the twenty-second of December reassuring the staff at Camellia Park.

The bitter weather had relented; the chances of a white Christmas had as usual receded as the big day approached. A watery sun climbed valiantly towards its midday zenith, the lowest of the year. There was even a little warmth in its rays, and the golf course filled with people as the morning wore on. The sky became increasingly blue behind the stark outlines of the leafless trees at the top of the course. Three miles away, May Hill looked green again, after the frost and north-east winds of the last week.

Chris found Alan Fitch planting two rowan trees behind the fifth green. He watched the methodical turning of the spade as the greenkeeper dug a hole, measured it against the root bole of the rowan and then carefully lowered the new tree into place. Pearson picked up the bag of leaf mould which Fitch had brought with him on the tractor and emptied it carefully into the space around the roots. 'You'll be missing young Hooper for this sort of work,' he said.

'Quiet time of the year, this. There's no mowing to do. I'll manage until he gets back,' said the taciturn Fitch.

'Be some time, I should think. The lad's smashed himself up quite badly, I hear.'

'Daft young bugger!' Fitch spat his disgust on to the roots of the rowan, then covered them quickly with compost.

'According to Mrs Nayland, he seems to have taken the boss's watch,' said Pearson, watching for a reaction from the man who refused to lift his face from the task in hand.

Fitch tamped down the soil around the rowan with the back of his spade. 'He told me that, when we saw him in hospital. Daft young bugger! He won't lose his job though, will he?' He looked up at the man standing beside him, revealing for the first time his

310

anxiety for his protégé.

'Do you think he killed the boss?'

'No. He's a daft bugger, but not a killer, young Barry.'

'It looks as if one of us did.'

'Ay. One of us here, or one of his family. He were a randy sod, and randy sods get thumped.'

'Or knifed, in this case.'

'Ay. I wouldn't have minded seeing the horny bugger getting a thumping, but I wouldn't have wanted him killed.' It was the first time Chris had heard the greenkeeper reveal such an open contempt for Patrick Nayland. Fitch's eyes were on the ground again, as he levelled the earth around the thin trunk of the newly planted sapling.

'As far as I'm concerned, Hooper will keep his job, if no serious criminal charges are brought against him.'

'He's a good worker, young Barry.' It was the closest Alan Fitch would allow himself to come to openly stated affection. 'But who knows what will happen now, with Mr Nayland gone?'

'Things will go on much as before, if it's left to me.'

'And will it be?'

For a moment, Chris was taken aback by the directness of this churlish worker. Then he told himself that Fitch was just not good with words, that he wouldn't have known

311

how to phrase his query more diplomatically. 'I think it will, yes. I've talked to Mrs Nayland, and she doesn't want to interfere with the way we do things.' He wasn't going to tell him about the partnership, of course. That could leak down to people like Fitch, in a month or two, when he began to implement the changes he planned. 'I think you can be pretty certain that your job is safe, Alan. Assuming that you didn't kill the boss, of course.'

Alan Fitch looked up sharply at him on that. He wasn't good at spotting whether people were joking or not.

Joanne Moss seemed to be a little on edge when Chris Pearson went into the clubhouse.

'I wish it was settled, all this business,' she said. 'I wish they'd put someone away for killing Patrick, and let us all get on with our lives.'

'Do you think they're getting near to an arrest?' said Chris.

'No idea. They were pretty cagey when they spoke to me on Wednesday. They clearly knew a lot more than they did when they'd seen me last week, but they weren't letting on exactly what, or how much. I suppose that's one of their techniques. I expect they sometimes pretend to know more than they do. They certainly got me on edge.'

'Young Hooper stole Patrick's watch,' said Pearson.

She looked at him sharply. 'Did he, indeed? I'm disappointed in him. Do you see him killing Patrick, though?'

'He might have. It might have been a mugging that went wrong. He might have panicked when Patrick resisted – lost his head and stabbed him. It looked to me like that sort of killing.'

'He doesn't seem the sort of lad to commit murder.'

'He didn't seem the sort of lad to steal watches,' Pearson pointed out grimly. 'And it seems he was on drugs. When they're high, people do unpredictable things, behave out of character.'

'I suppose so.'

Chris said casually, 'What did the CID people ask you about?'

'Nothing very much. They made me go over the discovery of the body again, asked whom I saw around the spot just before I found him.'

They were fencing with each other, testing the ground between them, trying unsuccessfully to pick up any clues as to whom the police suspected. Chris said, 'I suppose it could have been Alan Fitch. He's a dark horse, doesn't say much. But he has violence in his past, and from what little he does say, I get the impression he didn't like Patrick.'

'I still find it difficult to believe that anyone who works here killed Pat. What about the family? Don't they say that most murders are committed by people within the family? Do you think it might have been Liza Nayland?'

'I suppose it might, if she'd—' He stopped suddenly, not knowing how to go on with the thought.

'If she'd found out about Pat and me?' She gave him a bitter smile. 'It's all right, you can say it. The police were clearly thinking it was a possibility.'

'It must be, I suppose.' Chris looked bleakly past her at the array of neatly arranged kitchen utensils. It wouldn't suit his book if they arrested Liza Nayland, not with his partnership in the balance. 'And what about Michelle Nayland? I don't know her well, but I know Patrick had lots of problems with her, in the early days of the marriage. She seems a resourceful young woman, very protective of her mother. If she found Patrick was straying, she'd have been furious on her mother's account – furious with a man she already disliked and resented.'

'I suppose it's possible,' said Joanne. 'Somehow, I've never been able to see a woman killing Patrick like that.'

Which leaves Alan Fitch, Barry Hooper and me in the frame, thought Chris Pearson ruefully. He said firmly, 'I don't think we can

314

rule a woman out as a possible killer.'

It was at that moment that the phone rang and DS Hook said they would like to see him for a third time during the afternoon.

Chris Pearson wished in the end that they had come immediately after Hook's call.

His first reaction was that the three hours interval would allow him to prepare himself, to set out his stall as he wanted to present it to these shrewd, experienced investigators. But he had thought about his position so much that he could have done that in ten minutes. The extra time only seemed to make him more and more nervous as he speculated about what they were going to say and how he should react. Anxiety wasn't a usual condition for him, and he had discovered over the last week that he wasn't good at dealing with it.

He set out his office at the back of the clubhouse to receive them, tidying his desk until its surface held only the picture of his wife and children and the bright brass ink and pen stand which he never used. He straightened the big pictures on the walls which showed the course at various stages of its development, from farmer's fields, through the first brutal earth-shifts with the bulldozer, to finished course with its first few tender saplings and bunkers with pristine sand.

Chris decided he must take some more pictures, showing how the trees had grown and the fairways matured from meadow grass to something much better in the last few years. He got out the blueprint for a full eighteen-hole course and studied it for a few minutes, planning a couple of minor amendments, diverting himself happily with the thoughts of how he would press forward once this unfortunate business was out of the way. They'd have a club professional, once they got the full eighteen holes going. There was ample room for the shop he would need at the end of the clubhouse building.

He thought at first that he would sit behind his big desk to talk to the policemen, play the man at the helm dispensing lordly advice to his visitors, helping them where he could and being politely blank where he couldn't. Twenty minutes later, he was shifting the furniture again, bringing an extra armchair in from the small members' lounge outside so that they could sit more informally, equals discussing the regrettable death of the man who until last week had owned and controlled Camellia Park.

He felt himself becoming palpably more anxious as the time they had arranged approached. He even went out and walked briskly around the course, waving to the taciturn Alan Fitch, exchanging pleasantries with one or two of the golfers he recognized. He couldn't remember when he had last had time to kill, and he didn't enjoy the feeling. And he found that all the time his eyes strayed towards the entrance to the car park from the main road.

They came exactly as they had arranged, at three o'clock. He took them into the office he had so carefully prepared, seated them as he had planned, and said, 'We can chat here without being disturbed. And no one can hear us. The walls are pretty soundproof anyway, but I've sent Joanne Moss home a little early. It's Friday afternoon, after all, and she's a good worker, and it's only three days to Christmas.' He felt himself talking too much, saying more than he needed to say, filling up space with words whilst words were still safe.

Lambert said, 'We know considerably more than when we last spoke to you, Mr Pearson.' He contrived to make it sound like a threat.

'That's good. The investigation is progressing well, then?'

'Some of our new information concerns you. There are things we feel you should have revealed to us during our previous meetings.'

'Really? I can't imagine what you are referring to, but I assure you that this must have been an oversight on my part rather than any

317

deliberate wish to—'

'What is your present position here?'

'I am the General Manager. Chief Executive, if you like. I oversee all the activities at Camellia Park, both on the course and in the clubhouse. I reported to Patrick when he was alive, but in the new situation I shall—'

'I understood that situation had already changed your position.'

He made himself pause, telling himself that there was nothing to worry about here, that he could handle this easily enough. He nodded, forcing a smile. 'I hadn't planned to mention this, simply because I thought the information was still confidential. Obviously you have talked to Liza Nayland and she has told you that she proposes to offer me a partnership in the firm.' He waited for confirmation from the two observant faces opposite him, received none, and went on more uncertainly, 'It is very gratifying to me to have my commitment to the place and its development recognized in this way. Patrick was planning to offer me a partnership, and Liza has chosen to honour that commitment.' He knew it sounded stuffy and formal, but that was probably the appropriate note to strike about this.

'Have you anything in writing to prove that Mr Nayland intended you to become a partner in the firm?'

Chris made himself smile as he shook his

head. 'We didn't operate in that way. But there was an understanding from the early days that, provided things developed satisfactorily, I would become a partner in due course. It was his money which financed the whole thing, but my know-how which developed it. This place has been my whole life in the last ten years.'

They caught the emotion in his last sentence, noted the quick, nervous smile with which he sought to mitigate that intensity. Then Lambert said, 'You must have been devastated to learn that Camellia Park was to be taken over by European Fairways Limited.'

Chris felt the blood pound in his temples, even as it seemed to be doing strange things like draining from his face. He knew his voice was uneven as he said, 'You must be mistaken. There is no question of any take-over. Mrs Nayland and I agreed on Monday that I was to become a partner in the firm. She confirmed to me this morning that the lawyers have drawn up a formal agreement, which I think we shall both sign in the next few days.'

'The representative of European Fairways spoke to us yesterday. We have checked out what he said with other senior members of his firm. We are confident that Mr Nayland had agreed to sell out to them, six days before his death.'

Chris felt his world crashing about his ears. Just when things had been going so well, his brain kept repeating inconsequentially. He said, 'I knew nothing of any such agreement. It must have been just a tentative one. Informal. Incomplete.' He was groping for words. 'This is the first I have heard of it.'

'I'm afraid it had gone much further than that. Mr Nayland had made a verbal agreement. Terms had been agreed. The formal documents for the takeover are with European Fairways, who were expecting Mr Nayland as sole owner to sign them this week.'

'I knew nothing about this.' He repeated it stupidly. It seemed at this moment more important than anything to convince them of that.

'And was Mrs Nayland equally ignorant of the approach from European Fairways?'

'Yes. She wouldn't have offered me a partnership otherwise, would she?' Suddenly, he saw the chance of a way out. If Liza knew nothing about the sell-out, as she didn't, then perhaps he could convince them that he was equally ignorant. 'I doubt whether we shall wish to sell out now. We shall have to discuss any approach together, as partners. You must see that.'

He felt like a crab wriggling sideways, trying to make deep water and obscurity, to escape from the calm, unblinking gaze of this policeman who suddenly seemed so much older and more knowledgeable than he was.

Instead, he was pinned squirming to the hot sand, as Lambert said, 'When did Mr Nayland tell you that he intended to accept the bid from European Fairways, Mr Pearson?'

'I just told you, he didn't! I knew nothing about this!'

Lambert studied him for a moment, estimating his state of mind as calmly as if he were some biological specimen. 'Tell us about the row you had with Mr Nayland on the day before he died.'

'Row? What row was that?' He felt his pulses racing again; that seemed to deny him the capacity for rational thought, so that he had no means of devising a reasonable reply. 'Pat and I didn't row. We discussed policy, even had occasional disagreements, but—'

'You were heard shouting at Mr Nayland, in this very room.' Lambert looked round at the walls, with their charts and photographs, as if they could bear witness to that fateful exchange. 'He shouted back at you and things became more heated. The shouting went on for a good ten minutes. I'd call that a row.'

Chris tried desperately to think of a logical explanation, but all he could see was Patrick Nayland, yelling at him that he was going to sell, that it was good business, that he couldn't guarantee the future of his General Manager or anyone else at Camellia Park. He said, 'All right. We were arguing about this bloody takeover bid. But everything else I've told you is true. He had promised me a partnership. That had been our understanding from the start. It's why I took a smaller salary to do the job. It's why I stayed here when I had offers to go to bigger jobs.'

'And you didn't think it right to tell Mrs Nayland that there was a takeover bid on the table when you talked to her on Monday?'

Chris shrugged his shoulders hopelessly. 'I was amazed she didn't know. And I was only claiming what was my due. What was best for everyone. I'd have taken Camellia Park on from strength to strength, made it eighteen holes. I'd have made it one of the best golf clubs in the area.'

He stopped, not because his enthusiasm had run out, but because he realized that he was speaking for the first time of what might have been rather than what was going to happen.

Lambert said quietly, 'And Patrick Nayland was stabbed to death on the day after you had been told that all these hopes had been dashed. Were you holding that knife, Mr Pearson?'

'No.' He couldn't get out more than the monosyllable, and that in a voice so low that it would not have been heard if there had not been such absolute quiet in the room. Out on the course, a man yelled in triumph as a putt dropped on the last green, and there followed the sound of banter with his companions, an ironic accompaniment to the deadly serious events within the club-house.

Lambert said, 'You were seen re-entering the restaurant just before the body was discovered.'

It was quiet, almost matter-of-fact, and it took the shaken Chris Pearson a moment to appreciate the full implications. 'Yes. I expect Michelle Nayland told you that, because I remember her looking at me as I came back into the room. But it was quite a while before the body was discovered, as I remember it. Patrick wasn't down there when I was in the gents' cloakroom.'

'This is information you didn't offer to us in two previous meetings.'

'No. It would have implicated Michelle, wouldn't it, and I didn't wish to do that.' Even he was not sure as he said it if it was true.

Lambert ignored it. 'You had the opportunity to kill Patrick Nayland. And you have just outlined for us a very strong motive for murder. A motive you had resolutely concealed from us throughout our investigation.'

'I know. But I didn't kill him. And I don't know who did.' He felt tired now, incapable of any further prevarication to save his skin. He was waiting for the words of arrest.

Instead, Lambert said briskly, 'Don't leave the area without informing us of your movements, please, Mr Pearson. If you think of anything else which may have a connection with this killing, you should get in touch with us immediately. It is plainly now in your own interest to do so.'

Twenty-One

The Christmas lights were on in Gloucester. They winked cheerfully in streets both ancient and modern.

The shops were open late on the night of Friday the twenty-second of December, anxious to make the most of the great commercial festival that is the modern Christmas. Seasonal songs blared, hideously distorted, through speakers hastily rigged over the shopping malls. In the brightly lit caves of commerce, shop assistants with permanently painted smiles strove desperately to be helpful and cheerful at the end of their most exhausting day of the year.

At the lower end of the town, the medieval cathedral was floodlit, its massive elevations soaring in majestic permanence towards a navy sky which had not changed since man lurched upright from the primeval forests. The cathedral choir was singing the 500-year-old 'Coventry Carol', the lofty, almost unworldly acoustics preserving the existence of a minority Christmas until the world should return to it.

All this Lambert and Hook saw and yet did not see as they drove through the city. Their minds were concentrated fiercely on the interview which was to come.

Joanne Moss brewed the tea as she heard the bell ring at the door of the flat. She brought the tray in as she invited the two big men to sit on her sofa. 'You've probably eaten, but I've put some of my home-made parkin on, in case you fancy a piece. The golfers at the club put away a lot of it each week, but they're hungry men when they've played!'

She appeared perfectly at her ease, her hands steady as she poured the tea into the china cups. She noted that and was pleased with her own performance. It was surely important that she remained calm now. It was the third time she had spoken to them and she felt that all might be safely over after this.

For they had surely discovered nothing. In all probability, this would be the last time she had to deal with these two. Today, for the first time since Pat's death, she had found herself looking forward to a new year and a new period in her life. After what she had achieved, she would go forward with confidence.

She was conscious of the CID men studying her, waiting for her to settle, She put a small table beside each of them and placed the cups and saucers and the plates with the parkin upon them. She felt herself acting a part, playing the wholesome middle-class female she had never been, as she ministered unhurriedly to the needs of these strange visitors.

When they still did not speak, she said cheerfully, 'Well, what progress have you made? Are you anywhere near to an arrest?'

'Very near.' Lambert had not moved a muscle since he sat down. The steam rose unheeded beside him from the tea he would never touch.

She hadn't expected to hear that. She said lamely, 'That's good, then, isn't it? Get things all tied up before Christmas, perhaps.'

'Sometimes the most obvious solution is the correct one. That's why we're always interested in the last person who saw a murder victim alive.'

'Yes, I've heard that. But in this case—'

'In this case we had to be interested in the first person seen with the body.'

She tried not to react, forced herself to complete the sip of her tea she had already begun. 'But that was me, in this case, wasn't it? Or have you discovered some other—'

'When did Patrick Nayland tell you that your affair was over, Mrs Moss?'

The formality of the title sat oddly upon the brutality of the question. She said, 'He didn't. And you've got it wrong, it wasn't just an affair. Pat and I were going to be married.' She gazed past him, towards the point on the wall where the picture of she and Pat together had once hung.

'Other people had told you that he wasn't to be trusted. When did you find that they were right and you were wrong?'

He was making it sound as if everything was already decided. She knew she must cling to her version of events if she was to get away with it now. She forced a smile, made herself look from the blank wall into those all-seeing grey eyes. 'I don't know who you've been talking to, but they've given you the wrong idea. Pat and I were going to be married.'

'When?'

She hadn't expected that. She didn't have an answer ready for it, and she found herself suddenly without the energy to go on dreaming up lies. 'We hadn't decided when, exactly. It would have been after he'd told Liza. We couldn't make definite plans until then. Pat had to let her down gently.' Her voice almost broke on the last phrase, as she quoted her dead lover so exactly.

'You told us about the argument that Chris Pearson had with Nayland. Told us how their voices were raised against each other in what became a blazing full-scale row.'

'Yes.' For a moment, hope sang within her. 'I never told you that Chris killed him, though, did I? It wouldn't be fair of you to presume—'

'I think you discovered what that row was about, didn't you, Mrs Moss?'

'No. I heard the two of them shouting at each other, that was all. I knew it must be serious, because I'd never heard them so worked up about anything before.' Her lips set sullenly on that contention.

It was Hook who now said softly, 'He let you down, didn't he, Joanne? There's no need to protect him any longer, now that we know what happened. You pressed him about what was happening, and he told you that he was selling Camellia Park to a big company.'

His voice was beguiling with its soft Herefordshire accent, luring her towards agreement with every phrase. She had protected the bastard's memory for long enough. It would be a relief to tell them just how badly he had behaved. Her voice seemed to come from a long way away as she said, 'He wasn't just selling the golf course. He was selling out on me.'

Hook nodded sympathetically. 'He told you that, when you asked him about the row with Mr Pearson, didn't he?'

He seemed very concerned for her. This must be what counselling was like, she supposed. 'I couldn't help hearing what the two of them said at the end of the row. So when

I got Pat on his own, I asked him whether it was true that he was selling up. He said yes, it was an offer too good to refuse. He couldn't guarantee anyone's future, but he couldn't turn down the price he was getting. He was going to wash his hands of the whole project and move away. I thought at first that he meant with me.'

Her eyes brimmed for a moment with tears at the memory of that awful moment when the scales were stripped from her eyes, but she dashed them angrily away with the back of her hand. 'He said he was staying with Liza, that I should have known all along that it would work out like that, that I was a fool to imagine that it could ever have been any different.'

'And so you decided to kill him.'

Hook's soft tones made it a statement, not a question. There seemed no point in denying him. Joanne found that she only wanted to put her own case, not to deceive them any more. 'Not at that moment, I didn't. But Alan Fitch came in the next morning and saw that I was upset. He'd been trying to warn me about Pat for months, but I wouldn't listen. Now he saw that I would listen to him, and he told me about some of the other women that Pat had had a go at. Then I asked Michelle Nayland to meet me in a pub, because I knew that she hated him. She told me what he'd tried to do to her.'

'So you decided to be rid of him once and for all.' Hook made it sound to her the most natural, the most logical way to react. Confession was a relief, really. It seemed to Joanne now that the most important thing was to get the facts absolutely right. 'Not at that moment, I didn't.'

'But you took a knife with you to Soutters that night. You must have been thinking about it.'

Joanne nodded slowly. She seemed almost to be discussing the actions of someone else, now: someone very close to her, but not herself. 'I suppose perhaps I must have been. I put a knife into my handbag when I left the kitchen at Camellia Park. But I've often brought utensils home if I wanted to use them here. I've only a small kitchen here, you see, and we're very well equipped at the golf clubhouse.'

She nodded, a suburban housewife explaining the boring business of food preparation. Hook thought how carefully a defence counsel would explore this in due course, as he sought desperately to show a jury that this was an impulsive crime of passion, not a premeditated act. He said gently, 'Will you tell us exactly what happened in the basement of Soutters Restaurant, please?'

Her brow furrowed with concentration beneath the neat black hair, and she suddenly looked quite young, like a schoolgirl determined to give an accurate account of an incident which had happened nine days earlier. 'I saw Pat leave his seat at the middle of the table and go downstairs. I followed him down a couple of minutes later, on impulse. I met him coming out of the Gents. He looked so smug that I screamed at him. I was so furious that he stepped back a pace or two. I liked that. Liked the shocked look on his face.'

A small, unnerving smile crept over her features as she remembered the moment.

'And what happened next, Joanne?' Hook was as quietly persuasive as if he had been handling a difficult child.

Her face darkened. 'He said it was no dice. This dinner had now become not just a celebration of the first ten years, but a way of saying farewell to everyone. I said what about all our plans for the future. Why had he paid me more than the job was worth if he hadn't been serious about our future together? He laughed and said he reckoned it was money well spent. And I should reckon myself lucky; I'd been well paid for all the services I'd offered. Especially the ones in bed. That's when I stabbed him.'

With that last chilling simplicity, the smile came back to her lips.

'So you'd taken the knife down there with you.'

'I'd taken my handbag. I don't know when

I took the knife out, but it was there in my hand when I needed it.'

'What happened next, Joanne?'

'I don't remember anything else very clearly. I think I screamed at him about his other women and about Michelle as I went on stabbing him. I must have put the knife away in my handbag. But I don't think I realized I'd killed him then.'

'But you screamed, and brought the others.'

'Not then, I didn't. I heard someone coming, so I shut myself in one of the cubicles. A couple of people came in, one after the other. I don't know who they were, because I was keeping very quiet and planning what to do.'

Hook knew. Alan Fitch, who'd merely checked that Nayland was dead, and then Barry Hooper, who had removed the dead man's watch. He said gently, 'So what did you do, after you'd had this time to think, Joanne?'

'I came out of the cubicle, gave it a couple of minutes, and then screamed. Pretended I'd just found him, you see.' A smile of content at her cunning suffused her features. 'I almost got away with it, didn't I?'

She let Hook put the cups and the parkin back on the tray and carry it away into the kitchen whilst she sat staring past Lambert at the wall, still with that knowing half-smile upon her face. She made no attempt at resistance as Lambert pronounced the formal words of arrest and they took her out to the car.

Joanne Moss scarcely glanced at the handcuffs on her slim wrists as she sat in the back of the car with the silent Hook. She looked unseeing through the windows of the police Mondeo as Lambert drove slowly through the Christmas shopping crowds in Gloucester. The only movement of her head came as she raised her eyes to look towards the floodlit tower of the cathedral, as they passed it and moved into the darkness beyond the city. Bert Hook was happy that her last image of the outside world should be this unchanging one.

The choir was singing unaccompanied, its tones pure, almost ethereal. The sound of 'In the Bleak Midwinter' followed them into the night.